Jupiter 7
Space Monkeys

I0687687

Mat Roll

First Edition 2013
Second Edition 2015
ISBN: 0692215298
ISBN: 978-0692215296

Cover art & Layout design by Mat Roll

The characters and events portrayed in this book are fictitious. Any similarity to a real person, living or dead is coincidental and not intended by the author.

THE SPACE MONKEYS

WRITTEN BY MAT ROLL
EDITED BY CHERLY HAMLITON
ART BY MAT ROLL

Early editors and special thanks for helping me with
my story and being apart of it.

Richard Roll (Father)

Emiko Roll (Mother)

Mike Roll (Brother)

Tina Mayer (Big Sis`)

Tommy Change (Ichia)

Amanda Duncan (Colleen)

Jessica Maley (Mittens)

Chelsea Carr (Kat)

Celiest Douglas

Mark Vigor (Sam)

"Don't tell me what can and can not be done."

Mat Roll (Ichia Chang)

PROLOG

Jupiter 7

<u>Space Monkeys</u>

I've never really told my story to anyone before. Honestly not sure who would want to hear about a hopeless romantic. Who fights to save the Solar System and tries to meet the right girl in the process. I've always put my friends first and never myself, I'd take a bullet for any of them. I grew up on Mars in the city of Olympus. Olympus was the first colonized city on Mars, it has over 240 million people living there. Olympus is the most advanced city on Mars, it's surround by large atmosphere generators. On the outskirts past the atmosphere generators is Mount Olympus, it's the tallest peak on Mars. Its funny, at the top there is a spa resort. My parents are politicians, my father was governor of two states and now resides in the senate. My mother has worked with two different Presidents of Mars as an advisor. My best friend Mark and I grew up together, and did everything together. During high school we were both on the football team, robotic team, and in symphonic band.

Mars is basically the upper class, Doctors, Lawyers, Politicians and any one important. Earth upper and middle class and the moon was mostly middle class. Throughout the Solar System we have multiple Space Stations, the biggest one is orbiting Earth.

It's known as The International Space Exploration Station. Don't ask, some yuppie named it. Most people just call it ISE, kind of catchy. Jupiter has the second most Space Stations, and they harvest fuel for all humankind. After high school my uncle talked Mark and I into joining the Flight Academy for the Alliance Military. But our parents wanted us to be the next Presidents of Mars. Let's just say that Mark and I didn't listen to our parents and today they don't really talk to us much. But our moms still send us goodies every now and then. Moms are always the best, no matter what situation. Then came the unfortunate turn of events of the Space War. Safe to say human kind was at war with itself in space. The war actually only lasted two years well some say one year and two months. People and the Governments between planets realized the past mistakes on Earth. With new treaties, trade and space jump gates being built, the Solar System was working as one.

Not everyone was happy, out of the ashes came a new enemy. We call them Lab Rat Mafia and it's still unknown where they come from. But they are the real threat in the Galaxy. They are mostly humans, a few xenophobes, but they are a big bad group of mobsters. They take, steal, and hurt innocent people, just because they don't want to be under the man. The worst thing about The Lab Rat Mafia is their new form of weaponry, we call it Biologicals. They've created huge space monsters, just stupidly huge. At least their fighter pilots fight like a bunch of crop dusters. I can say I've been to four different planetary systems and Sol is the best one, with the best views. Parking next to Jupiter on a Friday night is the best relaxing medication you can get in my opinion. My name is Ichia Chang and this is my story.

5

Chapter 1

The end to a good day.

CRASH!!!!!! Skidddddd SLAM!!!!!! Echoes through a large hanger bay on the space station. Barrels and tubes are being hurled and scattered around as two space fighters and a bomber crash land, skidding into the hanger of the Space Station.

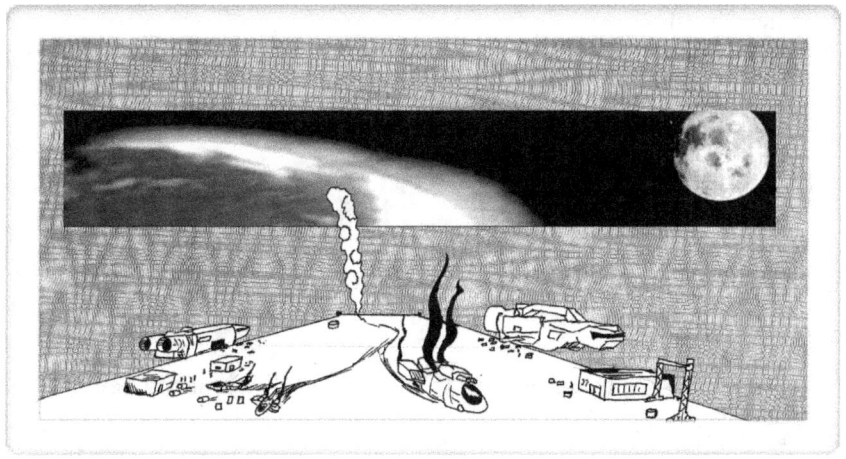

"GODS DAMIT!!!!! What the hell are you guys doing? You can't park there, they go on the other side!!!!" screams a mechanic holding his hard hat tightly.

"MAN PISS OFF! We just saved your parts and liquor supply." I said pulling off my helmet and slamming it to the cockpit counsel.

"You guys alright?" A young pregnant girl comes over, covered in grease and holding some rags.

"Wow you guys got messed up, heard you destroyed a Dreadnought." said the young girl pulling up her coveralls.

"Yea, you could say that." I said climbing down my fighter.

"Hey Mittens, what's my bill going to look like?" the bomber pilot asks as she walks over rubbing her butt.

"Looks like about a week's worth of work. I'll get you guys back out there in no time." Mittens said smiling, throwing a rag over her shoulder.

"Well I guess we can use some R&R, this would be a good time to look for a new recruit." I said to everyone unzipping my upper jump suit

A few hours later after cleaning up, I was back at my apartment watching the news and talking to Mark on my cell phone.

"Oh my god, how?" I said then looking down at my cell phone. Mark texts me, *"we made it in the news hell yea!"*

I look up again and see a video of us crash landing into the hanger.

"How the hell do they get these videos? Gods, it's on every channel." I said while searching through cable channels

8

I look down again at my cell phone, Mark text me. "dude lets meet up at Asian Boutique sometime!"

"I'm there." I text Mark back.

The next day I walked down to the hanger bay to see my broken fighter. As I walk into the huge hanger I could see Mittens attempting to pry off a broken panel.

"Hey let me give you a hand with that." I said, grabbing gloves off the work bench.

"Oh heyyy… what's up train wreck?" Mitten says smiling putting her hands on her hips.

"Not much, I figured I'd come and see the damages, see if I could cut costs." I said as I'm struggling to pry off the broken armor panel.

"Well it's not that bad, mostly armor repair, all your systems are good." Mitten says unplugging her com pad from the ship.

"How are you and Jeffery doing?" I ask tossing the panel into the scrap pile.

"We're okay, he's working hard as usual being a lawyer and all." Mitten says while pulling out tools from her hand bag.

"That's cool, hey what wrench should I use on this?" I ask pointing at the panel.

We continue to work on the fighters, replacing broken panels and the occasional bolt. Most of the repairs were rather quick just a lot of them. We worked late into the evening finishing up as much as we could.

9

"Hey thanks for the help, we almost completed all the repairs today." Mittens says taking a drink from her water bottle.

"Hey wanna get some pizza or something?" I ask Mittens wiping my hands off with a wet towel.

"Sorry can't Jeffery made plans for us tonight." Mitten says.

"That's cool, yea maybe another time." I replied.

"Yea well I'll catch you later." Mitten says as we walk out of the hanger.

Four days later I walk into the Asian Boutique. A young girl comes up to me putting her arms around my neck.

"Hey boy, where you've been?" the girl asks.

"Here, there, in a wall, and across the floor." I said smiling back at her with a goofy grin.

"Yea I saw that, shit don't feel bad at least your team didn't run into the door on takeoff." Said the girl then taking a chug from her beer.

"Hey Ichia, quit playing with all the toys and get over here!" Mark shouts across the bar.

"Alright, I'm coming, hey I'll talk to you later." I said waving to the girl.

"See ya." Replied the girl holding up a peace sign.

"What's up man?" I say to Mark while pulling out a chair at the bar.

"Not much, I got you tonight, what you want?" Mark says grinning.

"I'll take an RB & Vod." I said without looking at the specials, might as well splurge I thought to myself.

"Good choice my friend." Mark replied, typing the order in for the drinks on a small console.

"So, I heard we're getting a fifth person in the groupie? Sounds good to me, I just hope he or she is a good mechanic like Mitten's. Because we all know once that baby pops out, she's out of here." Mark said then taking a sip of his drink.

"Yea, I'm supposedly moving over to the Delphinus. They're looking for some extra pilots on the weekends." I said then taking a drink from my straw.

"Sounds like your uncle wants us to come back, must be getting lonely." Mark said.

"Yea, well they're giving me half off on my apartment bills, because I'm stationed on a military vessel. So on the weekends I'll be at the Delphinus, and during the week I'm at home." I said then taking a longer sip from by Ice cold drink.

11

"Looks like your fly time will be just a little longer depending on where the Delphinus is floating around. Better hope they're not parked out by Pluto."

"My luck it will be on the other side of the galaxy near M1 or something stupid." I said, then pulled out the straw and chugged the rest of my drink. It went down smooth as ice and didn't even leave that burning trail, I smiled.

"By the way check this out." Mark hands me a blue card with a crescent moon on the front, and a half naked cat girl on the back, licking her hand, and butt in the air.

I look at the flyer then look up, then look at the flyer, and up again.

"You gotta be kidding right, you know we can't go there. You didn't." I said with my arm on the chair and finger pointing at Mark.

"I know that man, old Joe gave it to me, he goes down there all the time." Mark said with a stupid smile on his face.

"Old Joe says a lot of things, but I guess he could go down there, he's a civilian still." I replied.

"Yea, I swear they need to get rid of that rule. I'd feel so much better about flying if we could go to a strip club." Said Mark as he order more drinks from the menu.

"Just out of curiosity how do you get there?" I asked tapping my fingers on the bar.

"Joe said it's a secret tunnel in elevator shaft six, down in sector six just as you come off of the express train." Mark said.

12

Mark and I talked on for a few more hours, later we departed to our apartments. As we left Mark said, "don't forget we're back on in the morning." I nodded and gave a thumbs up to Mark as we left to our apartments. Later I was lying in bed looking up at the ceiling, I couldn't fall asleep, most likely due to the liquor. I think we drank four or five drinks plus three shots of UV Cake. Hmm, I don't ever drink that much, but Mark had the bill so I guess it was okay to splurge for once.

"Damn it, why can't I fall asleep?" I said lying in my bed, arms crossed behind my head.

I looked over to right of my bed. Sitting next to my keys was the card I received from Mark. I picked it up, examined it, and thought about it. I kept looking at it wondering what it was like, going to a strip club or any adult club. As a military personal I was not allowed because of an incident back several years ago. All military personal where banned from Adult lounges on the space station, mostly due to the Mob presence down there. Lots of military people were disappearing, and high military officials were being used to smuggle in weapons.

"Shit, I wanna check this out." I said, getting up from my bed.

I glanced over to my closet, looking at a brown bag, then remembering. Colin gave me some old clothing of his. That's right, no one will know who I am if I wear this. There are no military logos on the tags or sleeves, this just might work. I threw on the jeans and the brown fleece hoody. As I went to put the bag away, a little green bottle fell out.

13

"Aspen? What's this? Oh its cologne, hmm, never heard of it before." I said to myself, while tapping some around my neck.

I left leaving with determination to find out what this place was all about. Knowing what to expect if I was caught, knowing the trouble I'd be in, I slapped my hat on and took the late night elevator train down to sector 6. Usually at that hour no one ever rides the train. Sitting on the bench looking out the window, I could see earth and the moon. The moon looked like it was trying to hide behind the earth, glowing ever so brightly. Finally I arrived in sector six and headed over to the old elevators. I pulled the door open to find a long, lightly lit hallway that curved to the left. The hallway was like walking in a horror movie fog, but in a fog of cigar smoke. At the end of the hallway was a little red light. I came to another heavy metal door, I turned the handle and peeked inside.

When it opened, smoke poured out. I walked in, it was like a night market back on earth. There were shops all along the path ways, mini bars, and food stands everywhere. I started to walk down the street, and there was the club that the card was from. As I walked down the street some people stared at me, and people where trying to sell things to me. Some creepy old lady tried selling me a bottle of clear moonshine. I only looked, I dared not to buy it because it was a rainbow clear color, kind of creepy.

"Cool, that's it." I said quietly to myself.

As I came up to the door of the club, a very very big bouncer came out.

"I've never seen you around here before." The bouncer said holding his hand out to stop me.

"Um. I'm new around here, oh, wait, here." I said pulling out the Flyer.

The bouncer took it from me, looking over it, and then looking at me.

"Well?" I ask smiling at the bouncer.

"You're good to enter, where did you get the flyer from?" the bouncer ask getting on his chair.

"Um, up in sector 22 of the station." I said pulling out money to enter the club.

The Bouncer gave me a ticket, and opened the door for me. As the door opened more smoke poured out like water out of a jar. It was like the smoke was a wall or a solid object. I stepped in and raised my right eyebrow with amazement.

"Daamnnn!" I said with my mouth open wide.

Looking around, in the center there was a stage and seats all around it, and around them were two more stages and booths to sit in. On the stage there where half naked women dancing and women in bathing suits serving drinks to people. I cautiously made my way to a booth in the left corner. As I went to sit down a girl passed me and gently brushed me.

"Hey baby, want a dance?"

"Um, I'm okay," I replied scratching the back my head, and staring a little south.

"It's okay, I'll stop by later then." She said and walked towards the stage.

Thinking to myself, dance? I'm lost, I better figure out what they do here so I don't get kicked out." I sat down into the nice cushioned leather seat, I bounced a little bit due to low gravity.

"Wow, the gravity is low in this area or something." I said enjoying the nice cushier seat.

Now comfortable in my booth, I looked around to see what everyone was doing. There aren't many guys in the club mostly women. Most of guys in the club are sitting with women, Or at the bar. The glass mugs are huge and there are Christmas lights hanging everywhere. Even the bartender is a girl, and her tip jar is over flowing. A younger girl comes up to me asking me what I would like a drink, and hands me a menu.

"Wow, you got Italian soda pop up here? How did you manage that? In space of all places?" I ask the young girl.

"Well in this sector you can get just about anything. You must be new around here," the young waitress says, holding her PDA and pen.

"Um yea kinda, well, I'll take a raspberry Italian soda pop, please." I said smiling.

A few minutes later she comes back with the drink. I paid her and tipped her. Looking around, I saw the Dj sitting there just playing music with girls all over him. I wish that was me if I ever got that good, thinking to myself.

All of a sudden a girl in a black laced dress sits down across from me, she's trying to tie her shoe lace. The booths' lighting was poor so I couldn't really make out her face.

"Sorry, darn things keep coming loose." The girl says.

My face started to turn red, as I watched her, trying to tie her laces.

"Um, you know if you tie it around instead of under they won't come off so easy." I point out.

"Well here, help me then." She says putting her feet on my lap. Turning redder than an apple, I tie her shoes for her.

"Hey thanks, isn't that like a military tie or something?" she pointed out. I gulp, thinking, *"oh shit, I'm screwed."*

"Um, I've always tied it that way." I said while scratching the back of my head smiling.

Before we could start to talk, the DJ called her on stage.

"Crap, well there goes the conversation. Stay here I'll be back in a few, and we can continue." she said standing up. Still there wasn't enough light to see her face. It was almost as if the lights dimmed when her face would begin to appear.

"Well, I'll be here." I said waving to her as she left.

As she got on stage, she danced around. She danced to some R&B with loud bass. It was still hard to see her face because of all the smoke. One guy walked up to her on stage, and she got on her knees and pulled her underwear string out and the guy put money in her underwear. Then a couple of guys near the stage folded money like paper air planes and were throwing them on the stage.

Then the Dj was like "Okay guys, if anyone can land one in her clothing you get a free dance on me!!!"

I thought to myself, *"this place is crazy awesome."* As the mysterious girl bent down with her cleavage out, everyone tried it. I thought to myself, "eh what the hell." So I folded a bill.

"Well here goes nothing." I said holding a greatly engineered arrow dynamic paper dollar bill airplane. I threw it like a bat out of hell, every one watched it. I threw it so hard it went around the stage, over the bar, caught some more air, turning again going over the waitress, over the bartender, and straight for the stage right into her panties. The girl on stage screamed.

"Hey!!!" Pulling the paper plan out of her panties.

"Looks like we got a winner!!!!" The Dj shouted through the Mic, pointing towards me.

I just slid down in my seat, trying to hide like a dog that did something wrong. The waitress came over to congratulate me. I received a ticket and free drink. Then the DJ walked over. "Hey, great shot, no one has ever been able to do that." The Dj said high fiving me.

"Just lucky I guess. Ha.. ha.." I said smiling back to the DJ.

After a few minutes, the young girl came back over to my booth and sat down.

"Hey that hurt, you almost got in my corn hole." She said as she sat down, still unable to see her face.

"Well, it was a good shot." I said smiling.

"Can you do me a favor my heel lace has come undone can you tie them again for me?" The young girl asked as she puts her leg up on my lap.

"Oh, oh okay" I stuttered and turn red as a ripe tomato.

"So…. you want that dance?" She said as I looked like a lost kitten, thinking to myself. *what does she mean?"*

"Um okay" I said shrugging my shoulders.

"Well come on." she says grabbing my hand.

Like being dragged by a monster, the girl took me into a room darker than the main room. The room was cooler, and the gravity was a lot lesser than the club itself.

"Here, sit." She said, pushing me down on the seat.

20 minutes later:

Now knowing what a dance is, we returned to the booth. Sitting next to each other like a couple, she put her hand on my leg rubbing it back a forth.

19

"So… have fun back there?" she asked me nudging her cheek on my cheek.

"Y-eah!" I Stuttered and smiled.

"You don't have to lie to me, I can tell it's your first time." She said while pulling out a bottle of water.

"Yea, I guess it's kind of sad, I don't get out much."

"My names Anesthesia." She said holding her hand out.

"I'm Ichia." Shaking her hand.

For some reason the light shifted towards her face. She had short dyed blue and blonde hair. Her eyes were as blue as the sky back on Earth, with a smile that could paralyze anyone who looked. We talked for a while, and then closing time came.

"Well, will I see you around here?" Anesthesia asked me.

"Probably not, I'm returning to work tomorrow, but it was fun, maybe I'll run into you somewhere."

"Well, see ya later." Anesthesia said. Giving me a big hug and kissing me on my cheek.

"Hey, don't stop wearing that cologne." She said as she winked at me.

I left and made my way home.

"Holy shit its 6am, I gotta be at the CIC at 6:45." I sigh and said "Crap." with my head down, standing in the middle of my apartment.

Chapter 2

"Ballz to the Wall!"

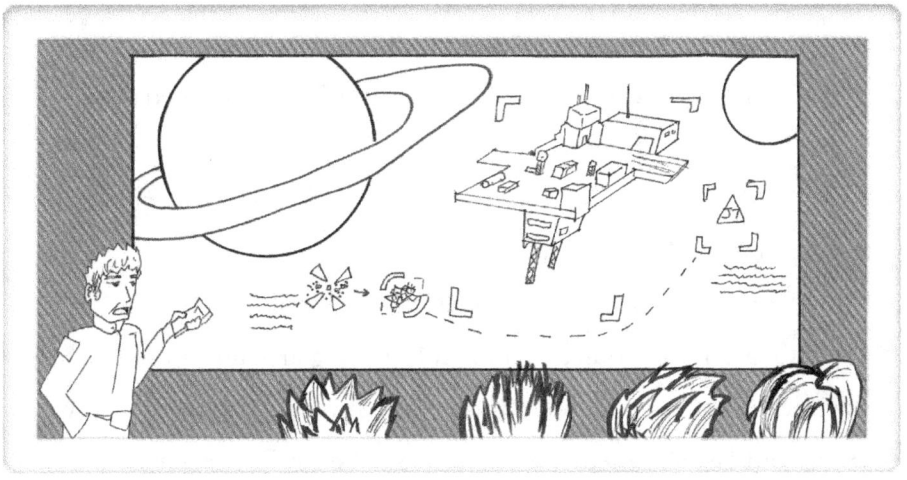

6:45am CIC: I was looking like Rocky The Raccoon as I entered CIC and sat next to my team.

"Hey didn't you sleep last night?" Mark asked.

"Not really." I said taking a sip of my coffee.

"You look like hell, long porno or something?," Lynsye said putting her arm around Missy.

"Yea, of your mom." I replied as Mark giggles.

"Hey only I can go down on my mom, you can choke your chicken all you want." Lynsye said smiling licking her lip piercing.

We were sitting in a small auditorium with a large blank screen in front, and four rows of seats that swivel. When the Screen turned on, it projected the map between Space Station 2-A4 and Jupiter.

"What the hell." Mark says.

"Good morning Jupiter 7." The master chief says.

"Oh shit." Mark mumbled.

A large tall man dressed in black decked out with medals, walked up to a podium.

"Ichia, you look like hell, what happened, missed the runway last night?" the Chief says.

"Um no sir. I almost did a week ago." I said.

"Okay enough bull shit, SS2-A4 orbiting around Jupiter has been having trouble with the locals, which you guys already know from your last shipment a week ago. SS2-A4 will be receiving a special package at 10:00 hrs, today. All you have to do is sit there and make sure they get the items. The Military is fitting the science lab with special defense systems so the scientists won't get robbed by pirates or whatever the hell is out there. There is a warning of Dreadnought in the area so keep a weather eye out. Damn things can come out of nowhere, any questions?" the Chief asks.

"Yea, where do babies come from?" Lynsye asked?

"From Marks ass, any real questions, comments, concerns, confessions?" asked the Chief raising a cigar to his mouth.

"I didn't know she was 16." Mark said.

"Wow someone's in a good mood." I said smiling.

"By the way Ichia, just because you destroyed a Dreadnought all by yourself last time, doesn't mean you can do it again. Delphinus is on standby, if a Dreadnought's reported, she'll be there. Watch your butts people, and good hunting." said the Master Chief.

07:36 hrs:

"Man I'm hungry as hell, hey Ichia let's get some Taco Bell before we go." Mark said.

"Yea, go ahead, you're going to stink up the cockpit if you eat there and we go out." I said checking my helmet.

8:00 hrs:

"Oh yea, this is great! Double decker taco's will always be my favorite!!!" Mark said with a mouth full.

"Yea, I'm going to check the flight plan again you enjoy them tacos pal." I said looking through my manual.

8:36 hrs:

In the suit room, everyone's getting their gear on. We pack extra oxygen, food packs, and water for our little endeavor. Then all of a sudden.

{*FFFFiiirrrrrrrttttttt!!!~~*}

"Aw, what the fuck man, come on." Lynsye shouted across the room.

23

"Yea, really, you know there's no fresh air around here." I said pulling the neck of my shirt to my mouth and nose.

"Hey I'm proud of my flatulence, want some more?" Mark said with his arms in the air.

{*FFFrrrraaapppppp!!!!~~~*}

9:36 hrs [Launch time]

Everyone sits in their fighters, ready to roll on the run way for launch.

"Alrighty, everyone ready?" I said, lowering my visor on my helmet.

"Man my stomach hurts like hell." Mark said draped over in his seat.

"Otay people let's fly." I said as I grabbed the throttle.

First a loud hissing noise, then the engines fired. Each ship gently takes off of the platform raising up. Then they drift out of the hanger bay of the space station.

"I.S.E. jump station, this is Ichia J-007 permission to jump?" I said over the com.

"This is Station, you are cleared for outbound jump to section SS2-A2. Be advised the Delphinus will be joining at 10:15hrs for reinforcements. Attack on Delphinus and your team is immanent." The Man said, from tower station.

"Hey guys, attack immanent, and the Delphinus is coming in too, why do they need us to go?" I say thinking aloud over the com.

"Yea. that is kinda weird, hmmmm" Missy says over the com.

24

"Well, either way we're getting paid right? Lets get going {*bblurp*}." Mark said over the com.

"Thanks for sharing." Lynsye said.

Over the com the station gave the countdown for launch.

5. 4. 3. 2. 1……

10:00 hrs {boom!!!}

The ships get sucked through a portal and flash out of space in Sector 4-A2.

"There's the station, this should be rather easy," I say looking over at everyone.

"Guys I'm getting a distress call from the station! Looks like a couple of fighters and one boarding craft." Missy says over com, while looking through binoculars.

"Yea, I'm getting the same thing here. I can't tell how many there are, lets get over there." said Mark.

At the same time a large, light flashed over us like a flash from a camera. It was a Dreadnought.

"Fiddle Sticks!!!!, Break! Break!" I scream while pulling back on the throttle lever and control stick.

"Hey, we need to get to the station. I can't tell how many baddies there are up there." Missy says.

"I got this, you guys head to the station I'll keep this thing busy."

"You're nuts, you can't take one of these again"! Mark yells to me.

"If we don't defend that station innocent people will die, NOW MOVE!!!!" I yell over the com.

"We'll be quick, remember don't be a hero and save some for us." Mark said pulling his controls right.

"More like save some for me!" I said smiling turning my fighter towards the Dreadnought.

My fighter does a 180 and screams towards the Dreadnought. The Dreadnought is throwing everything it's got towards my fighter. But due to the size of the fighter, they can't get a lock on me either. The Dreadnought dwarfs my space fighter. It looks like a Smart Car versus a battleship. I head under the Dreadnought to take out the door so it can't launch any support fighters. I take aim and fire two rockets and blow the door inward on the Dreadnought. Over by the space station, Lynsye and Missy bombard the boarding craft. Tearing it into pieces, as Mark dogfights the other two spacecraft's. I'm still dueling with the Dreadnought, now nearly depleted of rockets.

"Hell yea, this is easier than before, now to take out those gun towers." I said.

Flipping my fighter again, shooting every little tower, one rocket hits a large cone shape tank that starts an explosive reaction.

"What the hell? Time to go." I say looking behind my fighter.

The Dreadnought starts to combust and blows apart.

"We're coming buddy!!! What the, how, what, where, you destroyed it, how the." Mark said confused.

26

"All that in 15 minutes. Give me some of that coffee you drank earlier son." Lynsye says while putting her feet up on the console.

"Wait, 15 min" I said pondering. But before I could finish, a bright flash and the Delphinus jumps out of Hyper Space through the wrecked Dreadnought, cutting it into two large pieces with me right there.

"Crap, Crap, Crap, gotta get away, come on move, move," then nothing but silence over the channel.

"ICHAI!!!" the team screams. Mark calls the Delphinus, and they fly over to find him. Then two Dreadnoughts jump out of hyper space.

"Oh shit! Mark form up!" Lynsye shouts over the com.

"Warning! Do don't form up, head to point 6 6, we are going to fire Plasma Cannons," The Captain of the Delphinus says over the com.

Still alive but without a com I'm trying to flying half a space fighter.

"Come on, Damit!!! Oh crap they're going to fire the big ones," I said while punching the console.

Looking out of her gun cockpit Missy could see me, smoking and flying towards me were the two Dreadnoughts close behind.

"OH My Gods! Don't Fire!" screamed Missy.

But it was too late, The Delphinus fired both cannons destroying the Dreadnoughts, scattering flame and debris everywhere, with an impressive shock wave.

27

Chapter 3

You got to be kidding!

14:54 hrs

"Get the hell out of the way!" Lynsye shouted at people in hospital.

The team was pushing the carrier with their half dead friend to a waiting emergency room.

"How long was he adrift?" asked a nurse, who was trying to find my pulse.

"3 or more hours, should we take off his helmet?" Mark asked.

"No he could have a neck injury and we might have to cut it off," said the nurse.

"We'll take it from here," said the nurse, grabbing the carrier with other nurses and running into the emergency room, as they took my deadish body into the ER room. A battered, tired team just stood there in the hallway, helpless to help their friend.

17:00 hrs

The team was in the waiting room with their heads down. Missy fell asleep onto Lynsye. Mark was trying to keep awake, looking at a social network on his cell phone.

"Hey, here comes the nurse from earlier," said Lynsye says sitting up and gently waking Missy from her lap.

The nurse came in and closed the door behind her. As she went to close it, the Admiral walks in too, every one stands at a lazy attention.

"Well, how is he?" Mark asks.

The nurse sighs. "He's still in critical condition, we will be keeping him in ICU. He's in a minor coma, he did respond earlier, but that was over an hour ago." explained the nurse.

"Can we see him?" asked Missy.

"Yes I'll take you there," she said leading the way with her hand.

They exited the room and headed over to a different floor. They entered the room, and everyone turned white. The mood was more unsettling than a funeral home. I lay there with a dozen or more tubes coming out of my legs, chest, and arms. I could almost be mistaken as a science project.

"Man I've always wondered how they made Darth Vader." Mark said, and Lynsye punched him in the arm.

As the girls get all teary eyed, the Admiral walked over to my bed, and sat in the chair next to me.

"Your Mom and Dad are going to kill me when they find out what I let happen to you. It was my idea for you to join the Military, and after the War, I figured you'd quit, but you wanted to stay." The Admiral said with his head down.

29

"You know his parents?" Missy asked.

"He's his uncle, didn't you know that?" Mark said.

"Oh shit," said Missy.

4 days later.

"Well at last they took all of them tubes out of him, and he's in a better room," said Mark sitting on the couch with a magazine in his hands.

"You know what, we still haven't met the doctor that did all the work on him," Lynsye said, then taking a sip out of her coffee.

"Yea, your right," Mark said, then was interrupted by the door opening.

A young girl wearing a large white coat, with glasses and bright blond and blue hair comes in.

"I'm so sorry. I've been under the gun lately and never had a chance to come in and see him or you guys," said the young doctor.

"Yea, we were just talking about that," said Mark.

"It seems like there has been a rise in accidents, and homicides lately," said the girl looking at the team. Then she starts to walk over to my bed.

"He still had his helmet on so I didn't get a chance to see."

The doctor came to a pause looking at me. The doctor looked like as if she seen a ghost.

The team looks at each other.

"Have you guys met before?" Mark asked, as everyone looked at the doctor.

"Um..." muttered the young girl.

"Looks like love at first sight to me, hee hee," Missy says giggling.

"Um, no, no, um, I have to run a test here so I'm going to have to ask you guys to leave for a few minutes if you could please," she said to the team and pointed towards the door.

"Sure no problem," Lynsye said raising her eye brow.

Everyone gets up and leaves the room. Missy closes the door behind her. Then everyone jumps to the door and puts their ears on the door to hear what's going on inside the room.

The Doctor has her hands to her face looking at my comatose body.

"You gotta be kidding me," she says walking over to the bed.

"I saw you the other night, no it can't be. Military personal aren't allowed to even go to places like that," she said looking at me.

"Mmm. What? Mark is that you?" I started to come to.

"Oh shit!" said the doctor, as she grabs the chart and puts in front of her face. She turns towards the door.

"I can't let him see me," she thinks to herself and opens the door and everyone falls in from listening.

"Um, you can see him now, he's actually awake," the doctor says smiling as she walks into the hall and goes over to the nurses' station. Mark, Lynsye and Missy walk into the room, grabbing a part of me like a giant toy.

"We thought you were done," Missy said all teary eyed.

31

"Where am I?" I asked.

"You're in the hospital," Mark replies.

"Who saved me?" Looking around getting my eyes to focus.

"We found you adrift by one of Jupiter's Moons. The Explosion from the two Dreadnoughts pushed you way out," said Missy.

"Who did I get for a doctor?" I said looking at my hospital wrist band.

"I'll go get her," Lynsye says getting up and runs out the door.

"She?" I said raising an eye brow.

"Yea man, she's a hottie!" Mark says with his hand on my shoulder.

"Come on, Miss Doctor Lady," Lynsye say struggling.

"HEY! Come on, let go," The doctor says being dragged into the room.

As she was dragged into my sight, you could hear a pin drop in the entire hospital. My eyes opened up like I had a near death experience again.

"Hey guys, can we get a minute alone," I asked, everyone staring at the female doctor, or should I say Anesthesia. The stripper I met down in sector seven the other day.

"Ok?" Mark says. Once again everyone leaves the room. Lynsye closes the door behind her, and everyone looks at each other and jumps to the door and listens.

Back in the room we stare at each other. Almost as if it was first love, but that wasn't the case, maybe more like we both just saw a ghost.

"Anesthesia?" I said looking at her.

"Shit, you do remember me."

"Holy shit you're a," I say getting interrupted.

"What the hell were you doing down there. Why the hell, how the hell, oh my god, what the fudge? I need to sit down," the young girl says and sits next to my bed and looks at me. She sat with her hands on her face as if she was trying to hide from a photo shoot.

"Please you can't tell anyone, even them."

"Hey, I'm in the same boat. This is weird though, kind of funny," I said interrupting her.

"So how long have you worked down there and been a doctor?"

"I've been a doctor for about three years now. I came up with UV gel 34 for your skin."

"No kidding, I use that all the time when I go to the beaches on Mars. But wait, didn't you make out big with that? I mean you shouldn't have to work down in the slums if you made something that great."

"Wait, don't change the subject. What are we going to do about our little problem here," she said grabbing the side of the hospital bed.

33

Looking at her face, then looking a little lower at her name badge.

"I take it that your real name is Kat"

"Oh yea, Anesthesia is just my dancers name," Kat says rubbing her leg.

We chatted for a short little bit and she left the room. The team slowly walked back into the room.

"So what was that all about?" Lynsye asked smiling at me.

"Don't worry about it, she had to ask me some personal questions." I said with a goofy grin on my face.

"Pimp Down!" Said Mark.

The next day, Kat comes into my hospital room and sits next to me.

"Well you are being discharged today, I bet you're ready to go home," Kat says smiling at me.

"Yea, by the way I know this is going to sound strange, but since we kinda know each other a little bit already," getting interrupted.

"I know where this is going, don't even ask it," Kat says shaking her head.

"How do you know what I'm going to ask?"

"You're going to ask me out! yada yada blah blah. The answer is NO," Kat says to me with her arms crossed.

"Why, is it because I know you're a stripper?" I replied crossing my arms.

34

"That was uncalled for," Kat says in a bad mood, getting up and leaving the room.

"Why did I say that, I mean come on, she was really nice and ya done blew it, dumb ass," I said to myself hitting my hand on my head.

Later Mark came to pick me up, and as I rolled down the hall way, I saw Kat. She looked at me and turned away.

"I take it something isn't working between you to?" Mark asks.

"Yea kind of," I replied looking down towards the floor like I lost a battle.

Chapter 4

<u>The best seat in the house.</u>

The following day, really late at night, I came down to check out my fighter. I was sitting on the wing just looking around.

"What's up with you, you've been acting kind of weird. On top of that it's so late, what are you doing down here?" asked Mittens, hopping on the wing with me.

"Eh," I muttered sitting there sulking.

"Girl problems, yup I can see it, so who's the unlucky girl this time?" Mittens asked, putting her elbow on my shoulder.

"Don't worry about it, she's probably got someone else anyways," I said.

"Oh come on, you can tell me. Look what we went thru on your last relationship. I thought you were going to kill me with info I had on the last hoe. Come on, what's bothering you?" Mittens asks me with determination.

"Can you keep a secret?"

"Sure." said Mittens, eyes opening up like she's getting a gift of a life time.

"I mean, this could get me in some serious shit."

"You know I can. Wait, did they give you the wrong blood in the hospital and you have AIDS?" Mittens said smiling.

"What? No. You know the doctor that healed me?"

"Yea Doctor Katie Marilee," Mittens said.

"Well I did a bad thing and went to sector 7. I saw her there."

"Yea, so what, she was in the slums, probably at the old market place. I go there all the time to get medicine for Jeffery," said Mittens.

"Well, I guess you could say she has an extra job."

"Like what?" Mitten's asked.

"She's a stripper." Then Mittens slapped me across the face.

"Don't say that about her. She's a respectable woman, she created that cream that cured skin cancer," Mittens said, looking at me, angry and beating her fist on the wing.

"Here look at this." I hand her that card, and start to explain everything that happened that led up until now.

A few minutes later.

"Wow she's a stripper," Mitten says looking down her thermos.

"Yea," I replied with my head in my shirt looking like a turtle.

"Well, hmmm, never done that before, I guess this is all new territory for me," Mittens said, looking at me.

"I wanna show her there's more to life than being half doctor and half stripper."

"Maybe she's got real problems or something. Heck, maybe she gets off on that. You never know nowadays. Look at Lynsye and Missy, they're a gay couple. I can't believe they follow you, a male, into a fight some times." said Mittens

"WHAT WAS THAT?" Lynsye yells from across the hanger.

"NEVER MIND!!!! STAY ON YOUR SIDE OF THE HANGER!!!" screamed Mittens, sticking her tongue out.

"I need to find out something, I know she's better than that," I said hitting the wing with my fist.

"Oh no, what are you planning to do?" said Mitten's giving me a serious look.

"I'm going to go help her, I hope. Wish me Luck!" I said jumping off of the fighter and running to the exit.

"I hope I didn't induce anything stupid," said Mitten's shaking her head.

I run to my apartment nearly knocking down the door. I kick off my shoes and jump in the closet and pull out the old clothing from Colin.

"I hope I know what I'm doing," I said to myself throwing my clothing on like I'm going to war. As I get ready, I look outside of my window and I see the Jump Gate in orbit. Staring at it like it's trying to tell me something, I ran out of my apartment checking my watch.

38

"They close in less than an hour I can make it," I said to myself.

Jumping on the late night express train, I noticed the jump gate again. Thinking to myself maybe it's trying to tell me something still, but what? Looking around on the train, for once there were a few people riding it. Arriving at Sector six, I ran over to the elevator shaft.

"What the hell, its welded shut?" I said trying to tugging on the door trying to rip it open. I look around service area and see people heading towards another alley.

"There's must be another way in," I said jogging thru the crowd. As I was jogging thru looking around, I was in the slums of the space station. People were making deals for food, and other goods. People standing around fire barrels trying to keep warm. In one part, people were floating around because the station had no gravity in that area. I noticed a small alley with lots of smoke coming out of it.

"That's got to be it."

I went over to the alley and moved the dark red curtain and sure enough, there was the back alley street. Walking in and heading towards the club, I started to notice everything was already closed or closing down. As I came around the corner I heard a door bust open.

"I'm done working here, I'm tired of this crap and I paid you back in full. We're done! I'm no longer your slave!" a familiar female voice screamed.

"You're never free unless you're sold, and who's going to buy a cheap hussy like you?" a male voice said.

I looked around the corner and there was Kat surrounded by three large men and a guy dressed in a suit.

"Oh shit," I said and stepped back and knocked over some crates. The crates crash down and reveal me, dumb ass.

"Hi, I was just passing by and now I'm going to go, bye!" I said smiling, but as I turned to go the other way a bouncer came from behind me and grabbed me.

"Hey, what's the big idea!" I said trying to free myself from the bouncer.

"Who the hell are you? What are you doing in my alley?" said the man in the suit.

"I just took a wrong turn, I was looking for a hot dog."

"Oh my god, Ichia what are you doing here?" Kat says interrupting me.

"Oh, I see, boyfriend, you're not allowed to have one of those without my consent," said the man in the suit. Then he slaps Kat across the face and she falls to the ground.

"Take care of him boys," said the man in the suit, as he lifted a cigar to his mouth and grabbed Kat by the arm.

"Come on bitch, you belong to us, not this little gook," said the man in the suit, as he dragged Kat back into the club.

"Bullshit, jack ass!" I screamed and flipped the bouncer into the dumpster.

"She's coming with me!!" I yelled and pointed at the man.

"No one talks to me like that kid," said the man in the suit. The man pulls out a gun, and points it towards me. I stand my ground, fists tight at each side, waiting for my moment.

"You're in my world kid, I own this place," said the man in the suit.

"You're a cowardly, stupid, chicken curry-eating Dune Coon!!!" screamed Kat kicking the man in the shin.

I look to my right and see that a bar over the door is holding the roof over the man in the suit.

"Yea, and I own the space around Jupiter, Beyotch!" I said, and ran into the bar, collapsing the roof. Kat jumped out of the way and the man in the suit was crushed. I ran over to kick one of the bouncers in the head and then I grabbed Kat and ran like hell.

"I'll get you one way or.. or.. another kid, said the man in the suit.

"The only thing you're going to get is, thrown into space," I said and then I kicked him in the face.

"Let go of me," said Kat as she pulls her arm away from me.

"Come on, let's get out of here," I said to Kat pointing at the exit.

"I'm not going with you, I'm going to my home. I need to get away from here, and fast," Kat says as she picks up her purse.

"Listen I'm not looking to get laid, or have a girlfriend. Well, maybe a girlfriend. I wanna get you out of here too, to a better place," I pleaded to Kat and we both paused.

"You don't even know me!"

"Well that's a good thing, right? Let me at least walk you home." I asked as Kat shakes her head.

"You really are a tough one. What don't you understand? Look at what just happened, when he wakes up he's coming after me." Kat shouted at me.

"Well, with luck we shook him up enough where he should leave you alone." I said.

"He's a mob boss, he only fears the gods and demons," said Kat.

"Good, I just happen to be one of those. Now let's get outta here."

"Fine, you can take me home but that's it. After this don't try and find me or even come here again," Kat said crossing her arms.

"Well for your sake, I hope you stop working here."

We started to walk back out to the main street where I had came in from. It was rather dark with all of the bars closed, but the smoke still lingered in the air. The only thing lighting the way were single lamps every few feet.

"Which way from here?" I asked.

"Straight and to the right, I live in sector seven," said Kat

"In seven!" I said and paused.

"Yea, I live in the slums. I can't afford anything better like you probably can, Mister Military. I live in the Projects," Kat said to me.

I gulped as we headed over to the train station in Sector Six. For once the train was actually loaded with people. At first Kat was going to sit by herself, then she saw all of the old people, and bums floating around asking for change. She sat next to me instead. I rested my head against the glass.

"I hope that guy didn't see my face, he heard my namethough.

Eh, should be, with good luck he's paralyzed," I thought.

We arrived in sector 7. As we headed over to her apartment, we were walking to Main street. There were lots of medical vehicles moving in and out of the area.

Then we turned to her street and it was blocked off by the police.

"What's going on?" Kat asked one of the officers.

"Pressure Failure, not everyone managed to get out, but people won't be able to return home probably until tomorrow," said the officer.

"What?" Kat said, falling to her knees and starts to cry.

"I can't take this anymore," Kat said sobbing on the ground, punching her fist to the ground.

I picked Kat up off of the ground and walk her over to a bench by a digital park.

"Can my life get any worse?" says Kat wiping her eyes.

"Um" I tried to say something, but then I looked out of the large window in the street, and saw the Jump Gate again. I thought about it, I just might have a great idea on how to make her smile again.

"I know how to cheer you up, come on," I said kneeling down in front of her.

"Just, get me drunk and let me pass out and die," Kat replied.

"Um no, how close have you ever been to Jupiter?" I ask with a smile.

"What?" Kat says looking at me funny.

"Jupiter the planet?" I said.

"I've only seen it in photos, why?" Kat asks.

"Come on," I say holding Kats' hand walking back to the express train.

"Wait, quit pulling me, I can walk on my own you know. What do you have in mind?" Kat asks with a worried look on her face.

"You'll see," I said smiling at her.

We walk back over to the train station. We get on the express train and grab a seat.

"Where are we going?" asked Kat again, getting frustrated with me.

45

"You'll see, we're going to get off at the next stop, just follow me and stay behind me, okay?"

Kat looks at me like I'm crazy. We get off at the main hanger bay, where the military crafts are located. Walking up to the security gate, the guard is sleeping.

"Get behind me and duck." I said.

"What?" said Kat as I pushed her behind me.

"Hey, let me in," I holler to the Guard.

"Huh what? Oh it's you, what's up, what are you doing down here so late?" Asked the guard.

"I wanted to check something out on my ship, and talk to Mittens."

"Okay, you can go in," said the guard yawning falling back asleep.

Kat and I made it past the guard. We headed over to my fighter. I walked thru the supplies bunker, so no one would see us. Coming around Lynsye and Missy's bomber, we come up to my fighter.

"Wow, this is yours?" Kat asks.

"Yup, this my fighter, here hop in," I said and giving her a boost.

"Hey, don't look up my skirt." Said Kat.

"I'm not," I said, then I saw that Mittens was coming over.

"Shit, get it in,m" I said in a hurry pushing Kat into the cock pit, as Mittens came over.

"HEY! Ouch!" Kat fell into the seat.

46

"Hey Ichia, what the heck are you going on the flight deck at this hour again?" Mittens asked, as I smiled like a kid who stole candy.

"Did I see someone with you just a second ago? Asked Mittens, as Kat peaked over the console to see what was going on.

"Naw, you probably just saw my shadow or something."

"Yea, you're probably right, I'm tired tonight and this damn baby in my belly," said Mittens.

"So can I take her, I mean my fighter out for a spin?"

"I don't care, it's your ship, just don't break anything. It took me forever to fix your clutch system from last time. Oh yea, your new FTL drive is installed and running at hundred percent." said Mittens.

"Thanks Mittens I owe you one," I said climbing into the cock pit of the fighter.

"It's all good, use strip 3 for takeoff, see you later," Said Mittens waving to me.

"See ya Mittens."

"Wow, who was that?" asked Kat crouching down in the cock pit.

"A very good friend. Here, sit in my lap so we can get a move on," I said to Kat.

"I'm not going to sit in your, HEY" Said Kat as I closed the cock pit, almost hitting Kat's head.

"Just stay low until I get us out of the hanger, okay."

47

"Don't get any ideas." said Kat with an angry look on her face, sitting between my legs.

I turned a little red after she said that. I moved my ship into the third strip in the hanger and took off thru the tunnel. We were now moving fast down a long tunnel, making our way outside of the space station.

"Look ahead, there's the Jump Gate, get ready for a little jump," I said flying through free space, passing other ships, and small satellite billboards.

"Oh god, this is my first jump." said Kat clinging onto me.

"Is this going to hurt?" she asks.

"Don't worry, you won't feel a thing, just stay calm, you'll be okay," I said.

"Tower this is J-007 permission to jump to Jupiter please." I said over the com.

"J7 fighter 007 you are clear for outer rim jump to Jupiter," said jump operator.

"Ready?" I asked Kat.

"No." said Kat.

3...2.....1.... BOOM

"OH MY GOD, ARE WE DEAD?" screamed Kat.

"If we are, we have the best seats in the house. Take a look, come on look," I said softly, holding Kat.

Kat looks up at me, then turns around to see the gas giant Jupiter right next to us. We are in orbit around Jupiter, right in front of the great red spot. It almost looks like a beast was staring at us like we were nothing to it. Kat gasps, "Wow, It's beautiful. I've never seen anything like this," Kat said holding my hands tightly.

"Yup, this is what I get to see almost every other day," I said steering the ship.

"This is amazing, I've only seen pictures of Jupiter, I never thought I'd be this close to the planet."

"This is nothing, hang on," I said pulling on the throttle bringing the engines to life.

"Where are we going? Slow down!" said Kat clinching onto my shirt.

"We're going to the moon of Ganime, to see the ocean we're building out here," I said.

"Ocean?" Kat asks.

"Yup."

We fly away from Jupiter just a little bit and come to a small rock known as Ganime. On the surface you can see machines making the air breathable and turning the ice into water. The moon has a thin haze around it, also starting to form are clouds. Large lakes can also be seen from our view.

"Wow, that's amazing. Is that a planetary reconstruction crew?" Kat asked.

"You bet it is. This is one of the great things we are protecting out here," I said as Kat sat there and leaned into my lap, like a kitten getting comfortable on a pillow.

"I'm glad you brought me out here, this is so amazing." Kat said snuggling into me.

"So can we call this our first date?" I asked.

"I think so, no one has ever done anything like this for me before. Most of my first dates were at bars or restaurants," Kat said.

We flew around Jupiter's Orbit and drifted for a while enjoying the wonders of the gas giant.

"Well shall we head for home?" I ask.

"Sure, your place sounds good for tonight, since my home is out of air at the moment. I hope you keep your place clean," Kat said sarcastically.

"I try, the kitchen is clean, as for the bedroom, maybe a little iffy," I replied.

I fire up the FTL and jump us back to the space station. We land back into the hanger. We made it back at a good time, everyone on third shift is on their lunch break. I help Kat down from the fighter, and then walk quickly out of the hanger bay before any one comes back from lunch. We hopped back onto an empty express train, which is usually somewhat packed full of third shifters.

"Where is everyone tonight?" I said looking around at all of the empty seats.

"Yea, it's usually full, sometimes I get off at this hour from the hospital and ride this train home," Kat said.

As the train was going up to the station we could see the Jump Gate, orbiting the Earth, with the moon in the distance.

"You live up here? How much are they paying you?" Kat asks, walking on the balcony of apartment complex.

"Not enough, sometimes I don't know how I make it. Try to be quiet, my friend Mark has an apartment above me, he might come out and start asking questions," I said very quietly, pulling out my keys

"Oh sorry," Kat whispers.

I open the door and we enter the room. It's a little chilly, and the kitchen light is on and clothing is scattered around.

"Home sweet home, it's not much, but it's got everything I need," I said.

51

"Someone's a little messy," Said Kat looking around at all of the clothing scattered around.

"Well, I had to act fast to find you tonight." I said, picking up some clothing and throwing them into the corner by a basket.

Kat walks over to the large window in my apartment and looks out the window. She looks down and she can see the center disc of the station where the hanger and hospital is.

"So are we going to sleep together?" Kat asked turning around looking at me.

"Um no, you can have my bed, I'm going to sleep on my couch," I said while fluffing a pillow.

"Are you sure?" asked Kat.

"Yea, I figured you could use a bed by yourself tonight. Your day was a little rougher than mine. Oh, by the way I never asked, does your face hurt from being slapped? I totally forgot," I asked.

"I'm fine now. I was too pissed off and miserable to care at the time," Kat said as she slipped into the bed and took off her dress under the sheets, as I turned around on the couch taking off my hoody.

"Well, good night Kat," I said.

"You know I didn't say thank you." said Kat

"You're welcome, good night, I hope I see you in the morning," I said yawning.

"Don't worry I don't really have anywhere else to go," Kat said.

"Good point," I replied

We fell asleep. Kat was cozy in the bed while I was a little chilled on the couch. A few hours later, Kat woke up and tiptoed over to the fridge in her underwear to find something to drink. She opened the door; inside was beer, eggs, something in a can, and a head of lettuce.

"Great, he doesn't even have, oh good, he does have bottled water," Kat said as she moved the case of beer over. She found some bottles of water and had a drink. Kat looked over at me and noticed I was sleeping on the floor, without a sheet.

"What the hell, he must have fallen off the couch, he'll catch a cold," Kat said looking at me shaking her head. Kat looked around the apartment. Rubbing her hands and arms trying to get a little warmth, it was rather cold in the apartment.

"Good, he has this option in his apartment." Kat said while she turned off the gravity in the room to move me over to the bed. She gently picked me up and pushed me to the bed and laid me down. Then she turned the gravity back on, and went back to the bed.

"Okay, don't get any ideas buddy." Kat said while pulling the covers over us and holding me ever so gently in her arms.

Chapter 5

<u>My day off with I hope my new girlfriend.</u>

I woke up to Kat wearing my uniform fleece and cooking some breakfast. I look around and wonder how I got in the bed, and then I look back over to Kat.

"Hey, what's shaken bacon?" I said while yawning.

"Good morning, I figured since you were so kind to me yesterday, I'd make you breakfast," Kat said smiling and winking towards me wearing my fleece.

"Nice coat by the way," I said smiling.

"It feels nice too, oh, by the way I'm impressed you actually have food in your house," said Kat.

"Yea, it's all military food. It's okay, after a while you'll get sick of canned eggs and sausage." I said walking over to Kat, then leaning on the counter.

"So, how did I get into the bed? I thought I was on the couch last night?" I asked looking at Kat as she started to blush.

"Well, you were lying on the floor shivering, I couldn't let you freeze. So I turned off the gravity and put you into the bed," Kat said with a bright red face looking at the slowly cooking eggs.

"I told you, you're amazing. At first I thought maybe I sleepwalked to the bed," I said softly putting my arms around Kat.

"Hey, I'm still trying to cook here, don't get any ideas bud," Kat says holding onto my arms.

As we cuddled and cooked for a minute there was someone knocking on the door.

"Hmm, I wonder who that is," I said walking over to the door.

I open the door to find my entire team. Lynsye, Missy, and Mark were standing outside.

"Dude, you can smell the food all the way down the hall, what are you, oh." said Lynsye looking over at Kat, as if she already knew the whole story.

"What are you doing here doctor lady?" asked Missy.

"Please tell me you got pictures!!" said Mark, then Lynsye slaps Mark in the back of his head.

"It's not like that," I said scratching the back of my head, as Kat walks over.

"I guess you can call me his new girlfriend," Kat said putting her arms around my waste.

I turn towards her thinking to myself, really, with a smile on my face.

"Boy you're turning red there, do you have enough oxygen?" ask Lynsye.

"Come on in, I made a lot," Kat said.

Everyone came in. Missy and I pulled out the kitchen table from the wall and set up the chairs. Lynsye and Kat pulled out the plates and brought the food to the table, as Mark got the drinks.

"This looks really good for being military food," Mark said.

"Thanks," Kat replied.

"Yea how the hell did you turn military food into something edible?" asked Lynsye.

"And to top that, you made enough for seconds." Mark said.

"I like to cook when I get the chance, and I always make extra for some reason." Kat said.

"Come on, let's eat before it gets cold," I said smiling at Kat.

I looked at Kat and how everyone enjoyed her company. I felt I saved her life, and wanted to do something for her. Maybe take her to a Lunar game, or get her to move out of her apartment to mine. Then I thought maybe I'm thinking too much ahead, maybe I just better eat and figure that out later. I still couldn't stop looking at her. Staring at Kat, like an angel who just saved me from a crash.

"You okay? You haven't really touched your plate," Kat asked.

"Sorry, I'm just happy that I met you." I said, as everyone looked at us like we were two newlyweds.

"So when's the Wedding?" asked Missy, as Kat and I turn bright red, then everyone laughs at us.

After breakfast.

"Hey Ichia, on Friday we're getting our fifth person right?" asked Lynsye.

"Oh yea, that's right, thanks for reminding me." I said.

"Well, we'll leave you two love birds alone, see ya," Mark said walking out the door.

"That was a lot of fun, you have great friends," said Kat.

"They're more like family," I said placing the dishes in the washer.

"Don't you have any family?" Kat asked.

"My parents really don't talk to me much. They're upset that I joined the military after high school. They wanted me to stay on Mars and go to school at State," I said.

"Sorry things turned out that way," Kat said putting her hands on my shoulders.

"I try not to think of it. Anyway I have my own place, great friends and hopefully, well you know," I said looking at Kat.

"I wish I lived in a place like this, I'd be so much closer to the hospital." Kat said.

I turned to Kat, wiping my hands on a towel.

"I know we just met and all, but why don't you? I have plenty of room," I said.

"Listen I don't want to rush things, you're my first boyfriend in a long time," Kat said.

"It's okay, I just thought you might want to get out of where you're at. But you're always welcome to stay here," I said with a warm smile.

"Speaking about home, I'd better get back. I have to work at the hospital tonight," said Kat

"Yea, I have to get ready for tomorrow, we're getting a new team member," I said as Kat put a pair of my pants on.

"Hey, I'm going to borrow your clothing. Here, call me when you get back." Kat said kissing me on the cheek and handing me her doctor's card.

"Yea, here's my number, if I'm flying you can reach me here as well." I said holding Kats hand.

"Well, thank you for everything," Kat said smiling at me.

"No, thank you, I know things are going to be better," I said.

58

"Well, see you later, I'll call you when I get off. Maybe if you're not busy we can go out or something," Kat said throwing her purse over her shoulder.

"Sounds good to me," I replied, opening the door for Kat as she walked out. We walked into the hall where Lynsye, Missy and Mark were looking our way and turned around like nothing was going on.

"I get it, ha ha ha." I said.

"I'll see ya," Kat said kissing me on the cheek again. Kat walked away and for some reason I couldn't turn away from looking at her walk away.

"I saw that," Lynsye said poking me in the shoulder.

"Saw what?" I asked shrugging my shoulders.

"You were looking at her butt," Missy said.

"Yeah, so." I said.

"How was it?" asked Mark.

"GODS DAMNIT! WE DIDN'T DO ANY THING!" I yelled.

"Geez, calm down kid, we're just kidding," said Lynsye grinning with her arms crossed.

9:00pm Oh how the time flies

So I'm sitting on my bed, closing my duffel bag which is packed with snacks and extra clothing.

"Alright, all packed for my weekend. I wonder, what," I said being interrupted by the phone ringing.

"Yello?" I said.

59

"Hey it's me," Kat said sniffling on the other end of the phone call.

"Are you okay?" I asked standing up from my bed.

"I got a slight problem, you still got room over there?" asked Kat.

"For you, of course I do, what's up?" I asked.

"Can you come over now, please?" asked Kat sniffling.

Thinking to myself, "wow she said please," something must have went wrong?

"Yea, I'll be over in a few minutes."

"Okay thanks, I'll see ya," said Kat.

"Alright see you in a few," I said hanging up the phone.

I jumped to action, grabbed my keys, my brown hooded fleece and went out the door. I locked my apartment door quickly and ran down the hall. As I locked up and ran away Mark just happened to see me run away.

"The wedding must be over," said Mark to himself.

I jumped on the express train and headed over to sector seven. As I went to sit down, I leaned back on the bench and read a sign that said, "Keep Clear."

"I keep trying," I said to myself.

Arriving at the Sector Seven Train Stop, I hopped off of the train and jogged over to where Kats apartment is. Running over, thru the main street I stopped.

"Wait, I don't even know which one it is, I'll call her."

I pulled out my cell phone and called Kat. She gave me directions to the back of the third complex on the right. Then I headed up to the fifth floor. Finally getting up to the fifth floor I tried to catch my breath.

"Damn. *Heave Heave* That's a lot of stairs," I said trying to catch my breath.

I continue over to Kats apartment and find that the door is open slightly, I knock on it and it opens. Kat is sitting a chair in the middle of the room.

"Hey, what's up?" I ask.

"Things are getting worse," Kat said while sobbing with her face in her hands.

"Hey, it's alright. I'm here what can I do to help? First of all what's going on?" I asked trying to calm down Kat.

"Remember last night?" asked Kat wiping her eyes.

"Yea, there was a breach," I said.

"Well, they are evicting everyone, on top of that, they won't give us our deposits. I don't have enough for a new apartment. I have to renew my Ph D. license before I can go back to work tonight. For some reason they said I didn't re-file it last year. Then I promised two of my patients that I'd be in tonight before they were discharged. My life was just flushed down the toilet in less than twenty four hours," Kat said rambling on. I was looking over her license renewal information.

61

"Hmmmm, I got this." I said pulling out my phone and sending a couple of texts to someone. As Kat kept crying, I kept my hand on her shoulders, lightly messaging them.

"I take it those two boxes are your belongings," I asked Kat.

"Yes, Why?" asked Kat looking up at me, with teary eyes.

"First, you are coming with me but before we leave. In about." I said was interrupted by the door opening.

"Hi, you are Mr. Chang?" said a short man with a beanie on his head.

"Yup." I replied

"I'm so sorry, I didn't know this was…" the man said then I interrupted him.

"Just give me the damn money." I said.

"Uh.. uh here sir. I'm very sorry please it won't happen again. I'll make sure to file my new goods to the military for our next shipment," said the man.

"Good, I'll see you in another week, behave yourself." I said to the man, and then the man bowed and walked out quickly. Kat sat there looking like "what the hell." She looked in her right hand, it was two thousand dollars in cash, which was her original deposit.

"What the hell, was that? How, who, what are you," Says Kat standing up backing away from me.

"I'm helping you out. Come on lets go to my place," I said picking up the heavier box.

"W-wait, Why?" asked Kat.

"It's simple, I really like you, Duh," I said with a goofy face.

Kat wiped her eyes looking at me, not sure what to expect next from me. I clearly had a unpredictable plan to help this girl I enjoyed being with. She picked up the other box and didn't even turn to look back at the apartment. As we got onto the train to go to my place, she leaned her head on my shoulder.

"I hope I know what I'm doing," Kat said.

"Yea, me too," I said.

We finally got back to my apartment. We set the boxes down and sat down on the couch.

"So, what exactly did you do?" asked Kat.

"Well, I looked over your bill and I knew the name of your leaser. I've been doing him favors keeping his shipments safe from the pirates around Jupiter," I said.

"It's sad, I wonder how many people he ripped off?" asked Kat.

"Who knows. All I know is if I see him in a convoy I'm not going to double my efforts to help him out." I said looking at Kat and holding her hand.

"You wouldn't happen to have a washing machine and dryer would you?" asked Kat.

"Yea, I do it's in the wall by the bathroom, I have to wash some clothing. We can put ours together. The washer takes a little bit, but the dryer is fast," I said picking up a basket of clothing next to the couch. We started to put our clothing into the washing machine. I showed her how to work the machines.

"How do I use your shower?" Kat asked.

"Oh, push the button that looks like fountain, and the shower will come out of wall by the toilet," I said pointing at the console.

"Oh I see, thanks, and no peeking," Kat says pointing at me.

"I'll try," I said smiling.

Kat goes into the shower, and I think to himself. "This is the first girl to ever shower in my apartment." I walked over to the fridge to get a drink. I opened the door to look for some milk.

"Damn, it's out of date. I'll go run out to the store real quick." I said.

I left a note on the couch for Kat letting her know I went to the store. Lucky the store was on the same floor of the station. I jogged over to the market passing the video game store, passing the flower shop, then stopping. Thinking that might be a good idea on the way back. I kept going, and some people waved to me.

"Hey looking better Ichia," a man said sitting on a bench in front of the store.

"Thanks," I said jogging into the store. As I walked in I saw Mittens with Jeffery.

"Hey guys, what's up?" I asked.

"Not much just feeding my army here," Jeffery said laughing.

"Ha ha, yea well you're not the one with a bomb ready to pop out," Mittens said holding her precious cargo.

"Good to see you guys out and about," I said.

"What are you up to?" Mittens asked.

"Oh, I just wanted to get some milk," I said.

We talked for a little bit, and I bought some milk and headed back to my apartment. But first I stopped by the flower shop and picked up two tiger lily flowers for Kat.

"For a special someone, Ichia?" a young lady asked.

"Yea, for a change," I said.

"That's good to hear, here you go, have a good one," the young lady said handing me my change and receipt.

"Thanks," I said then jogged back to my apartment.

Arriving back home, I came in and Kat was already dressed for work.

"Hey, there, what do you have there? Oh, for me?" Kat asked with a savory look on her face.

"Yea I figured it might cheer you up a little more," I said while pouring some milk into a glass.

"I'm happy already with what you've done. What makes me more happy is that you got some more milk. I like to have a little after a hot shower," Kat said.

"Why's that?" I asked taking a drink from my glass.

"It makes my breasts bigger." Kat says smiling.

I laugh and milk comes out of my nose. Kat laughs at me, and brings me a paper towel. She wipes the milk from my face.

"Even with milk on your face you're still cute. Well ,I'm going to take some to go, I'm going to be late for work," Kat said pouring milk in to a water bottle.

"What time do you get off?" I asked.

"Around 11pm, but sometimes not until 2am," Kat said.

"Alright well give me a call when you get out." I said.

"Okay, see ya" Kat said, going out the door.

I stood in my apartment. "Wow smells like female perfume in here now," I said.

Chapter 6

The New Comer.

I jumped out of my fighter after landing on the Delphinus, standing and looking up at the hanger. The hanger was huge, like being inside of an enclosed football field, but with ships going in and out. I headed over to the Master Chiefs office.

"Good morning commander," said the Master Chief

"Morning, I'm checking in to pick my team member."

"Yea, he or she will arrive at 15:00 hrs, and your rack is in 108. Also your uncle wanted to talk to you as well," the Chief said shuffling papers.

"Ok thanks Chief."

I headed down to the crew quarters.

"Wow, I forgot how big this place was, and cramped," I thought to myself in a cramped elevator. Leaving the elevator, I headed down a small hall way to room 108.

"Ah, room 108," I said looking at the door.

"Commander Chang, Engineer Colby? Hmm, okay?" I said unlocking the sliding door.

I came into a very small room with two racks. The racks have sliding doors for privacy and the top on is closed. Next to the racks is a mini bathroom and shower. Each rack is small and compact but complete with fridge and mini micro-wave.

"Well this is cozy, I'm guessing Engineer Colby took the top bunk," I said sitting down on the bed.

"I guess I'll start unpacking my things." I open a drawer and look twice.

"Panties? What the hell," I say as the door to the room slides open and a girl with short red hair comes in.

"WHAT THE HELL! WHO ARE YOU AND WHY ARE YOU IN MY UNDERWEAR!!!!!" she screams at me.

"Whoa!!! Wait, wait, wait, this ain't what it looks like it is," I tried to explain. Then the girl comes up to me and decks me across the face and kicks the drawer shut.

"What are you doing here? Never mind I'm going to the Chief to get a different room!!! Don't touch nothing! ASS HOLE!" she yells as she locks the drawer as I'm trying to pull myself off the floor.

"What the hell was that?" I said, staggering up, and the girl leaves the room.

"Gods damn, who was she? I thought it was only one sex rooms?" I said to myself.

I put my stuff away in the other drawers. Later on I get a text from Lynsye. "Hey get down to the galley, I found our new Team Member."

"Great, get to meet the new recruit with a bump on my head, I sigh, I'll talk to Master Chief later," I said locking the bunk room door.

I follow the wonderful smell of the galley through the ship. Coming into the galley, I grab a plate of the special General Tso Chicken and some iced tea. I walk out of the galley to the food court.

"Hey Ichia, over here!" Lynsye shouts while waving.

"Hey guys, what's up....." I stall, as the girl who just laid my ass out on the floor is sitting with Lynsye.

"Oh Shit!" the girl and I both say.

"Wait you're my new boss... Perv," the girl says to me.

"Whoa, hold up. I was assigned to that room and I just

69

happened to open that drawer because it was on my bunk." I said slamming my food to the table.

"Uh uh uh um....." the girl starts to get teary eyed.

"Good going Chang, you made her cry," Lynsye said.

"I'm sorry, I," I said then being interrupted.

"No I'm sorry, its just been hellaitous two weeks, I shouldn't have hit you like I did," the girl says sobbing.

"Its okay, I'm sure I deserved itm" I said.

"You guys probably don't want me any ways... I'll just," the girls says. Then I interrupted her.

70

"Shut up and drink you tea, what's your name anyways?" I ask taking big fork full of chicken.

"Casey Colby," Casey replies as she wipes her eyes with her sleeve.

"What flight group did you come from?" I asked.

"The Alpha, or as they say, the Alpha Male Squad," Casey replied taking a drink from her tea.

"Those guys are morons! They have the worst record ever!" Lynsye said.

"What were you doing on that team anyways?" I asked.

"I was suckered in as the mechanic, but they made me a pilot. I'm a good pilot but I'm better at fixing and building things," Casey said

"You fly a Rapier right?" I ask.

"Yea, RP40." Casey replied

"We'll make you better," I said smiling at her.

"Really? I'm good but I really need help on the flight tricks and stuff" Casey says.

"Are you talking like special maneuvers?" I ask.

"Yea, I can do 180's all day, but like the crazy dives, and pull outs. Hit the break kind of maneuvers, forget it," Casey says as she takes a drink from her juice box.

"We'll treat you like family, and not a piece of meat like the Alphas... oh shit, speak of the devils." Lynsye says taking her feet of the table.

The team looks to the right and the Alphas are walking out, tall and stupid. The Alphas walk in like they own the place, they walk over to the next table and start laughing at me and my team.

"The Heck You laughing at bitch?" I said leaning back in my chair.

"Your new recruit, you can have her dead weight ass, she just gets in the way," the leader says.

"The only dead weight around here is you, at least that's what your wife said as I was banging her with my strap on." Lynsye says.

"Oh, you wanna talk shit." the leader yells.

"Lets go Tiger Lilly!!!!" Lynsye yells kicking chairs out of the way, jumping onto the table in the middle of the galley.

"Behave yourselves!" says the Admiral standing in the door way of the galley.

"Oh shit, it's your uncle," Lynsye says.

"Crap," I mumble.

"Jupiter 7 Report to the bridge, your skills are needed," says the Admiral.

The team clears their food and follows the Admiral to the bridge.

"Well, I need the best, and the craziest team we have," the Admiral says with a face that could almost break a smile.

"What's going on?" I ask.

"Well, apparently the Lab Rats are out for revenge along with a new battle ship they've acquired. I need your team to knock out their relay dish and destroy their fuel depot.

Then we can clean up with the Delphinus. I'm sure you heard about the breach on the station. Yea, that was the Lab Rats stealing a new weapon from the mob. Not to mention, surveyors are mentioning scratching sounds, not sure if it mechanical or biological,"

"Well whatever you need, we can handle it," I said walking next to my uncle.

"Good, review the maps and briefing and report to the hanger at 03:00 hrs," the Admiral said.

"Yes sir," the team replied.

The team begins to walk off the bridge and the Admiral stops me.

"How have you been?" the Admiral asked.

"Well alright, mom says hi," I replied.

"I'm glad you're here, nice to have family onboard again," the Admiral said.

"Yea, I do miss the routine sometimes, have you heard from my dad?" I asked.

"He's still mad at me, he'll never let it go that I talked you into joining the military," my uncle says, looking at his watch.

"Well I did it for myself, I didn't want to be a politician," I said.

"Ha, yea that would just be curse in itself," said the Admiral.

"Well I'm going to go prep, I'll see you Uncle Hitoshi," I say saluting him.

"Good hunting," Hitoshi says saluting me back.

73

02:00 hrs

"So what do you think we'll find?" Mark asks me while suiting up.

"No clue, probably the usual, same thing different day," I said.

"Yea, crappy pirate pilots, and missiles that go boom," Lynsye says strapping her belts on her suit.

"Wow, you guys sound so confident," Casey says.

"We like to think of ourselves as the ghost busters. Someone saw a roach on twelve," Mark says leaning over Casey with his leg up and elbow on the wall.

"Never heard of the ghost busters, who are they?" Casey asks.

"Duhh FUCK?" the entire team says at the same time. You could almost hear a mouse fart it was so quite.

"Um, should I know this..." Casey says and pauses.

"We need to have a movie night Ichia," Mark says shaking his head.

"Yea sounds like it," I replied.

"Better get your new wife Ichia, hahahahah!" Missy says.

"Ha. Ha. Ha. Let's go people, we don't get paid by the hour," I said leading my team out of the ready room.

03:00 hrs

I look around at my team as everyone checks their consoles. Then I look out the hanger door towards the earth and the space station.

"I wonder what she's up to? Need to keep my head clear." I think to myself.

"Officer on Deck," The video engineer says.

"At ease people, Ichia is your team ready?" Admiral Hitoshi asks me walking over.

"Yes sir, we are packing major heat and with our new team member we're gonna blow them out of the stars," I reply.

"Good hunting people." The Admiral says.

Chapter 7

Saturn: Burn Baby Burn.

Jumping in just over Saturn's northern pole in the aurora. Jupiter 7 forms ups.

"Where's the party at?" Mark asks.

"Look over there," Casey says.

"Look at the size of that thing! That's two times the size of the Delphinus maybe bigger," Lynsye says.

"Whateves, the bigger they are, the bigger the boom. Mark, Casey, take out the relay, I'll handle the fuel depot and Lynsye, Missy give'em the Clap," I said forwarding power from my engines to my shields.

"10-4 little buddy!" Lynsye says.

"Rock n Roll," Mark says.

The team jumps in different directions, Mark and Casey head low to take out the relay. Meanwhile I'm causing a ruckus at the fuel depot. I'm flying super close to stations ground level, while ripping apart large drums to cause a massive explosion.

As I fly low, my finger is on the trigger. I guess I need to just tape it with the amount of spray I'm letting out here.

"Ichia don't get burned down...... OH SHIT!!!!! They're launching fighters!!!!!!!" Missy says turning the bomber hard right.

"Relays toasts we're on our way Missy!!!! Casey says over the com.

Missy and Lynsye take the first wave of the fighters head on. Missy is flying the bomber like a B52 in WWII and Lynsye is dropping fighters like flies in the gunner chair. Casey's covering Marks' back while taking out lead fighters. Mark hits the brakes as Casey uses the engine wash to cause two fighter to collide.

"Woo, that's how we roll!! Mark shouts.

"Hey, where's Ichia?" Casey asks.

"I'm a little busy at the depot!!!!" I yell through the com.

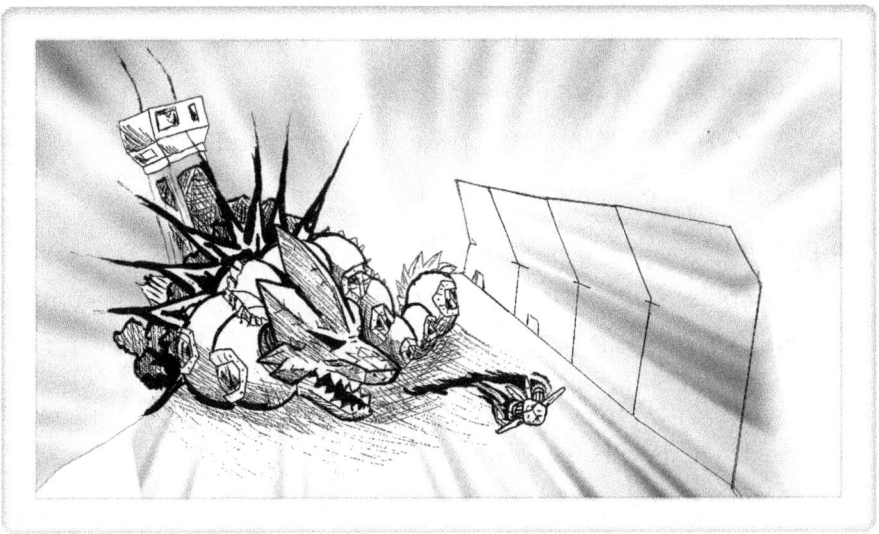

77

Everyone looks towards the depot and there's a large metallic snake creature chasing me. As I fly around, I'm firing missiles at tanks to damage to the snake-like creature. From the distance, it looks like a snake chasing a mouse.

"Holy Biologicial BATMAN!!!" Lynsye shouts.

"Help would be nice!!!" I yell over the com avoiding the large creature as it thrashes towards me.

"We're on our way!!" Casey screams.

Mark and Missy stay back to hold the fighter as Casey does a 180 and drops to me like a bat outta hell. I'm hauling ass in a long trench, with the pedal to the metal and the creature keeps snapping at me like I'm dinner. From up above Casey opens fire with everything she has. Casey manages to cause an explosion that knocks over large towers of fuel and impales the creature. The creature is squirming like a worm on a hook, I come around and fire a rocket right down its throat. The creature eats the rocket and turns its head like "huh", then its head blows off.

"Good shot!" Mark says.

"Woo Hoo, Yay!" Casey screams with her hands up in the air.

"Everyone back the hell up!!! That mother ship thingy is turning this way," Lynsye says.

"Delphinus, now would be a good time!!!" I say over the com.

"Fire Package acquired," a voice comes over the com.

A bright Flash appears next to the Large Mother ship and another flash appears on the opposite side.

"Oh Snap! Gang Bang!!!." Mark says over the com.

78

The team gets to a safe distance to watch the mother ship get ripped apart, then over the com a raspy voice comes over.

"Seven...... Jupiter 7!!!!!!!!!!!!! I'll have my revenge on all of you!!!

"Who the hell is that?" Casey asks.

"Sounds like a new fan," I said

"Hey look there's something escaping the ship!" Mark points out.

Everyone looks over to the disabled ship and a large object that looks like a knife detaches and fires upon the Alliance destroyer.

"It's getting away, go after it!" I yell.

Jupiter 7 floors it to the enemy ship. It starts to open a jump gate and starts to drop mines.

"Shit, break off people break off!!!" I yell as we all pull up and 180 away from the mines.

The ship jumps into hyper space and mines explode.

"What the hell was that?" Mark says.

"Dunno, but we may need to look into it," I replied.

"Jupiter 7, good work, head to the Delphinus for the debriefing," a voice says over the com.

"On our way," I say turning my fighter towards the carrier.

Chapter 8

The truth be told.

The team is sitting in the ready room looking at photos of the mission.

"I take it the science department is going to keep the large snake," Casey asks.

"Yea we've never seen any biologicals like it, and that's starting to worry me," the Admiral says.

"And what was that voice over the com?" I asked

"Dunno, all we know is that they know your team by name," the Admiral says.

"Hmm, that doesn't sound good, should we lay low?" Lynsye asks.

"All Alliance people love you guys, I wouldn't worry about it. We'll be home within the hour, get some rest, you guys deserve it," the Admiral says.

Later on in rack room, the Jupiter 7 team is hanging out in mine and Casey's bunk room until they get back to the station.

"Please don't tell me you're giving up your apartment for this, Ichia," Lynsye says.

"No no, just for a while, I think my uncle wants me around." I replied.

"Hey good flying today Casey, you're pretty hot with a fighter." Mark says.

"Um... thanks," Casey says with a confused look on her face.

"There's dumb, then dumber, then stupid, then Mark, you'll get used to it." Missy says as Casey giggles.

"Hey, I'm just saying" Mark says.

"Yea, thanks for saving my butt out there today," I said to Casey.

"Hey, you saved me from my old team, we're even." Casey says.

"Chinese tonight guys, it's on me," I say to everyone holding up my credit card.

"Hell ya!! Lynsye says.

"I'll get the tip," Missy says.

A little later the Delphinus enters the space of the Space Station. It comes through the colossal doors of the space station. It dwarfs any ship in the hanger, it clears everything by mere meters. At the docking port, people are hooking cables and hoses to the Delphinus as it docks with the space station. Jupiter 7 flies their crafts to the military hanger. Upon landing, Mittens walks over to the team.

"Wow, I'm impressed, nothing looks to be broken," Mittens says with her hands on her hips, head turned and sarcastically smiling.

"Haha, you just like working on our shit," Lynsye says.

"Ha, you guys always pay cash, so yea, I love your shit," Mittens replies.

"To bad you can't fix the water pressure in the showers," Mark says.

"I'm not a plumber," Mittens replies.

"Speaking of shower I don't know about the rest of ya, I smell funky," I say throwing my helmet over my shoulder.

"You're always funky," Mittens says.

"Hater," I replied walking towards the main structure of the stations. Everyone closes down their ships, secures them, and then they head to the showers.

"No peeking mister, just because we're on the same team," Casey says to Mark.

"Hey, I just want to shower," Mark says to Casey.

Casey smiles at Mark and afterwards everyone heads up to my apartment.

"Hey, is Kat off work yet?" Lynsye asks

"Should be, I've been texting her but she hasn't replied." I said.

We stop at Lucky Garden Chinese, pick up more than we need in food. and we head to my apartment. We're joking and goofing around in the hallway all the way up.

When we arrive at the apartment the door lock is broken.

"What the hell?" I said as the team looks at each other.

We rush in, there's clothes all over the floor. Don't remember them being here before. Smell of perfume isn't here, why's lipstick on the mirror? I still don't understand. My pictures aren't on the walls.

"I don't understand," I say stunned, dropping the food to the ground.

The team notices dents in the wall, the furniture is knocked over.

"What the hell?" Mark says

"My shit's all over the place, why's this happening to me, what did I do?" I asked falling on my knees to the floor.

"I don't think you did anything. Look at this Ichia," Casey points to lip stick on the mirror.

I crawl over to the mirror, and look closer. HELP S7 HEL, is written in pink lipstick.

"SHES BEEN KIDNAPPED!!!!" I say surprisingly.

"What!" everyone says.

"Wait, you think it's the pirates?" Lynsye asks.

"Yea, they did mention our group by name," Mark says.

"Shit, are they going after our families?" Missy says getting teary eyed holding her hand close to her chest.

"GUYS, GUYS WAIT A MINUTE!" I yell punching and breaking the mirror.

Pulling my hand out of the broken glass I fall back to the floor.

"There's something I need to tell you guys, this could get me Court Marshaled," I said dazed.

"What the hell did you do?" Lynsye says kneeling and sitting next to me on the cold floor.

"Hey, we got your back man," Mark says putting his arm around me.

"Remember that card for the moon bunny you gave me weeks ago?" I said looking at Mark.

"Yea..... Wait.... You didn't," Mark says with a pale face.

"Yup, I did," I said lowering my head.

"Asshole, didn't invite me!" Mark says.

"Hey, this is serious Mark. Ichia what happened? You went to sector 7, we can't go there. How and why did you go?" Lynsye says in a serious voice looking at me.

"I was curious and I had some civilian clothing. What do you want? I wanted something different. I was so tired of being hurt, I figured what the hell." I said, and I explained everything that happened right up until the day we all had breakfast.

"Look, we know your love life has sucked in the past, but if you're going to do something like that, you might as well as throw yourself into space," Missy said crossing her arms looking at Lynsye raising her eye brow.

"You guys don't understand what I've been thru. Ok, I've been cheated on, lied to, I've almost killed myself twice.

84

Thanks to Mittens for saving my ass and knocking sense into me. I was heading to a really dark place, and I'd wake up in corners of my apartment with liquor in my hand," I said beating my head against the wall.

"You two looked close for a while back there," Mark said sitting crossed legged next me.

"Yea, long ago right before her and Jeffery got together I was going to express myself, but couldn't do it. I like Mittens a lot and owe her, but her and Jeffery hit it off, she got pregnant and got married in like three months. I hurt myself in that one, I don't blame her, she's a great friend." I said.

"Ouch, been there, you can't tell someone you have feelings for them. But you'll do anything to help them with whatever they need. It hurts more not knowing if it would ruin your friendship. I know it's like a curse some times," Casey says kneeling down holding my hand.

"Jesus why didn't you come to us?" Lynsye asks.

"You guys were all gone, and I was by myself," I said.

"I was around," Mark says

"No, you weren't. You were with that Alex girl until she dumped you for that officer, ass hole," I said.

"Damn, you're right man, I'm sorry bro," Mark says.

"It's alright." I reply.

"Um, no its not, where's Kat at?" Lynsye asks me.

"Only one place, Sector 7, and that's where I'm going."

"We're going with you, I got some spare clothing we can all wear, be right back," Missy says running out.

Lynsye sits with me on the floor, Mark and Casey start to clean up a little bit.

"Ichia, I'm so sorry. I didn't know you were going thru life like that," Lynsye says holding me.

"I'm still here right, what's left of me."

"You and Mittens would have been great together. I bet she would of said yes." Lynsye says smiling at me.

86

"Dunno, don't ever tell her ok."

"I won't," Lynsye says as Missy shows up with a huge suitcase.

"Alright bitches, get dressed!!!" Missy says opening the suite case.

"Where did you get all this clothing from?" I ask.

"Shit you ain't the only one that goes down there. They have better drinks than we do up here," Missy says with a priceless grin on her face.

"Then why were you yelling at me about it?"

"Hheeehee" Missy laughs at me.

Everyone grabs some clothing and gets dressed. Looking like mine workers, we all head out to the elevators.

"Um, how are we going to get in there unnoticed?" Mark asks.

"Just act.... well just don't be like a tourist," Lynsye says as she lights a cigarette.

We ride the elevator down to level 6 and take the back smokey tunnel right into the market.

"Holy crap, it's hard to breath down here," Casey says trying to cover her mouth.

"So what's the plan boss?" Lynsye asks me.

"Well, I know which place it is, we're gonna have to break her out," I said.

"We're going to need a distraction, go look for her at the bar you were at. Mark go with him, Casey come with us, we're going to make some noise," Lynsye says.

"You sure?" I ask.

"Yea, just text me when you find her, we'll do the rest," Lynsye says, high fiving me.

"Let's do this, Chinese is getting cold back at the apartment," Mark says rubbing his stomach.

Mark and I head into the bar where I first met Kat. We have a seat and grab a couple of drinks.

"This place is da bomb!!! I wanna come here every day! So how can we find her? These bouncers are bigger than a bear," Mark says looking like a kid in a candy store.

"Simple, just follow my lead, we are going to get dances." I say.

"Dances, what's that?" Mark asks.

"You're gonna find out shortly," I say as two girls sit next to us.

"You two looking for a little fun?" one girl asks.

"I don't bite too hard," the other girls says.

"Sounds good to me," Mark says with a big grin on his face.

"Yea, lets go," I say.

We head back to the little room. As we do the door to the manager's office is open. I peak in and see Kat tied in a chair, then a bouncer slams the door.

"Mark, its game time," I said pulling out my phone, and send a text to Lynsye.

Over on the other side of the market Casey is watching the alley while Lynsye and Missy are preparing for mischief. Lynsyes' phone starts to vibrate and she looks down at it.

"Alright, game time! Casey are we clear out there?" Lynsye asks.

"All Clear!" Casey whispers.

Missy grabs a rope and starts to unwind it towards the end of the alley. Meanwhile, Lynsye starts a small fire, then pulls a large lever.

"GO! GO! GO!!!" Missy screams.

The three run like hell towards the bar, knocking people over in the crowd of people. All of a sudden a large explosion rocks the area, then followed by another large explosion. Everything starts to free float, the gravity has been disabled. Alarms go off and lights start to blink, then the large sound of metal ripping.

"Oh shit! The explosion was too big, it ripped the hull of the station!!!" Lynsye says with wide eyes floating.

Back at the bar, I knocked the girl off of me, and Mark did the same. We knocked the door down and the bouncer was right there. We started beating down the bouncer, then a gun when off.

"Well, well, well, its lover boy!" A well-dressed man says holding a gun towards me.

"That's Mister Lover boy to you, ass hole. I won't let you hurt her or anyone else anymore." I say with my fist clinched.

"Hahahahaha you're funny kid. Without me no one could live. The Alliance wouldn't be anything without the black market. I may only be one of many in this market that run things, but you'll never stop us all," the man says laughing.

Then a voice comes over a speakers system.

"Warning Hull Breech, Hull Breech minimum safe distance in five minutes."

"We gotta find em!" Lynsey says whacking a bouncer with a baseball bat.

Back in the little room.

"Well, looks like you've caused a minor setback, Ichia Change of Jupiter 7."

"Shit, he knows your name" Mark says.

"Good, then you'll always know who took a stand for a girl I love," I say looking at Kat. She is passed out floating in the room.

"How about we make a deal, you do a few runs for me and she's all yours. I'll never bother you again," the man says.

"You're crazy, I'll never help you," I reply.

"Maybe this will change your mind," the man says as he shoots towards Mark and misses him.

"Whoa, someone's shooting in there." Missy says.

"I got this" Casey says grabbing a large oxygen tank.

"Damn girl you're nuts! I love your style!!!" Lynsye says throwing Casey the baseball bat.

"Wow! I actually missed, I never miss," the man says.

"Ichia, don't make a deal with this jerk off, I'll take a bullet for you and Kat. Don't lose her. I've never seen you happier than now man," Mark says pleading with me.

"Have it your way," the man says.

"NO!!!" I scream as a large oxygen tanks blows thru the wall.

The tank blows thru the wall, blocking the shot from the Man.

As it passes in front of the man, I pull out my gun. Everything is moving in slow motion as I raise my gun. The man in the suit is knocked over by the spinning tank of oxygen. He spins towards me.

"Smile, you son of a bitch!" I said looking down the site of my gun.

I pull the trigger and put one right between his eyes. His brains and blood splatter all over the wall.

"Now that's how you shoot someone!!!! GOD DAMN I'm glad we're bro's, brother!" Mark says hopping in mid air.

Over the Speaker system.

"You now have 2 minutes to reach minimum safe distance," after another loud explosion.

"GRAB KAT, ICHIA!!!!!!!!!!!!!" Lynsye screams.

I grab Kat and hold her tight as I kick off the wall, then air swim out of the bar.

"We're not going to make it!" Missy says looking around as the rip in the hull gets bigger.

We're huddled around, looking for an exit. Casey notices a mini speeder.

"THERE!!!!" Casey screams and points to the speeder.

We all jump over to it.

"Ichia, hang on to her I'll fly this thing!" Mark yells.

As we take off with the speeder, racing away from the market, a huge chunk of hull rips off and several bars, including the one we were in blow into space. Then as everything goes into space we are racing away. The suction is pulling on us, then we all notice the closing gate ahead.

"Hang on!!!" Mark screams pushing the speeder to its limits.

"AAHHHHHHH" the team screams as we just beat the closing gate by inches. Mark tries to stop us but we hit gravity. We speed out of control and crash into a large heap of garbage.

"CRASH!!"

"Oh damn!" Mark says lying on his back.

"I think my life just flashed before my eyes," Casey says standing up.

"Huh, where am I Ichia?" Kat says waking up.

"You're okay baby, I'm right here," I say holding Kat in my arms tightly like an amazing book.

"You guys saved me?" Kat says looking at everyone covered in garbage.

"I'll never let anyone hurt you, I promise," I say holding her tightly.

"Aww, they are so cute," Missy says with a banana peel on her head.

"Yea, um guys, we need to get a move on. The 5-O is coming!" Lynsye says.

"Shit! Hey let's take the service tunnel!" Missy says.

We all sneak past Fire Rescue and head into the service tunnel. We climb the long, low, lit stairs back to the main hanger bay.

"I knew you would come," Kat says looking at me as she holds my hand.

"I had to, I'm not going to lose someone I care about," I said.

"Yea, we kind of know the whole story. Don't worry Doc, you're safe with us. Just don't cheat on him or break his heart," Lynsye says giving her the thumbs up.

"I don't think that will ever happen, not after this, I'm in love," Kat says.

I miss a step and trip.

"Whoa buddy, hang in there!" Mark says and everyone laughs.

After a long long walk, we finally get back to my apartment.

"Finally we get to eat!!!" Marks says.

"Is that all he thinks about is food?" Casey says raising her eye brow.

"Yup, he has no brain, just his stomach," Missy says nodding her head.

Everyone laughs and grabs a plate of food. Everyone's exhausted and talking about miscellaneous things as Kat and I stare each other.

"Well hey, let's have movie night this weekend." Mark says.

"Yea, let's introduce Casey to Ghostbusters." Missy says.

"You've never seen Ghostbusters?" Kat says.

"Nope." Casey replies.

"Oh yea, I'm off Saturday, we're doing movie night and its Christmas Eve too!!!!" Kat says.

"Well, let's leave these love birds to clean their apartment," Lynsye says walking towards the door.

"Night guys, thanks again," I said.

"Hey don't worry about it, we are a team, remember," Lynsye says with her hand on my shoulder.

Everyone leaves, then we stare at each other and fall into each other's arms.

"Let's take a shower," Kat says to me, I gulp and smile.

I don't need to go into detail about what happened here but you can use your imagination.

Meanwhile in the hanger bay.

"Hey wait, where are you staying tonight Casey?" Mark asks lightly stepping to Casey.

"Well, I was going back to the Delphinus," Casey says yawning.

"Alright look, don't take this the wrong way, come on back to my place. It will take you like another 45 minutes to walk over there any way," Mark says holding his hands up.

"Look you're cute, but I'm really not interested," Casey says crossing her arms.

"NO, no, I'm not trying to hit on you," Mark says.

Casey looks towards the Delphinus and looks towards Mark.

"Fine, but your place better be clean pal," Casey says shaking her head.

"Oh yea, always, come on lets go," Mark says to Casey.

The two walk through the food court over to another set of apartments. Mark opens the door to his apartment and leads Casey in.

"Wow, I'm impressed, you're a total Jock," Casey says looking around at the weight lifting equipment and protein shakes neatly stacked on the shelves.

"Hey, I'm a gentlemen," Mark says with a goofy grin on his face.

"Well I'm going to steal your shower no peeking, remember I have a gun," Casey says.

"Promise, scouts honor." Mark says smiling with his hand over his heart.

"What the hell was I thinking?" Casey says walking into the shower.

"Man she is cute, maybe she'll want something that will help her sleep." Mark says to himself looking at the kitchen. Mark grabs some mixes and whips up a recharge drink. A few minutes later Casey comes out of the shower.

"Alright, my turn. Here I made you a recharge drink and set up the pull out couch for ya," Mark says taking off his shirt.

Casey looks at his muscles thinking to herself, holy crap he has a washing rack on his chest.

"Um.. okay thanks," Casey says in a daze and blushing.

As Mark jumps in the shower, Casey couldn't help but prowl around the apartment. She looks at the photos of him and Ichia. Mark has photos of them as kids and thru high school and military training. Next to the photos are the medals he was awarded.

"Wow, he has a humanitarian award, he seems so stupid though, but cute, and this drink is really yummy," Casey says blushing a little drinking the smoothie.

Mark came out of the shower, and Casey is already passed out on the couch.

"Yea, we are all tired." Mark says looking at Casey.

Mark turns off the light in the kitchen and goes to bed. The next morning Casey is still sleeping on the couch, and Mark's up already working out on his mini gym. As Mark is working out, he sets a weight down to hard.

"Oops" Mark says.

Casey jumps up.

"What who wha…..? Oh, its just you." Casey says looking at Mark.

"Sorry, I was trying to be quiet." Mark says.

"Yea, big fail there," Casey says sitting up yawning.

"Hey come on, cut me some slack, I know I act dumb sometimes," Mark says looking down.

"I'm sorry, I'm just not a morning person," Casey said.

"Hey, wanna get breakfast, there's a good Coney Island around the corner," Mark says.

"Sure I could use some food, anyways breakfast is the most important meal of the day," Casey says.

The two head over to the restaurant in the food court.

"Hey Marky Mark, what shaken, whoa can't remember the last time you brought a lady with ya," the waitress says with an order pad in hand.

"Oh no, it's not like that," Casey says waving her hands.

"Yea, she's our new team member on Jupiter 7," Mark says.

A couple of customers stand up and congratulate her. One lady comes over to them and tells her how Mark and Ichia saved her daughter's life from pirates attacking a medical ship. The two finally eat breakfast and walk out of the food court.

"Well, I have a lot to do today, I'll be in the hanger bay later if you want to stop by," Casey says.

"Oh yea, you're checking our fighters out today, yea, I'll stop by," Mark says putting his hands behind his head.

Casey turns red looking at his muscular arms.

"Ok….. see ya," Casey says walking away red as an apple.

Chapter 9

New love birds on the station.

Later on Casey is running diagnostics on all four fighters. She sits crossed legged with a can of Sodi Pop next to her and a sucker in her mouth.

"Hey, what's up," Mark says to Casey coming around the fighter.

"Hey, what's going on?" Casey replies waving at Mark.

"Nothing, just seeing if I can lend a hand." Mark says.

"Um well maybe, can you pull out the main jump drive on bomber?" Casey says.

"Yea sure," Mark says taking off his top shirt, now only wearing only his tank top.

Casey stares and the sucker falls out of her mouth. Mark helps her plug in cords and different cables to all of the ships. She continues to walk around each ship and tweaks little things here and there. As she works, she keeps staring at Mark, and as they work on, she flirts a little bit. At one point she hands him a large cable to hold the hood up with and slaps him on his butt. Mark notices Casey staring at him so he flexes every now and then. Mark uses his strength to replace large shocks on the landing gears. As Mark holds the shocks Casey bolts them in. They move on to Plate Repairs and she sits on his shoulders screwing in new plates.

The two finish up on the updates and minor repairs. Casey slides down right in front of Mark, within a few inches. They're so close they can feel each other's breaths.

"Hi," Casey says in a calm voice.

"Gulp, um hi," Mark replies.

She couldn't resist the temptation. She closed her eyes and right then and there her mind was blown. She kissed Mark, then they fell to the floor of the Bomber making out.

"I've never been kissed like that, you're amazing," Mark says holding Casey brushing her hair around her ear.

"I don't know what it is about you, but I really like you," Casey says trying to catch her breath.

"Um, so wanna be my date to movie night?" Mark asks.

"I'm the main guest, remember," Casey says.

"Well, can I at least be your wing man that night?" Mark asks blushing.

"You can be my wing man any time cutie," Casey says as she starts to kiss Mark again.

Outside of the hanger, Mittens had lent a few tools to Casey earlier and was heading over to see how it was going.

"Well let's see how the new girl returns my tools," Mitten says while she throws her Coach tool bag over her shoulder. She comes around to the fighters looking around for Casey.

"Where the heck is that girl?" Mittens says walking over to the bomber and looked into the cock pit. She doesn't see her there either, and then Mittens walks over to the bay door of the bomber and gasps.

"Oh shit!" Mittens says surprised to find Mark and Casey making out on floor of the bomber.

"Ugh, oh my god!" Casey jumps off Mark falling onto her butt.

"Mittens! Wha, what, what are you doing here?" Mark ask while lying on the floor looking up at Mittens.

"Well, I was going to collect my tools but looks like you two were running diagnostics on each other," Mitten says, as she pulls out her phone and snaps a photo of the two.

"Hey, why did you take a photo?" Casey angrily says.

"For future reference and just the look on your guys faces....

Priceless. I can't wait to show Ichia," Mittens says laughing.

"Oh come on, don't show him yet, it just happened." Mark says getting up off the floor.

"Well I'll keep it for a good time to come. Oh hey, where's my tools newbie?" Mittens says putting her hand on her hips.

"They're on the table over there," Casey points as Mittens walks to the table.

"Wow, you cleaned them too?" Mitten says holding one in the air inspecting it.

"Yea I always clean what I take, I was going to bring them back to you but I ran into a little speed bump," Casey says.

"You rock girl, thanks, you can borrow my tools any time you need em," Mitten says putting tools into her bag.

"Question why are you using a nice Coach Bag to put tools in?" Casey asks scratching her head.

"Ha, I can answer that. Old girl here is a high roller married to a lawyer. She's on a different level than us, but still works with us, right?" Mark says smiling arms crossed.

"Ok troll! Just cause I'm from the upper class you don't have to rub it in," Mitten says pulling her purse over her shoulder.

"Nothing wrong with that, I wish I could afford nice thing like that," Casey says staring at the purse.

"Maybe one day you can come over. I have a few extra I've never used in my closet," Mitten says to Casey.

"Sweet, definitely," Casey says smiling.

"Hey, did Ichia invite you to movie night?" Mark asks.

"Nope, what you guys going to watch?" Mittens asks.

"Ghostbusters, Casey's never seen it," Mark says

"Really, Wow," Mittens replies.

"Why does everyone say that?" Casey says putting her hand on her head.

"Whateve's girl, don't let it get to you. Maybe I'll crash movie night," Mitten says walking out the bay door.

"See ya," Mark says then he turns to Casey, and gives her a hug.

"What's the hug for?" Casey ask enjoying the hug.

"No reason just wanted a hug," Mark says smiling.

Chapter 10

Saturday Night Christmas Eve, who you going to call?

It's Saturday night orbiting the earth at 3,300 feet. The ISE Space Station stands tall. The hustle and bustle of the station keeps going, people are rushing to make their last Christmas purchases. But on 43rd floor of the space station, a couple prepares for a wonderful evening with friends, cleaning and rearranging their living room so everyone can enjoy the featurette. Meanwhile two of the guests can't figure out what to wear.

"Have you seen my bra?" Casey asks Mark pulling her panties up.

"I can't find my shirt!" Mark says throwing the sheets back on the bed.

"We're going to be late!" Casey says frantically looking for her bra running around in panties.

Meanwhile back on the 43rd floor.

"Wonder where Casey and Mark are?" Lynsye says.

"Yea, it's not like Mark to miss a free meal. Let me send em a text to see whats up," I said pulling out my phone.

Suddenly there's a knock at the door. Kat goes over from the kitchen to answer it. As the door opens Casey's in half of Marks uniform and Mark's wearing flip flops, gym shorts and a tank top.

"Wow.... really guys," Missy says while shaking her head.

"Well, do the curtains match the rug, Mark," Lynsye says holding her 40 high.

The two new lovers turn redder than an apple.

"Nice, love's in the air around this station. First me and Ichia, now you and your name is?" Kat asks

"More like her legs!." lynsye says

"I'm Casey, new pilot and engineer," she says shaking Kats hand.

"Come on guys its movie time!" I say giving Mark a high five.

"I'll explain later," Mark whispers into my ear.

Everyone gathers around the mini video screen, and I hit play on the remote. Everyone looks like kid at a magicians show, waiting for that puppet to come out, as we are watching the film enjoying several alcoholic beverages. Kat had made several dozen pot stickers, along with boneless chicken baked with a light batter. Next to Lynsye and Missy was a cooler full of beer and wines. In the future, beer is known as Sodi Pop, Sodi Pop has changed quite a bit. It comes in several different flavors and it's carbonated.

By the end of the film we are starting to re-enact scenes from the film. Casey is standing on the couch with Kat.

"Oh my god, save me, save me, it's horrible, who we gonna call?" Casey says slurring and stumbling behind the couch.

Lynsye and I come up wearing back packs. I'm holding the vacuum and Lynseye is holding a blender.

"See you on the other side RAY!!!! Lynsye says.

Hours after drunk fun, everyone exchanges little gifts and trinkets. In the near future, space is very limited so gifts are usually small. Mark hands Casey a small box. As she unwraps it and opens it, it's a mini Coach change purse.

"Oh my god, how much did you spend?" Casey says looking at Mark.

"Don't worry about it," Mark says giving her a hug.

Kat sits on the bed with me, she has her gift in her lap and begins to open the gift which is gently wrapped in a colorful paper and topped with a pre made sticky bow. She slowly opens it, feeling a little shy due to this being the first Christmas in a long time she has actually spent with someone. She takes off the paper and comes to a white box with a lid. She looks up at me and smiles, and then she takes off the lid. To her surprise she looks inside and it's several different Scrunchies, a Watch, and a Doctors pin. She jumps up on me and gives me a big hug.

"Thank you so much, I've been a doctor for over two years and I've never purchased my officer pin like everyone else," Kat says to me.

105

"Well I noticed you didn't have one so I thought it would help, along, with the Scrunchies." I said.

"Well, they are a girl's best friend, here your turn," Kat says handing me a little colorful bag with a Santa and reindeer on it.

"You didn't have to get me anything," I said looking surprised at Kat.

"Come on, open it," Kat insists.

I open the bag and it's filled with paper. I slowly slide my hand into the bag. I look like a kid reaching into a cereal box looking for the toy. I pull out a bottle of my favorite cologne and fancy watch that has multiple moving parts and you can see right thru it.

"Thanks, I was running low on this," I said.

"Yea I noticed that too, and I didn't see a watch anywhere so I thought maybe you could use one," said Kat holding me low and then coming up giving me a long kiss.

Everyone begins to pass out around the apartment. Lynseye and Missy pass out on the cushions on the floor, Mark and Casey are cuddling on the couch. Kat and I are sitting up in the bed looking at our friends.

"I'm glad I know you," Kat says to me holding my hand.

"I'm glad you trusted me," I say kissing her on the cheek.

"I kind of feel like parents, all our children are sleeping," Kat says smiling.

"Yea, they usually take care of me. I'm the one that used to be on the floor screaming fire the cannons," I said to Kat as she giggles.

"Its nice and peaceful, I can't remember when I've see the orbit so clear of space ships," Kat says looking out the window over the bed.

"Yea, but its better with you here," I said softly as we lay and snuggled into the bed.

Chapter 11

<u>Silent Night</u>

It's about 3 a.m. and everything is beyond peaceful. The Station is orbiting the earth. There's no space traffic, the jump gate is not even activated. Back in the apartment everyone is snuggled up together. The mini Christmas tree is still lit on the kitchen counter. Throughout the station you could hear a pin drop, the only thing running round are the mice. Even in the hanger bay nothing moves, all ships are docked, some ships are actually lined with colorful Christmas lights. The hospital is quiet, the staff on duty is gathered drinking coffee and talking about good times. In the food court nothing is open except for Mc Donald's, which is a 24/7 Kiosk of food. The world surrounding me is beyond peaceful as I lay next to my beautiful girl friend, Kat. I sleep soundly holding her tight, free of tyranny and oppressions from all evils.

Suddenly *CRASH!!!* The entire station shakes violently, everyone is thrown in the apartment. Alarms and a sirens are going off. Power and gravity begin to fail.

"What the fuck!!" I yell while crawling on the ceiling, everyone in the apartment looks around in confusion.

Everyone in the apartment stumbles around as the room loses gravity. Everyone looks around holding their heads, having a minor hangover.

"Hey, look out the window, holy shit!" Mark says amazed looking out the window.

As we all huddle to look out the window, a large heavy armed freighter has crashed into the space station. The massive ship has ripped into the hull of the station. People, presents, Christmas trees and lights are drifting into space.

"Oh my god!" Kat says stunned looking out the window.

"Holy shit, they're launching fighters!!!" Lynsye says pointing.

"People, let's move everyone to their fighters," I yell stumbling in the gravity free room.

"I'm going to head to the Hospital," Kat says grabbing her medical uniform.

Everyone works their way out of the apartment and everything is total chaos. At first we were able to run through the hallway down to the stairwell. Then gravity would give out in the stairwell. As we lifted off the stairs, everyone frantically grabbed the railing trying to pull ourselves down the stairs.

"Looks like the upper floor is cut off from getting to the hanger bay," Missy says.

"Shit that means we're the only military close to the hanger bay, shit!!" Mark says as we are all running down the stairs.

"Ichia!!!!" Mittens screams, running holding her stomach from bouncing the baby around too much.

"Mittens!!" I stopped and waited for her.

"What the hell's going on!!" Mitten says trying to catch her breath.

"We're under attack!!! A large freighter crashed into the side of the station and it's launching fighters," I said.

"Oh my god," Mitten says jogging with me.

"I know, it's fucking Christmas!!!" I yell while running.

We all arrive at the hanger bay and take cover behind soda and snack machines. Two of the main hanger bay doors are heavily damaged. Fighters are taking out everything that's docked. People are attempting to run, but are being gunned down on the deck. Fighters are also attacking the main structure of the station. Assessing the situation of how to get to our fighters, I come up with the best plan I could.

"Alright, looks like we're the only ones that made it down here. Lynsye, man the cannons on the bomber, protect the Hospital, take out as many of those ass holes as you can. Casey, Mark and I will take on the fighters and get them out into space. Mittens you contact my uncle on the Delphinus, tell him to jump in ASAP!!!" I said commanding my team.

"Lets do it!!!" Mark says throwing his fist in the air.

"Let's rock this shit," Lynsye says lighting a cigarette.

"Good luck guys," Mitten says giving the thumbs up.

Everyone runs to their spots. Casey, Mark and I are running through flying debris, machine gun fire, and rockets. Lynsye slides down with Missy to the lower deck. Fighters come around and open fire on them. Missy pulls out her side arm and starts firing back.

"Woman, you need a bigger gun!" Lynsey yells pulling out her shot gun and opens fire on the fighter and keeps running.

"Come on, hurry up Lynsye, move that ass!!" Missy yells, covering her.

The two get into the bomber, Missy begins the launch sequence. Lysnye jumps right into the big gun. The Bomber looks like a warped Warthog with a big glass bubble on it and two huge twelve inch cannons. Lynsye locks and loads it and starts spraying everything that comes towards the hospital. Meanwhile, on the other side of the platform, me, Mark and Casey are trying to get to our fighters.

"Damnit, they got us pinned down!!!" Mark yells ducking down.

"Look over there," Casey points at a bunch of civilians using their own firearms to shoot at the enemy fighter.

"Hey, cover us as we run to our, fighters!!!" I yell to them.

"We got your backs, get to your fighters!!!" a civilian yells as they start drawing the attention of the enemy fighters.

We storm towards our fighters. As we do, a fighter notices us and turns fiercely towards us. Casey notices the fighter coming after us, she runs to the left away from us.

"Hey babe, where you going?!!!" Mark yells at Casey while running.

"Go, he's right behind us MOVE!!!!!" Casey screams pointing, jumping and running towards a fuel tanker.

"What's she doing?" I yell as we keep running through the gun fire.

Casey slides over to a fuel tanker and kicks the switch up into place. The switch activates the compressor that pressurizes the tank so it can push out the fuel. She put it to the max and locked the excess release. Casey grabs the hose and straps it down as the fighter comes in closer. She kicks the release and the pressurized fuel comes out like a high pressure spray, and Casey is running like hell away from the tanker towards her fighter. The enemy fighter opens fire at her, and as it does, it ignites the fuels and creates a fire storm.

BOOM!!!! Mark and I are thrown high into the air, and land hard next to our fighters. The enemy fighter catches on fire and crashes into the hull of the space station.

"Damn, what the hell was that?" I said collecting myself off the floor.

"Me, making a big boom," Casey says as she runs and slides next to Mark.

"Damn girl, you're awesome!" Mark says.

"Alright people, let's get into our fighters and take em out!" I said.

"Rock and Roll, stay low, and turn and burn, these bastard will never know what hit em." Mark says to everyone as they jump into their cock pits.

We burn the deck by taking off and racing towards the bay door of the space station, clearing a hole through enemy fighters. Casey is the first to breakout with Mark right behind her. Casey gets out, does a 180 and is in horror over what she sees.

"Oh my god," Casey says tearing up and holding her hands on her face.

In front of her ship, the freighter has pulled away from the station and enemy fighters are attacking the station. Smaller ships are attempting to launch and can't get away as they are being shot down.

"Casey, snap out of it!" Mark shouts as he shoots down two fighters around her.

"Payback time! I'LL KILL ALL OF YOU!!!" Casey screams opening fire on everything that moves.

Mark and Casey start shooting down every fighter they come upon. Then a bright flash, a Dreadnought comes out of hyperspace, and the large freight begins to open fire on the space station.

Meanwhile back inside, Mittens gets to the radio room.

"May Day, May Day, Alert ready 5, ISE under attack. All military report to the station. Heavy damages and extreme losses, anyone come in!!!" Mittens screams over the com.

"This is Delphinus we're inbound 2 minutes."

"This will be over in 2 minutes! Gods hurry the FUCK UP!" Mittens screams and runs back to the hanger.

Meanwhile I'm being chased by five fighters and currently chasing two around the center of the space station. It looks like a game of cat and mouse, every time I come around to the hospital, Lynsye tries to shoot down a fighter behind me.

"Can you guys launch yet?" I yell over the com.

"I'm trying, this is a bomber, it takes longer than a diesel truck!!" Missy says kicking the side of the console.

"Ichia come around again, but come really low I'll get a better angle at them." Lynsye says.

"You better be locked and cocked when I come around!" I yell.

"Don't know about cocked!" Lynsye says as she turns the gun towards where I'm coming from. She gets low, face right up to the target and lines it up ready for the kill.

"Come on, come on don't freeze, HERE WE COME!!!" I yell

over the com.

"Come on baby, show me that sweet spot." Lynsye says sarcastically looking like a cat ready to pounce on a mouse.

I fly low to the deck of the space station. I'm flying in between freighters and large crates. The fighters behind me are in a perfect line and Lynsye opens fire taking out three of them. The other two fighters break off. I pull up and go after two more fighters which are attacking civilian transports that are trying to take off. I come around and take them both out, head on. I've managed to round up the fighters inside the station. Missy and Lynsye finally take off.

"Alright, let's get outside. Mittens, get the main cannon online for the space station," I say over the com.

"Ten steps ahead of you." Mittens says into her headset running up stairs.

I get to the outside of the space station and I'm confronted by a Dreadnaught.

"Shit, here we go again." I floor it and begin to take out the Dreadnaughts' main systems. I work my way underneath taking out the bay doors and shield generators.

"There you go again, hero." Lynsye says.

The rest of the team frantically fights off as many fighters as they can while I'm dealing with Dreadnaught. Meanwhile, Mittens smashes the door in to the main cannon room on the space station. Mittens jumps into the controller's seat and starts up the main battery computer. She brings the main cannon computer online and fires up the secondary reactor on the space station. As the gun charges, the power on the space station fades, and all lights dim.

"This is tower we have another enemy inbound, heads up!"

As I come out from under the disabled Dreadnought, three more appear.

"Frack me!!!" I say surprised, Then a bright beam of light rips through them like a hot knife through butter. The Dreadnaughts begins to implode and crash into each other.

"Whoa, Mittens got the main gun online!!!" said Mark.

"Form up guys, lets push these bastards back to whatever black hole they came from!" I say over the com.

We form and begin opening a carpet of fire into the last wave of enemy space craft. The enemy fighters begin to retreat, along with the heavy freighter. Before the freighter can escape, the space station blasts it with the large canon, shattering it into millions of pieces. The debris from the explosion destroys many of the fighters as they jump away.

"Come on guys, we ain't letting these sons of bitches get home!!!" I yell over the com.

We chase the enemy fighters, shooting them down one by one as they try to escape. It's a free for all because the enemy fighters won't turn to fight. We are actually outnumbered four to one and the Lab Rat Mafia keeps running and jumping into hyperspace. We hit the brakes after the last fighter is destroyed.

"See, that's why they call em Lab Rats, they run like rats!"

Lynsye says putting a cigarette in her mouth and lighting it.

"That was intense, and we cleaned house quick," Mark says breathing heavy.

"Yea, but look at the station, its all messed up," I say.

"Hey Ichia! you still alive out there?" Mitten says over the com.

"We don't die that easy, all enemies have retreated," Lynsye says over the radio.

"Better get back, casualties are bad and there's not enough hospital help." Mittens says.

"We're on our way," I said flying towards the heavily damaged space station.

Upon landing we can see the damages are extreme, people lay dead everywhere. Fires are burning out of control all over the place. We land back on our platform, people gather to help us out of our fighters, and hand us bottles of water.

"You guys are HEROS!!" a man screams. A small crowd cheers, but it soon goes away as everyone is stunned again by the damage and death. As we make our way to the hospital, people are carrying the injured from the hanger deck. The Hospital is in total mayhem, people are lying everywhere. Nurses and doctors are operating in the hallways. The smell of human flesh or burgers is in the air, we try to help where we can. Giving people water, one doctor instructed the team to give everyone morphine in one room. Then an officer came up to them. It was the same guy that took Marks ex.

"Oh great, you," Mark says' huffing from carrying people.

"Look, I'm sorry but we need your help. People are running out of air on levels 44 to 52, please help us. We need all the extra hands we can get." the officer pleas.

"Ichia, you and Mark go, we'll stay here and help where we can." Lynsye says grabbing a first aid kit.

"Right," I replied.

We follow the officer. Running through the halls people are lying everywhere, people are screaming and crying. As we run, several large explosions go off in the space station, knocking everyone to the floor, making ceiling lights and tiles crash down.

"Shit, this thing is decompressing bad," I say to Mark.

"We better get some suits if you know what I mean," Mark says.

We get to level 44, and grab suits from the Fire & Rescue. We start to enter low oxygen areas and pull people out one by one. Mark enters one room with his suit, a family is sharing one Oxygen can. I help Mark get them out of the room, Mark holds the broken door open as they slide out. I hear a family beating on the wall screaming at the top of their lungs.

"HELP! WE'RE TRAPPED AND THE AIR'S ALMOST OUT!!!"

"Mark get a serpent cutter!!!" I yell to Mark.

"Be right back baby!" Mark says storming back to fire and rescue.

"Can you hear me?" I ask to the wall.

118

"Yes!" a voice says from the wall.

"Stay calm, try to breath easy, we're going to get you out, I promise!" I say holding the wall like its the most precious thing I have.

"Come on MARK!!" I scream.

Mark comes around sliding in like a baseball player coming into home base.

"Got it!!!, Back up dude," Mark says as he uses the Flaming Laser torch to cut out the wall. The Torch turns the wall into molten metal, enough to start cutting through it.

"Medic, we need oxygen tubes!!!" I yell to the Fire and Rescue people.

"Come on Mark, rip that wall, we gotta get those people out of there," I say anxiously waiting as Mark cuts.

"I'm going as fast as I can bro!" Mark says focusing all his energy on the cutter.

A small team of Fire and Rescue come over to assist, along with a news robot which is recording everything. Back at the Hospital, Casey's helping Kat with a patient who is bleeding everywhere. They both look up at TV monitor for a second.

"Hey that's Mark and Ichia!" says Casey.

"Looks like they're trying to rescue people," Kat says as she stares at her boyfriend beating the wall with a sledge hammer.

"Come on baby, save em." Kat says.

"Almost there, get ready Ichia!" yells Mark.

Then a large tremor shakes that part of the station.

119

"Hurry, there's a rip in the wall, the airs going out!" a family member screams from inside the room.

"Fuck! come on you piece of SHIT!!!!" Mark screams as I beat the crap out of the wall.

As Mark finishes the last cut, I jump and rip a part of the wall off. As I come back to the hole we made, I see the family in their apartment. As I go to grab them, the back wall of the apartment breaks out and blows out into space. The whole family gets sucked out into space like rag dolls. Mark grabs me, as I grab one of the family members.

"NO!!!! HANG ON KID!!!!!" I scream as Mark pulls on my legs.

"COME ON PEOPLE PULL!!!!" Mark screams to Fire and Rescue people.

Casey and Kat watch with amazement what's going on LIVE on TV.

"I'M NOT LETTING GO! HANG ON!!!!" I scream to the little girl.

The little girl is screaming and trying to hang on to my hands. I'm hanging on with everything I've got, but it's not enough. the girl starts to slip.

"MARK. HURRY THE FUCK UP!!!!" I scream as I lose my grip of the little girl. As I lose my grip, I look into her eyes see the fear of the young child. The fear is all too real, as if it froze me to death. Just before she gets sucked into space, Lynsye pulls up in the bomber with the door open. They catch the girl like a baseball into the bay of the Bomber. Lynsye gives me the thumbs up. Mark and Fire Rescue pull me back in and seal the wall.

"GOD DAMNIT!" I'm screaming and punching the wall.

"Hey, you did what you could, Calm Down!!!!" Mark yells at me holding him back from punching the wall.

Mark lets go of me, I stagger stand and then kick a garbage can on the floor. Then I fall to the floor going into a panic, screaming. Mark comes over to me and pulls me off the ground.

"Come on man, we got more people to save." Marks slaps me across the face.

"What the hell, we had em," I said.

"We got one, that's better than nothing, now let's get to the next floor!" Mark says pushing me from behind. We grab more gear and start heading to higher levels to get people evacuated.

The Delphinus pulls to the damaged side of the station, then opens its lower bay, and docks with the space station covering the hull like a band aid. Hours later, after helping trapped people, Mark and I walk and stumble back to the hospital. Kat and Casey come up to us with a big group hug.

"Oh my god, you're amazing!" Kat says to me while kissing me.

"You two are brave as hell," Casey says kissing Mark and clinching onto him tightly, crying.

"Looks like we made the news again Ichia," Marks says holding Casey.

The Admiral walks in with Mittens, Lynsye, and Missy. We

121

stand in front of the Admiral, beat, bruised, and tired.

"Jupiter 7, I can only say thank you and great job. You saved the lives of thousands," Admiral Hitoshi says holding his hand out to me.

I walk over to my uncle and give him a hug.

"I couldn't save them all, sir," I said holding my uncle.

"You did great, and that little stunt Lynsye pulled to save that girls life, Amazing. It will go down in the record books for best save ever," the Admiral says.

"MITTENS!" a man yells looking around franticly in the hospital lobby.

"Jeffery!" Mittens runs over to her husband.

"Oh My God, I was on the 77th Floor, I couldn't get down until they freed us, Ichia got us all out," Jeffery says holding Mittens in his arms.

"Thank you Ichia." Mitten says to me teary eyed, holding Jeffery tightly.

"You don't need to thank me, Mittens," I replied as I smile back at her, holding Kat.

We walk out of the hospital looking for a quiet place to collect our thoughts. We walk over to our fighters, and as we walked over, there's a soda machine tipped over, cans are all over the place. Mark and Casey grab a bunch of cans. We get over to our fighters, sit in a circle and pass the cans of soda around.

"Well Ichia, we're gonna have to crash at your place for a little bit" Lynsye says taking drink of the pop.

"Why?" I ask.

"Levels 44 and up to level 47 are uninhabitable until engineers can fix the station," Lynsye says.

"Man, all my stuff, my weights," Mark says holding his hand on his head.

"Yea, you guys can stay. We'll just have to make more room," I said.

"Looks like our kids are coming home with us tonight," Kat says smiling to me.

Everyone is just sitting in a daze from the attack.

Chapter 12

Second wind.

We all walk together through the halls back to my apartment. As we walk through, people are thanking us for saving them. Word had spread quickly through the space station that we were the only Military personnel that made it to the hangers. Our group came to the balcony overlooking the shopping district of the space station. We leaned up on the fence and couldn't help but look at the one part of the station that didn't get destroyed or even touched. The shopping district is like a seven story shopping mall with many wings. There's movie theaters, clothing stores, and much more. On every level of the district there are small parks. In the center of the district is a medium park. The park is actually lit up with Christmas lights and trees, even the ponds have been artificially frozen over.

Around the district is transparent aluminum, and you can see the Earth and Jump Gate.

"Wow, this area wasn't even effected by the attack," Kat says holding my arm.

"Yea, its so peaceful, and the lights are beautiful," Missy says holding Lynsye's waist.

"Merry Christmas guys," I say to everyone holding Kat closely.

"Here's to loved ones lost tonight," Lysnye says pulling out a flask and taking a drink.

"Pass that here," Casey says taking it from Lynsye, and then everyone else passes it around and takes a drink.

We stand there to take in the moment for a little longer, then begin to head back to my apartment.

"At least the gravity is back on," I said opening the door.

We all walk into the apartment. The apartment is trashed, and everything is turned over. Everyone starts putting things back together, turning over the couch and tables. As we're putting things back together and pulling out the beds, I sat in the corner for a second.

"Hey babe, are you ok?" Kats says kneeling to me.

"I can't get that little girl or her family out of my head. All I can see is their faces as they where pulled out of the apartment," I said, starting to sob.

"Hey, hey, you did what you could. Thanks to Lynsye, you at least saved one member of the family. This way that family name will be able to be carried on," Kat says hugging me tightly.

Everyone looks at their friend worried, as I shake in the arms of Kat.

"Hey I'm here and I'm not going to let anything happen to you, I love you." Kat says to me holding me like a fragile painting.

I look up at Kat like I'm seeing an angel, I brush her hair around her ear and pull her closer and kiss her. Everyone stares with a warm feeling running through them, from the couple on the floor reassured that nothing could ever break them apart.

"Come on babe, let's go to bed." Kat says standing up with me.

Kat lays me on the bed and takes my socks and shirt off of me. She tucks me in gently and kisses me on the head.

"Nite everyone," Kat says to everyone in their beds.

"Nite everyone," they reply as Kat turns off the kitchen stove light.

As everyone falls asleep I just lay on the bed, eyes wide awake. Tears begin to run down my cheeks, as all I can think of is what happened earlier. I lay next to Kat, she still holds me tight but I can't breathe. I feel as if a part of me blew out with that family. I begin to question myself, what if I could have changed the outcome. After a few hours, I got up from the bed and went to the bathroom. I stood in front of the mirror looking at myself wondering what I've become. As I stood there, I kept splashing water on my face, hoping the cold water would clear my mind, but it doesn't have any effect. Kat wakes up and comes over to me in the bathroom. She puts her arms around me holding me tight.

"Come back to bed babe," Kat says softly into my ear then kissing my neck gently.

I keep resisting her, but she eventually manages to get me back to bed. As she takes me back to bed she turns on the vent system in the apartment, to create a little background noise. Kat gets under the covers with me and sits on top of me and stares at me.

"Come on, get off of me," I say.

"No, you need me, the trauma from today is tearing you apart and I want to help you," as she holds me tightly.

"All I can hear is that bursting sound of the oxygen leaving the room." I say tearing up.

"They're in a better place and the daughter will be taken care of, I promise. Grace Hospital has the best in every department. She will be taken care of." Kat whispers into my ear.

"I just feel so, " I say as Kat interrupts me by kissing me and starts to grind on me.

We have quiet intercourse silenced by the air vents, while our friends sleep in the room peacefully.

The next day Lynsye and Missy were the first to get up and head out. Mark and Casey stayed behind with me and Kat. Kat and Casey made breakfast, while I was still lying in bed, still stunned by the events of the attack.

"I've never seen him like this, besides when his heart was broken back in the day," Mark says to the girls.

"Kat, what should we do?" Casey asks Kat.

"I don't know, we had sex last night and he seemed okay, but this morning he looks really bad," Kat says as the two stare at her, like what!

"Well, sex will make any guy forget what's going on around him," Casey says.

"True that," Mark says grinning.

"I'm going to check on that little girl later today and I think

I'm going to introduce Ichia to her, maybe that will help the shock," Kat says to Casey.

"That's a good idea, might work," Casey says while putting the eggs onto the plate.

Kat walks over to the bed to check on me.

"Hey babe, time to eat," Kat says leaning over kissing me on my cheek, but I lay there unresponsive.

"Hey, come on snap out of it," Kat says shaking me.

"I'm not hungry," I say softly.

"God damnit, get up!" Kay says raising her voice pulling my arm.

"GET OFF ME!" I yell and rip my arm away from Kat.

"Hey, she's trying to help you!" Casey yells at me.

"Yea, come on man, this aint you, snap out of it bro," Marks says.

"Just leave me alone, I'm not worth saving," I say with my face in the pillow.

"What the fuck get up! I'm not letting you go down a dark path, gods damnit! Now get the fuck up outta the bed," Kat yells, then punches me several times in my side.

"Screw this!" Casey says grabbing the pitcher of water.

"Oh shit," Mark says as Casey dumps the ice cold water on me.

"AHHHH!" I jump up out of the bed almost as if I was going to jump on Casey. Before I could think that thought, Kat decked me across the face knocking me into a shelf.

129

"Ugh," I sigh trying to get up, then getting knocked out by my dictionary.

"Crap, I didn't mean to kill him." Kat says frantically checking my head.

"Is he okay? I thought he was going to kill me," Casey says.

"I've known him all my life I've never seen him like this, this is retarded." Mark says.

"He's unconscious, that dictionary hit em hard," Kat says.

"Here's some ice," Casey kneels down with a rag of ice.

"So what should we do doc, he's kind of self-destructive right now," Mark ask Kat.

"I don't know, he needs all of us right now," Kat says.

They pick me up, laid me on the bed, and tuck me in. Kat cleans up the mess from me falling and starts to hide the knives and my firearm, just in case. Mark takes the firearm from Kat and places it in his Gym bag.

"Guys I'm gonna go for a walk, I need some air, you need me to pick anything up?" Mark says to the girls

"No I'm good," Kat says

"I'll take a six pack of Orange sodi pop," Casey says.

"Ok I'll bring some back," Mark says hugging Casey and kissing her on the cheek.

Mark heads out towards the mall, he jogs thru the central park. He comes to the park where the Red Cross has setup some shelters for people who can't return to their homes.

Unbelievably, people are celebrating Christmas with whatever they have.

Some families have drawn pictures of Christmas trees on tents. Mark comes over to a small kitchen that's serving food to anyone and everyone, and Lynsye and Missy are helping out.

"Hey, what's up player?" Missy says to Mark as she stirs a big pot of soup.

"Not much, how did you guys get involved in this?" Mark asks.

"Well, they said they needed help, so we threw on aprons," Lynsye replies with a cigarette hanging out of her mouth.

"That's awesome," Mark says.

"What are you doing?" Lynsye asks.

"I'm just out for a quick jog, Ichia is really taking yesterday hard," Mark says leaning on the table.

"Yea, yesterday was rough as all hell," Missy says.

Mark stays for a little bit, and hangs out helping Lynsye and Missy. They continue to serve meals to people. Mark helps out by cleaning up garbage and emptying the heavy trash cans. The tables that are setup are simple picnic tables, each table holds eight people, and all twenty tables were full of people. Most people didn't even let the attack scare them.

A lot of people where thanking Mark, Lynsye and Missy for their service in the Military and for saving the Space Station.

Word really had traveled fast, how Jupiter 7 was dressed in pajamas and bunny slippers, beat the evil Lab Rat Mafia and saved as many lives as they could. Meanwhile back at the apartment, I finally came to and was sitting up, and Kat was feeding me breakfast.

"Sorry for jumping at you Casey," I said.

"Its okay, I know you're really depressed over that family," Casey replied while eating.

"Ichia, please listen to me, I'm here for you and all of your friends. None of them have stupid egos that are gonna bring you down. We're going to help you thru this, one way or another, ok," Kat says to me.

"I love you," I say to Kat, and Kat smiles like she just won the lotto.

"Aww, I love you too," Kat says and kisses me.

Mark comes back with a selection of beverages for everyone. We all sit watching Christmas Celebrations on the TV. Lynsye and Missy crash in the bed taking a short nap.

"Man we need to go to Disney World, remember them days, Ichia?" Mark asks.

"Yea, those were some fun times. The fireworks were the best," I replied.

"I've never been there before," Kat says.

"Me either," Casey says.

"Oh Snap, group trip," Mark says hugging Casey.

"Yea if we can afford it, it's so darn expensive to go, but it would be worth it," I said.

We continue to watch TV and pass out on the couch. Hours pass, everyone is exhausted from the previous day, and still passed out. Later on everyone wakes and I started looking for food in the apartment.

Nothing but condiments filled the fridge and ice fills the freezer. We decided to head down to the food court to see if anything is open. We walk through the station and down to the food court. The only thing still open is Mc Donalds.

"You think we could get something a little healthier?" Mark says.

"Not on Christmas night, everything else is closed, only the robots stay open during the Holidays," Lynsye says.

"Well, it smells like chicken," Missy says.

"Well it is all real food. I eat here a lot, and McDonalds does have the best semi-real-beef burgers, unlike most restaurants on the Station," Kat says.

"Yea, well on Mars you can get a real burger, just have to take a loan out on your house," Mark says.

Everyone orders from the Kiosk and little boxes of food come out like soda cans. We grab our meals and sit in the main food court area next to the fountain which has a good view of the hanger bay.

"What a day," I said, then took a bite into my double cheese burger.

Chapter 13

Into The Fire.

"Oh my god! It's hot as hell on the station today," I said to myself sitting on the wing of my fighter, drinking a bottle of water.

"Yea, no kidding. They said the Sun's acting up, and the solar flares are messing with our temps on the station and space crafts," Casey says holding a towel on her head.

"Yea, I talked to my mom the other day, I guess Olympus hit 121 degrees and the low was 100," Mark says.

It's two months into the New Year, and for the last few weeks the temperatures throughout the Solar System have been extremely high. Earth, The Moon, and Mars planet temperatures have risen three degrees in the last week. So far only sixty deaths are related to the heat. Local scientists have been sending probes to the Sun, but they only can tell that Sun Spots have been disappearing and Solar Flares are happening more often than normal.

The Science Academy has sent a team to the Sun, to run a closer look. They sent the Star Ship Requiem to help lead the investigation. Only few ships can withstand that kind of heat. Meanwhile, back on the space station, I stalk the job board hoping for work. The job board is a large network of Kiosks that are everywhere in the Solar System. They look like giant Information touch screens, like something you would find in a mall, but it's like five foot tall. Pilots or Military can pick up extra work from them time to time. The last job we had was before Christmas, and we didn't get paid for the attack on the station so money is beginning to come up short.

"You know if you keep staring at that you'll go blind," Mittens says walking up behind me.

"Yea, well you're married to a Lawyer. I'm not, so money is a little hard for me Miss Upper Class," I said taking a drink from my water bottle.

"Don't hate, look I owe you any ways, you dragged my drunk ass home two days ago. By the way, that was an awesome club we went to on the Moon, don't remember much, but I know it was fun," Mittens says giving me a thumbs up.

"Yea, not to mention you threw up in my fighter, and in all the halls all the way up to your apartment, and probably on Jeffery that night too," I said smiling.

"Yea, we won't talk about that," Mittens says holding her index finger.

"I have photos," I reply sarcastically.

136

"Well I guess I owe you, so if you need cash or something let me know," Mittens says putting her elbow on my shoulder.

"You know they never prepared us for this at the Academy," I say to Mittens.

"Yea I know, you ever think how far we've come. I remember meeting you and Mark for the first time," Mittens says as she jumps up onto the ledge to sit.

"Good Times... lots of drinking and...... Hey there's a JOB!!!!!...What, already taken, what the heck!!!!!" I jump up and kick the job board.

"There's gotta be some way to make money around here," I said beating my head on the job board.

"Male stripper, be Marks manager," Mittens says kicking her feet up and down on the ledge.

"Yea..... no," I say as we both laugh.

Stalking the board was getting old, and getting me nowhere, so I decided to go see the love of my life. I took a stroll over to Grace Hospital, to see Kat and pester her for a while. I walked into the Hospital and the hustle and bustle of people running around. I walked up to the information station to ask for her location. The receptionist pointed me to the ICU, the same place where we met for the second time. I started to get a chilling feeling I when walked in to the ICU, remembering what happened when I almost died of oxygen loss.

"Hey, babe what are you doing here?" Kat comes up to me giving me a big hug.

"Well, I'm bored and figured I'd bother you," I said.

"Well I'm just doing rounds. We had a big emergency rush from the Military. The Entire crew from the Requiem will be up here shortly," Kat says.

"What, wasn't that the science crew that was sent to the Sun to find out what's going on?" I ask Kat with my hands in my pockets of my hoodie.

"Yea, they said the Solar Flares were too intense," Kat says.

"Doctor, the Psychiatrist will be here shortly for the patient from the Requiem," A young nurse said to Kat handing her a chart.

"Thanks," Kat says to the girl.

"Psychiatrist, I though they all suffered from heat exhaustion?" I ask Kat.

"Yea, all but three where having a real melt down," Kat says.

"Did the military debrief them?" I asked.

"Not yet, the ambulance brought them right in, the Star Ship is still out there orbiting the Sun. What do think is going on?" Kat asks me.

"Not sure, but can I sit in with the Psychiatrist?" I ask with a little smile.

"I don't see why not, he's a good friend of mine. Actually here he comes." Kat points to a middle age doctor coming up to Kat and me. Plain and simple, call him "Mr. Handsome Dr."

"Hi Kitty Kat, how ya been, still looking outstanding as usual," Says Mr. Handsome. I think to myself, "who the fuck is this guy," and I'm giving the Eminem look of I'm going to beat your ass then sing about it on my next album.

"Hi Richard, how have you been?" Kat says rolling her eyes.

"I'm doing better now, who's this, is this, the patient?" Richard asks.

"No, I'm her boyfriend," I said crossing my arms.

"Oh hi, nice to meet you. Wow, I didn't think you where taken Kat." Richard says.

"Yup, couldn't be happier," Kat says sounding perky to Richard, and slaps him the chart.

"What's going on with this patient, lets see..... Big yellow eyes? Is this a joke? I thought this mission took place on the Sun," Richard says.

"Yea several patients are screaming about a monster or something," Kat says.

"Monsters on the Sun sounds a little hokey if you ask me," Richard says.

The patients are being brought in and most of them are burnt up. But a few look like they've seen ghost, they are shaking like a diabetic needing insulin. As they walk in, the Admiral walks in behind them.

"Ichia what are you doing here?" Hitoshi says taking his hat off.

"Uncle hey, um I want you to meet my girl friend," I said pulling Kat over.

"Oh wow, I'm impressed, a doctor, your parents will be happy. Mam, we know each other already, good to see you again," Hitoshi says to Kat.

"Yes, Hitoshi it's been awhile since you've been here," Kat says.

"What, you two know each other already?" I ask with my eyebrow raised.

"Well she's the best, and can fix up any human," Hitoshi says.

"Admiral, we can start when you're ready," Richard says standing in front of an ICU room.

"Yes, let's get started," Hitoshi says walking into the room, I follow my uncle and Kat as they walk into the room.

"Um.. sorry, no civilians in here kid," Richard says to me.

"He's far from a civilian. I want his opinion on this matter, he's coming with us," Hitoshi says to Richard.

"Oh, is he in the Military?" Richard says with a stupid look on his face.

"Yea, I saved the Space Station on Christmas Eve."

"You're from Jupiter 7. Wow," Richard says surprised.

"Yea, wow let's get this started," Hitoshi says crossing his arms.

We walk into the room and Richard closes the door. Hitoshi and I sit on the couch in the room.

Kat begins to monitor the medical equipment, she's checking pressures and the amounts of medication going into the patient. Richard is examining the Patient, checking for scars or burns. He uses his flashlight to check the reflexes of the patient.

"Lieutenant Smith, can you hear me?" Richard asks, the patient just sits there shaking.

"Lieutenant Smith, what is todays date?" he asks again as the patient continues to shake and just lay in the hospital bed.

"Lieutenant Smith, do you recall what happened on your mission?" Richard asks, the patient still doesn't respond. Then as the doctor goes to ask another question, from the window a space craft casts a shadow thru the window and into the room. The Patient starts to scream.

"AAHHHHHHH Don't let it get us!!!!!!!!!!! STOP! STOP! STOP! ITS GOING TO KILL US ALL!!!!!!!!" The patient screams and starts to go into shock. Hitoshi and I are standing up, startled by the screaming.

"I NEED A CRASH TEAM ASAP!" Kat calls over the intercom.

"Help us hold him down," Richard yells as he tries to hold down the Patient.

I jump over and hold the patent down with one arm, making Richard look like a weakling.

"SMITH, WHAT HAPPENED, WHAT DID YOU SEE?" I yell, then Hitoshi pulls out his lighter and lights it in front of the Lieutenant.

141

The light immediately grabs the attention of the patient. The patient starts to calm down and follows the light as Hitoshi waves it back and forth.

"What did you see out there on the Sun," Hitoshi asks holding his lighter.

"Bigggggg cccccrrrrr creature, massisssive. Yellow eyesss Yellow Eyesss.....ugh" the patients starts to go into shock again.

"SHIT!" I yell trying to hold him down. The crash team shows up and helps me hold him down while they start to inject drugs into the patient. Lieutenant Smiths eyes are bleeding and he is foaming at the mouth, and starts to go limp.

"We lost him, try the paddles, but his heart is gone from the stress." Kat says, as the crash team tries to revive him. As they try to revive him a Nurse comes in and calls for Kat, another patient is having an episode.

"What, come on lets go. Richard stay here we'll be right back." Kat says.

Kat, Hitoshi and I run over to the next room down the hall following the nurse. We enter the room and the patient is freaking out, screaming about yellow eyes.

"What the hell is going on?" I ask.

"We need another crash crew to the ICU room 144," Kat yells over the intercom.

"This is weird, I've never seen anything like this," Hitoshi says.

"Nurse, I need you to put the other patients from the Requiem on a heavy sedative, make sure they all go to sleep mode," Kat says to the young nurse.

"Yes mam, I'm on it," the girl says as she runs out of the room.

The medical staff and Kat try to revive the last crew member that had an episode, but they were unable to. In the ICU, the mood was a little unsettling like waiting for something else to go wrong. The entire staff went back to working quietly and they went about their business.

"Uncle, let me and my team investigate the Sun," I asked my uncle.

"Your ships can't handle that heat, plus I need to get this information to the council ASAP," Hitoshi says.

"Uncle come on, you get the info to them I'll worry about heat-proofing my fighters,"

"Okay, you work on that. I'll talk to the council and let them know that the Lab Rats may be causing this extensive heat wave," Hitoshi says putting his hat on.

"Thanks Uncle, I won't let you down," I say shaking his hand.

"Hey, it's getting hairy. I need to head to the ER, another craft working around the Mercury mines has had a Sun incident," Kat says to me.

"No problem babe, I'll see you later tonight, ok." I said holding her.

"I love you," Kat says to me as we kiss. Richard was in the background glaring at us.

I head back down to the main hanger bay with all kinds of ideas. I come up to my platform area frantically looking for Mittens. The rest of the team is sitting on their fighters watching a football game, wondering why is he running around like a moron? I come around a corner of a hanger and run into Jeffery.

"Whoa man, you okay?" Jeffery says to me.

"Yea, *huff huff*, where's your wife homie?" I ask trying to catch my breath.

"Right here-what's up? Why are you out of breath?" Mittens says coming out of the office all dressed up. Wearing a short black dress with a diamond necklace and earrings, Coach purse to match.

"I need your help right now!" I said.

"Um I'm going out, see my dress and my nails." Mittens says holding her hand up showing off her bright pink nails.

"We have tickets to the game tonight and we're running a little behind," Jeffery says with his hands in his pockets

"Look, there may not be a game in a few hours, or maybe next week." I said.

"What's going on?" Mittens asked.

"Lab Rats are causing this heat wave. Multiple ships have come under attack and everyone's screaming literally about yellow eyes." I said.

"Are you serious?" Jeffery asks.

"Yea, I just left the Hospital. My uncle's on the way to the council, and Mittens I need your money, I mean Jefferys money to equip my fighters with heat shields ASAP." I said.

"Money?" Jeffery says.

"I told Ichia I'd help him out if he needed it." Mittens says while rubbing Jeffery's back, smiling.

"Well, at least it's going to someone I like and not an old boyfriend or something," Jeffery said.

"Yea thanks, old boyfriend, come on," Mitten says heading back into the office.

"Sorry for ruining your night Jeffery," I said.

"Don't worry about it, you're probably about to save billions of lives and my baby is going to help you do it. Not to mention you saved me and you've always have been there for her," Jeffery says putting his hand on my shoulder.

"Alright, knowing you, we are probably running out of time. Let's run over to the parts yard and get some goods." Mitten says pulling up her overalls.

Mittens hugs Jeffery and gives him a kiss. We don't waste time, and take a hover cart to the parts yard. On the way there we are discussing the temperatures they will have to deal with, and how to apply the shield and armor to the fighters. Arriving at the parts place all the workers are focused on the football game.

"Hey, Bitches we need parts!!!!!!" Mittens yells to all the workers.

"That's one way to get their attention." I said.

145

Mittens goes over all parts needed for the upgrades, she's grabbing heat shields, mini air conditioning units, coolant, and canisters. The parts yard crew is adding it up and the bill comes to $5,000, Mittens looks at me.

"That's two dresses, or four purses, or 50 bottles of Jacky. This better not be a false alarm." Mitten says with her arms crossed and head turned sarcastically.

"I'll get you back, I promise." I said smiling at Mittens and scratching my head.

We run back to the hanger bay with a boat load of parts in the cart. The cart is over-loaded, I'm even sitting with parts on my lap. As we pull into the hanger bay we notice a huge freighter on fire. The fire and rescue freighter is trying to spray down the flames. We look in awe going "holy crap something crazy is going on out there." We finally get to my platform, and we dump the parts right in front of the Jupiter 7 team.

"Whoa, what's with all the armor, Ichia?" Casey asks.

"Guys we got a job, and its gonna get hot," I said.

"Hot, its already hot, what's going on?" Lynsye asks.

"I went to see Kat at the Hospital, and the entire crew from the Requiem was either killed or injured. All I know is there has to be something attacking people out there and damaging the sun. My uncle is talking to the council and getting support. We need to take all of this equipment and make our fighters as heat proof as possible," I said.

"Well, I have a feeling we are going to be fighting near or rather close to the Sun. We can't use missiles or bullets, and how do you plan to keep the fuel cool enough so it doesn't explode?" Lynsye asks crossing her arms with a cigarette in her mouth.

"Well, that's why we have an engineer," I say looking over to Casey.

"Me, hehehe, finally, I get to build something, yay!" Casey says hopping in the air.

"Yea, I only fix things I can't manufacture," Mittens says.

"Yea, you pick things up and put them down," Missy says chuckling at Mittens.

"Really, did you have to go there," Mittens replies with her hands on her hips.

147

"Ok, people we got a Star to save, Casey and Mittens you two work up a plan to make our fighters heat proof. The rest of us will start taking off armor and weapons. We don't have a lot of time as you can see from the last ship that entered the Station," I said to everyone.

The team goes to work, Mark and I begin by removing all the weapons from the fighters. Breaking out ratchets and using small roller cranes to remove missile pods and machine guns. Our work is delicate and time consuming, if we drop any of the weapons they could explode. Also parts for RP40's are hard to come by, they are actually old fighters, but these have been upgraded beyond their original capabilities. One major advantage is the RP40's have a small shield generator. They are faster and deadlier than most models out to date. The latest fighter, the Raptor RX, it is the fastest, and most durable fighter, it just uses a ton of fuel.

"Ichia, what are we going to use to fight with?" Mark asks me while carrying two missiles on his shoulders.

"Yea, what are we gonna use, foul language?" Lynsye says carrying a chain of bullets.

"Shit didn't think of that. Hey Mittens, what can we fight with that won't blow up on us?" I ask pulling a chain winch.

"Hmmm that's a good one, I'll run back to the parts hanger in a little bit, we're almost done with how to make this work," Mitten says as she's drawing blue prints.

The team and I have three fighters completely stripped down for upgrades.

148

We completely stripped them down in under two hours. We decided not to touch the bomber since the large cannon dome would never withstand the heat from the Sun. Mark, Lynsye, Missy and I sit on the side watching Mittens and Casey use their brains.

We stand watching them like a poker tournament. The two girls working on the blue prints are sweating and working diligently and as fast as they can. The clock's ticking and something is destroying ships in the fleet and possibly harming the Sun.

"Hey Ichia, I'll be right back. I'm going to go get us more water," Lynsye says.

"Yea, I'll go with her," Missy says as they start to head over to exit.

"Well, all we can do is wait for these two geniuses to come up with a plan." I said.

"Can you imagine fighting on the sun?" Mark says to me.

"It's gonna be hot, who knows what we'll find," I said.

"Better get some sunglasses you know," Mark says,

"Yea, that and some sunscreen. Heck maybe a radiation suit while we are at it." I said, taking a drink from my water bottle.

I get a text from Kat, it says. "Heads up more burned up ships are coming in, love you baby be careful out there."

"Gods, I love her," I say to Mark showing him them text.

"Yea, she's great man, I'm happy for you." Mark says lighting a cigarette.

Mark and I pace back and forth waiting for Mittens and Casey to come up with a plan. Lynsye and Missy come back with their large cooler, loaded with Ice, Water, and beer. They pass around drinks while watching the two girls talk and figure out the best idea to keep everyone safe. Hours begin to pass by, Lynsye has passed out in Missy's lap. Mark is working out, doing miscellaneous work outs, from crunches to lifting missiles like they are weights. I'm staring into space waiting for someone to bring me out of it. Then as I look to my right there's another freighter on fire, worse than the last.

"Gods damn," I said, then jumping over to the girls working on the blue prints.

"Look I don't want to rush you ladies, but look, another freighter just showed up looking like a Barbecue that went wrong," I said pointing at the flaming ship.

"We're going as fast as we can, we need more time," Casey says.

"Mark and I will head over to the parts place to look for weapons. Um Mittens," I said smiling.

"Bitch... here's my credit card," Mitten says to me whipping out her black credit card.

Mark and I hop on the hover cart and head over to the parts depot. Cruising through the station we notice that lots of people are all suffering from the heat. People are laying in the parks or sitting by fans. As we drive, buildings in the distance are starting to look like mirages.

"Are you seeing this?" Mark asks me.

"When did we get to the desert?" I replied.

We arrive at the depot and everyone is still watching the game.

"Yo, I need something that won't blow up in the heat!" I yell to all the lazy workers.

"That's one way to get their attention," Mark says.

"I learned it from a good friend," I said putting my thumb up.

"What can I get you?" a man covered in dust ask us.

"Well, I need a weapon that won't explode under extreme heat," I said.

"Hmmm. ever head of rail guns? They're actually new and haven't really been used. To be honest, they were built at the end war but never equipped to anything. Just need to put them on a small shield generator and you can use em. They're basically magnetic laser guns that use built up plasma and leftovers from a shield generator.

They have three firing types too, rapid fire like a machine gun, straight beam, or if you can fly good, cross the beams to make a bigger one," the man explains.

"Sounds good to me, how much?" I ask.

"Well we only got six in stock and they're hard to come by. But since you guys come here often I'll give you a little discount $1,000 per one, so $6,000," the man says as I shit myself.

"We ain't got a choice Ichia," Mark says.

"We'll take em," I said gulping as the man runs Mittens credit card.

"Yup, she's gonna kill ya," Mark says.

"Yea, she's gonna beat me to death," I said imagining Mittens flogging me with her purse.

The part dealers help load the rail guns onto the hover cart and Mark and I head back to our space crafts. Speeding through the station, another freighter is broken in half and burning up. We look at each other with long faces. We pull into our area and walk over to everyone.

"We got guns," Mark says.

"We got a plan," Casey says.

"Alright, how hard is this going to be?" I ask, then I take a drink from my water bottle.

"Well Casey has it mapped out very good. The good news is that you guys have shield generators. We'll have to crank the voltage a little, but it will run the coolers keeping you and your fighters chilly.

Also by turning up the voltage, the Shields should be a hair stronger, and that leaves a good amount of power for whatever weapons you purchased," Mittens explains leaning over the blue prints.

"We are going to be using rail guns," I said.

"WHAT!!! Them ain't cheap! How much did you put on my card....." Mittens yells

"Um $6,000," I said with a stupid grin.

Mittens throws a water bottle at me and it nearly takes my head off.

"Oh my gods, you blew my whole allowance," Mittens yells at me.

"Um, can we get back to saving the world, because if we don't you may not have an allowance left," Casey says putting her hand on Mittens shoulder and points to another burning ship entering the hanger.

"We will install the coolers first, then armor," Mittens says upset, crossing her arms huffing.

We go to work on the fighters, placing coolers, which are mini air conditioners inside the hull. We run lines as Mark walks up with two heavy air guns. Lynsye and I hold one of the coolers as Mark and Mittens ratchet them in. Casey is working on the programming in the cockpit of the Rapiers. Casey is typing in lines of code and pre-setting the computers, so all we will have to do is tell the machine what temperature we want. As we finish bolting in one cooler, Missy begins to plug the cords in one by one.

Within a few hours we have managed to upgrade all three Rapiers. We stand back and look at our fighters, covered in white armor instead of the old beat up Military Grey.

"Now we look sexy," Mark says throwing a rag over his shoulder.

"I think the proper phrase is we' brought sexy back." I said grinning.

"Well, I think we need to give the Rail Guns a test, what do you," Mitten says being interrupted by a large crash, and explosion.

As we were talking, a large cargo freighter came out of hyperspace burning up, and crashed into one of the gates on the space station.

"Um, no time for a bench test people, we gotta roll," I say.

"Sounds good to me," Casey says.

"Take the service tunnel out, its huge and it's the closet exit," Mittens says pointing towards a large circular grate.

"Thanks Mittens for everything," I say climbing into my Rapier.

"You and I are going to have a long conversation when you get back Mr!" Mittens says to me as she pulls several levers to open the service tunnel.

The ships lift off of the ground like an angel, then turning towards the service tunnel and rushing into it. Flying in a straight formation we come out of the tunnel. As we come out of the tunnel, I do a 180 and look at the damage of the last ship.

"Wow, looks bad," I said.

"Yea looks like a Barbeque gone bad," Casey says.

"FTL up, let's jump to the Sun guys," I said.

"Wait, wait, before we do, everyone open up your glove compartments," Lynsye says over the com.

Everyone opens their glove compartments, and sitting inside is a little green case. We all open the cases to find a pair of sun glasses.

"These are cool!" Casey says putting on her huge lensed sun glasses, looking like a pop star.

"Wow Lynsye, aren't these the type you always wear?" I ask.

"Yup, I figured ya'll are heading to a bright place. Figured I'd help where I could. Watch your butts out there guys," Lynsye says.

"We will thanks, let's do this!" I said pulling the FTL lever in my cockpit.

The ships flash like a bright snap from an old camera flash, and disappear.

Chapter 14

Great Balls of Fire.

We jump into orbit around the sun, it's like a burning ball of fire.

"Wow, never been this close," Mark says.

"We're about to get closer, let's head to the surface," I said pushing on my throttle.

We flew to the surface, flying a mere 300 to 600 feet over the surface of the sun. It looks like a fiery ocean with giant flames shooting out constantly.

"Wow, the rapiers are taking this a lot better than I thought, the temps are somewhat holding. But we're not going to be able to stay here too long," Casey says.

"Yea, my shields are taking a beating, I'm at 88 percent already," Mark says.

"Yea, mine too. This is the area where most of the ships were attacked," I said.

We continue to fly around the surface looking for any signs of life. As we circle around, a distress call comes over the radio.

"May day, May day, this is The Calipso, something is pulling us into the Sun, Please anyone HELP!" a frantic voice says over the com.

"That's our call, everyone lets jump out of orbit and cool off and dive over there," I said.

"Yea, that should allow our shields to regenerate a little bit," Casey says.

We pull up away from the surface and our shields begin to replenish. As we approach the distress call, we can see a large battleship being pulled towards the sun by a bright tentacle.

"What the hell is that?!" Mark says looking in disbelief.

"Quick, lets dive to the surface and cut whatever is grabbing the Battleship," I said.

We dive towards the surface of the Sun. As we approach the surface the tentacles are still pulling the battle ship towards the sun.

"Here goes nothing," I say pulling the trigger on my control stick.

As I pull the trigger, the rail guns light up and fire laser blasts. The laser blasts get absorbed by the large tentacle.

"Ok, plan B," Casey says pulling her rail guns into position to fire. She switches from blast to beam.

She pulls the trigger and a large beam forms in front of her ship and it rips the tentacle into two, and the battleship is freed. As the tentacle falls apart, a loud *shreek* rips through the area like a whale screaming under water.

"Holy Crap! What's that?" Mark says looking around.

All of a sudden, bright balls of fire fly out of the Sun. As they fly out they take the shape of a dragons. They begin to flap their wings and head towards us.

"What the hell, that's a new one, everyone let's take em head on," I said, putting the pedal to the metal.

"Wow, I've never seen anything like this!" Casey says firing towards the dragons.

"This is insane, there must be dozens of them things, keep shooting," Mark says.

As we shoot them, it doesn't take much to knock them down. As we blow through them, the dragons attach themselves to the ships. Mark pulls back from the group to clear off the dragons that have attached themselves to our ships. As Mark's picking them off, a larger dragon begins to chase after him and is spitting fire towards him.

"Oh shit, help would be nice," Mark says dodging and avoiding the fire balls from the dragon.

"I'm coming around baby!" Casey says as she cuts through several dragons with her rail guns.

She gets behind the large dragon that's chasing Mark, charges her rail gun and takes a single shot. The dragon breaks apart and falls into the Sun, then two more begin chase her. She forms up with Mark and they start heading towards me, and I'm already under attack, being chased by a dozen.

"Hey, let's play chicken with these suckers!!" Mark yells over the com.

"Hell ya, I'll break right you break left!" I yell.

"Right, I go right and you go left!" Mark yells.

"Your left, my right....right!" I yell back.

"Screw IT!!!!" we both yell.

I break hard right and Mark breaks hard left with Casey right behind him. The dragons collide and make a huge ball of fire.

"Oh yea, that's how we roll bitches!!!" I said.

"Um, thats not good, look out guys!!!!" Casey yells over the com.

The big ball of fire starts to form into a huge Hydra with wings and all the other little dragons are being sucked into it. Heads start to come out of the main body, a total of eight heads come out. The wing span of the hydra is ridiculously huge. After the first set of wings come out, another pair of wings come out along with a long tail that looks like a fiery flail.

"Holy crap, everyone head away from the Sun, damn its getting hot!" I said, flipping my fighter around.

"Yea, my shields are about gone!" Casey says.

"Yea, mine too," I said flooring it to escape from the surface of the sun.

"Watch out guys, break away," Mark says as the hydra's eight heads breath fire towards us.

We are unable to get away from the Sun, and we end up taking the Hydra head on. Diving towards the Hydra we attack each head. As we shoot the heads off of the body they come back again. As we pass around the Hydra, the heads try to snap at the fighters but miss by near inches. We are trying to tangle the heads, but they move like water through each other and we are unable to tangle them.

"Man this sucker is tough! Not to mention my shields are gone!" Mark yells taking off his shirt.

"We gotta try to head away from the Sun, my systems are starting to overheat!" Casey says taking off her shirt too.

"I'll get it to chase me, you two try to replenish your ships. Damn its hot in here!" I said charging my rail guns.

"We'll break away as you get its attention." Mark says.

"Here kitty kitty kitty." I said flipping my ship 180 and firing the fully charged rail gun.

The beam splits six of the eight heads off and part of the body. As the Hydra tries to recover, it starts to fall towards the Sun. Then a giant tentacle comes out and blocks Mark and Casey's escape route and pulls them back.

"Holy Crap my ship's burning up!" Casey screams, trying to recalibrate her fighter.

"Bank to the left to get away from this arm," Mark says

pushing her fighter with his.

I come around, starting to shoot the tentacle, then the tentacle grabs the hydra and pulls it under. As it pulls, the hydra is screaming trying to get away from them tentacle.

"That's what they call rape!" I said trying to head higher away from the surface of the sun. As we try to get away from surface, a large solar flare blocks us from going anywhere. We are trapped in a giant fiery dome.

"Holy crap!!!" I yell, shooting the flare wall

"We're trapped" Mark says looking for an exit.

"Guys, we got something big coming towards us!" Casey yells over the com.

We pull as high as we can, but the heat is just beating down on the fighters and the hull is heating up. We look down towards the sun and a dozen tentacles come out of the surface in every direction, then it's followed by a defining scream. We all hold our hands over our ears as we watch in horror as a large creature emerges from the surface. The creature comes out drooling fire, and is shaped like a giant ant. It has huge jaws with claws coming off its chest. It's eyes are bright yellow, so bright they stand out from the Suns light.

"Holy shit.... okay I'm down for options," I said.

"We're going to burn up here, my systems are over heating!" Casey says taking off her pants.

"This is Jupiter 7, is there anyone out there that can help us out?" Mark called over the com but there is no response.

161

"The solar flare must be blocking our signal," Casey says.

"Guys, this thing looks hungry." I said pulling off my shirt and tucking it under my seat.

Before anyone can say anything the creature charges towards us like a lion leaping at its prey. We dodge the creature and get behind it, as it slams into the solar flare and turns. As it turns we lay down a line of fire towards its face but it only angers the creature further. The creature dives towards us again with its claws out attempting to grab us. The creature misses grabbing me by mere millimeters, it crashes into the surface of the sun creating a huge tsunami wave of fire.

"Shit! Pull up people!!!" I scream pulling back on my throttle control.

We all escape the wave, but the creature comes back throwing huge balls of fire towards us.

"This is getting retarded, we gotta do something or were gonna be cooked," Casey says.

"Hey I got an idea, let's focus our rail guns," Mark says.

"That's a great idea, but can we stay still long enough? Watch it! another wave!!!!" I yell as we all pull up again.

"It's getting hungry!" Casey says

As the wave passes under us the creature tries a sneak attack us and nearly jumps on top of us. We pull away shooting in every spot we can. My ship stalls as we back off.

"SHIT!!!" I said kicking my console.

"ICHIA!!!" Mark and Casey scream as the creature jumps to swallow me in his ship.

I look up, eyes wide open and start to hold my breath. All of a sudden the monster is knocked back by several large explosions. The Solar flare is broken apart and still continuing to fire, it's Lynsye and Missy in their bomber high in orbit over the Sun.

"Hurry up guys, fall back!!!" Lynsye says.

We start to fall back away from the surface.

"Guys it's now or never, form up!" I said sitting in my boxers and shoes in my fighter.

"Right! now or never." Casey says wearing only her bra, panties and shoes.

The half-naked team pulls around and we form up on each other's, wing tip to wing tip, we form a triangle. As we form up, the monster regroups and turns towards us drooling fire. Looking hungrier than before, it growls and snaps towards us.

"Charge up main beams," I said.

"Light that sucker up guys!" Missy says.

The creature leaps towards us. The rail guns light up and create a center beam between the fighters. The beams come together to form a bright blue ball, then like a spear of light, a beam charges towards the creature ripping it in half. The beam is so strong that it punches a hole into the Sun, the hole starts to suck the creature in as it tries to get away.

"Holy crap, do you guys see this?" I said.

"Yea, that's crazy!" Casey says looking in amazement.

"Let's get outta here," I said, turning my burnt fighter around.

We head away from the sun. As we get into a safe orbit, our shield generators are badly damaged, we can't recharge our shields, and the coolers are barely working.

"I feel like I'm flying a soup can, and my FTL is toast." Casey says.

"Yea my FTL is down too." Mark says.

As we sit there, several freighters jump into orbit with us. Along with the freighter, several military battle ships arrive too.

"Little late, you guys missed the fun," Mark says over the com.

"Good work, the Frigate Charleston will tow you back to the station," a voice says over the com.

"Thanks for the lift." I said sitting in my fighter head leaned back.

The Frigate hooks the three fighters together and jumps us back to the space station along with bomber right behind.

"Jupiter 7, can you guys fly and land your fighters on your platform?" a voice over the com says as we enter the Stations orbit.

"Yea, we can still sorta fly," I said trying as hard as I could to keep it straight.

"Yea, I can still steerish," Casey says attempting the same thing.

We detach from the frigate and fly disheveled into the station towards our platform. Smoke is pouring out of our engines, and fighters are violently shaking. I'm the first to approach the platform, I attempt to pull up but the fighter won't respond to my controls.

"What the hell, come on, gods damit!" I yell pulling the flight stick as hard as I can.

"Dude, pull up!" Mark yells.

"I'm trying, she won't respond, SHIT!" I yell over the com while kicking the dashboard.

It's too late as I fight my fighter. I hit the deck like a rag doll hitting the top of a slide and scrape across the floor of the space station. People frantically move out of the way of the out-of-control fighter, and the burnt parts that fly off of it. Inside the tumbling fighter I'm desperately trying to reach for the ejection handle. I pull myself forward as hard as I can, and pulled the lever.

Just in the nick of time I'm rocketed out of the fighter right before it hits the center wall of the space station.

"Holy shit!" I said to myself while hanging on to my seat.

"Did he make it, did he make it?" Casey says landing her fighter.

"Hell ya, he ejected just in time, my man!" Mark says as his fighter engines cut out and slams onto the deck.

"Hey did you guys see that!!" I said over the com, piloting my chair back to the deck.

"You're going to be on the six o'clock news for sure," Missy says giggling.

"Hey it's not funny, Ichia you alright?" Casey says stepping out of her cockpit looking up at him coming down.

"Yea I'm good, little shaken, but damn, talk about a Hail Mary, I need a change of underwear," I said landing my seat gently on the deck floor.

I land and everyone comes to me, along with dozens of spectators who saw the landing. I pull off my helmet and look towards the wall where my fighter crashed.

"That was too close," I said.

"Hey bud, how ya feeling?" Mark asks helping me up off my chair.

"Well, looks like I'm out of a fighter," I said.

"Yea, well you can man my other cannon on my bomber, so you're not of work yet," Lynsye says.

As we converse over the fighter issue, the crowd grows bigger. Fighting through the crowd you hear a voice yell, "Move out of the way," and calling for Ichia. People are pushed out of the way and Kat appears from the crowd.

"You survived the crash, thank gods!" Kat says running to me.

"Come on, can't kill me that quick," I said, grabbing Kat into my arms as I kiss her.

"Hey!" Mittens yells.

"Oh shit," I said.

"Yea oh shit, you guys wrecked everything, and you're all naked!" Mitten says and starts to laugh very loudly, holding her gut.

Everyone takes a step back and looks at each other. I'm only wearing my shoes and boxers. Mark is wearing his shoes and a banana hammock. Casey is only wearing shoes, panties and a bra. We all look at each other and start to turn red.

"Um… OH MY GOD, LOOK PEOPLE, ITS ANOTHER MONSTER!!!!" Casey yells pointing towards the gate of the space station.

Everyone turns the other way, looking for the so called monster. As they turn back to look, we are gone.

"Phew, I didn't even realize we were half naked," Casey said in relief.

"I thought something felt funny," Mark says putting on a shirt.

"I'm just glad you guys are ok, the news media had the entire fight on camera. At one point I thought you guys where done," Kat says holding my waist tightly.

"Well Lynsye and Missy saved our butts from orbit," I said.

"Hey, it's all about team work, if we aren't all here it's not going to work," Lynsye says.

"I agree," Casey say as the Admiral walks in.

"Hello everyone, good job out there," Admiral Hitoshi says looking around.

"Thanks," we all say, standing at attention.

"Well you guys did a great job, the military wants to give you thanks and a little reward, along with the Mercury Mining Men. They heard about how much you spend on your fighters so they are going to donate the funds to you," Hitoshi says handing me some paper work.

"Cool, unfortunately I'm going to have to hand it right back to Mittens. She helped pay for everything," I said when everyone looks at him and sighs.

"For once I thought we were going to have real money." Mark says.

"Hold it right there, Ichia," Jeffery walks in with Mittens.

I stop and look towards Jeffery and Mittens.

"Just give her back half and I'll count the rest as a donation from my Attorney's Office. You just saved the lives of billions and you deserve something." Jeffery says with his hand on my shoulder.

168

"Are you sure, I mean you work hard for that money," I said as everyone looks at me like, "what the hell."

"I'm sure, life is more important than money," Jeffery says pulling Mittens closer as she blushes.

"Just bring me a bottle of Jackie and we'll call it even," Mittens says smiling holding Jeffery.

"Thank you, I don't know what to say," I said.

"Thanks Jeffery, we've been working so hard to actually make it out here, looks like we have a chance for once," Lynsye says pulling off her sun glasses.

"Any time guys," Jeffery says.

"In the meantime we're down a fighter now," I said.

"I'll have to go over there and salvage what I can out of the wreckage." Casey says.

"I'll go with you later if you want," Mittens says.

"Cool, thanks," Casey replies pulling up her shorts.

"Well, my fighter is kind of ok, the engines cut out while I landed," Mark says scratching his head.

"The bomber's always good to go," Lynsye says lighting another cigarette.

"And my fighter is burned up really good, so I guess that gives us one and half fighters and a bomber," Casey says leaning on Mark.

"Well, let's get you kids debriefed on this mission and you guys can have some time off," Hitoshi says.

"Sounds like a plan to me." Missy says.

Later that evening, back at my apartment, Kat and I cuddle on the couch.

"Wow, what a day," I said.

"You're telling me, we used about twenty gallons of burn gel and new skin." Kat says with her head on my shoulder.

"Yea, it got a little hot up there." I said gently combing my hand through her hair.

"I was so scared as I watched the monitor, I almost gave someone the wrong medicine," Kat said softly.

"Honestly, I wasn't scared, worried but I wasn't scared. Somehow I knew I'd make it home to be next to you and hold you," I said looking down at Kat.

"Liar," Kat said giggling holding me tighter.

"If I ever die, I'll be alone, it's one thing I've always known for some reason." I said.

"Well, you're never going to be alone, I promise. I love you," Kat said softly, getting closer to me.

"I love you too," I said kissing Kat.

Chapter 15

Sausage Gravy and Biscuits.

A couple of days later everyone met at the Coney Island at the food court.

"Oh yea, I slept good last night," Mark said while scooping up a fork full of eggs.

"Yea, same here," I said.

"So what's the plan for today?" Lynsye asked leaning back on Missy.

"Well, Casey, Mark and Mittens are going to salvage what they can from my crash. I was going to head over to job board to see if there is anything going on." I said taking a drink from my coffee cup.

"At this point we better take any job we can get," Lynsye said.

"Yea, new fighters aren't going to be cheap," Mark says.

"Yea, the new ones are too expensive and it's too hard to find an old goodie," Casey said.

"Maybe I should get a part time job," I said looking into my coffee cup.

"What! Yea, the last time you did was in college, that went well, remember," Lynsye says.

"Yea you burned all the food on the grill," Mark says laughing.

"Ok maybe not a good idea," I said.

"Just go over to the Job Board, here's five bucks, get a drink and sit there. You always have better luck at getting them than us," Missy says.

Everyone finished breakfast and headed on their way. I start to make my way down to the job board and make a quick stop at the hospital. I'm waved in by a nurse and I head over to the Intensive Care Unit to see Kat.

I walk through the hallway and see Kat standing at the counter, writing on a pad of paper.

"Hey beautiful," I said.

"Hey baby," Kat says giving me a kiss.

"Here, I brought you lunch," I said holding up a brown paper bag.

"Aw, what did you bring me?" Kat ask looking into the bag.

"Pudding snack, banana, and your favorite egg salad sandwich," I say smiling.

"You're the best boyfriend ever!" Kat says with a giggle, hugging me.

"Dr., room twelve needs the medication," a nurse interrupts us.

"Oh I'm sorry, I'm on my way, duty calls," Kats says.

"Go on, I'll see you tonight when you get home," I say to Kat.

"Love you," Kat says hurrying away with a needle in her hand.

"Love you too." I said standing by the Nurses station.

I head back to the main hallway to get to the elevators that go to the job boards. Stepping onto the elevator I look out the glass, I notice a reflection of the people standing behind me as they look at their compads and then at me. They whisper, "Hey that's the guy that saved the station."

A girl dressed in military uniform and a large red scarf stares me down as I look out of the elevator window approaching the main deck.

I leave the elevator and walk down the ramp towards the Job board. Slowly following me was the girl with the big red scarf.

I stop at the vending machine and put in the five dollars to get my favorite mineral drink, Pocari. The machine vents out my drink and I walk over to the ledge in front of the job boards and hop up on it.

"Damn, nothing, not even a delivery mission. Maybe the Lab Rats have scared everyone out here," I said then take a drink.

"Hey you're Chang, right?" the girl with the big red scarf asks.

"Yea that's me."

"Oh good, I've been looking for you lately," the girl in the red scarf says.

"Um, I have a girl friend," I said raising my eyebrow towards the girl.

"No, I need service," the girl says.

"Um, I'm not a male stripper," I reply.

"NO NO NO I need your skills," the girl starts to raise her voice.

"I'm just kidding," I say smiling, hopping off the ledge holding my hand out.

"I'm Ichia Chang of Jupiter Seven."

"I'm Colleen Duron of Saturn Five," she says shaking my hand.

"Saturn Five, we've helped your group before. You guys are the Marine Scientists, you guys took out that Lab Rat base on Titan. It was like six of you against like two hundred, right?" I asked.

"Actually four," Colleen says crossing her arms grinning.

"Wow, I've heard you guy were bad asses," I say taking a drink from my bottle.

"Well, I've heard and seen a lot of you lately, that last fight you all had on the Sun was wild. Never seen anything like that before," Colleen says.

"Yea, we took a chance and it did cost me my fighter, but everyone is safe." I say leaning on the ledge.

"Yea, no one deserves to get hurt by those bastards," Colleen says.

"So you need my services, what can Jupiter 7 do for you?" I ask.

"Well, this is a non Lab Rat Incident, this one is more Mafia. The stupid Mafia stole a water producer to make illegal alcohol and sell it on the black market," Colleen says.

"And that's a bad thing?" I ask.

"Yea, it is when that water producer belongs to poor people in the deserts of Mars who can't get water like the rest of us," Colleen says putting her hands in her pockets.

"Yea that's bad, well we're in, let me know what you need us to do and we'll do the best we can to help," I said.

"Sounds good to me, how soon can you be ready?" Colleen asks.

"Ha ha, um, yea, let me check on that," I say scratching my head.

"We're not planning to raid their frigate until the moon is dark in two days," Colleen says.

"Cool, that should give me time to get at least one fighter running along with the bomber. Hey, if you not busy now, come on down I'll introduce you to everyone," I said.

"Sure I got free time, my team's all still in bed, bunch of lazy asses some times. All they do is eat, sleep, shoot, and shit," Colleen says throwing her hands up in the air.

We start walking over to the deck where my team is working hard.

"How long have you been in the grind?" I ask.

"Eight years, seen a lot of stuff, two wars and a lot of death," Colleen says looking forward.

"Well you look different from most people," I said looking at her large eyes and angled face, not to mention cat like ears.

"Ha, I'm actually half human and Nephilum," Colleen says smiling at me.

"Whoa, you're a cross breed? I've only heard stories about your kind," I said in a amazement.

"Well, you're the first to appreciate it, most people make fun of me being half human and half cat. Although I can run faster and jump higher than most," Colleen says.

"That's awesome, I wish I had skills like that," I say.

"No you don't, trust me," Colleen says giggling.

Casey and Mittens are going through the scrap they managed to collect from my fighter. They lay everything out, and as they do Mittens looks up and see me walking with Colleen.

"Uh oh, here comes trouble, Ugh," Mittens says standing up holding her stomach with the baby inside.

"Who's that?" Casey asks.

"Dunno, never seen her before," Mittens says.

"Hey guys, how's it going." I ask.

"Not so good, only managed to get a few things, most of it burned up in the wreckage. So who's your friend?" Casey asks taking a drink from her water bottle.

"This is Colleen from Saturn Five, She's asking for our help for her mission," I said.

"Saturn Five, isn't that the Marines?" Mittens asks.

"Yup, S5 hoorah," Colleen says smiling with her arms behind her back.

"Great, Jar Heads," Mittens says.

"Hey, better than being a grease monkey," Colleen says.

"Alright kids, I know Fighter Pilots and Marines never mix, but let's change that," I said.

"Fine, I'm Mittens best mechanic on the station," Mittens says.

"I'm Casey, newest member of Jupiter Seven, I'm a pilot and engineer," Casey says.

"Aren't there a total of five in your team Ichia?" Colleen asks.

"Yea the other two girls are off somewhere, my buddy Mark, not sure," I said as Colleens phone starts to ring.

She answers her phone, and I glanced at the damaged parts.

"Well, it was great to meet you, I have to run. So, I guess I'll see you in two days?" Colleen says.

"Have to run already?" I ask.

"Yea, the usual business," Colleen says shrugging her shoulders.

"Yup, just email me the job info and we'll meet you at your platform," I said shaking Colleen's hand.

Colleen walks away and I turn towards Casey and Mittens and all of the broken parts laying on the floor.

"So, what's not broken?" I say smiling.

"Marines, really, you must be desperate," Mittens says crossing her arms.

"Hey, we are broke, down a ship and I'll help whoever we can to earn some cash," I reply.

"Well either way, we still have to fix my ship and Mark's. My ship will be an easy fix, Marks is bad but I can have her running with Mittens help by tomorrow evening," Casey says holding a big wrench over her shoulder.

"Yea I'm free, Jeffery's on Mars for a hearing, so I'm all yours Casey," Mittens says leaning on a counter.

"Hehehe, if I was Lysnye I'd take advantage of that," Casey says giggling.

"Ha, I thought my jokes where bad," Mitten says.

"Anything I can do to help?" I ask.

"Yea, go find Mark, We sent him on a smoothie run, and he's still not back," Casey says.

"Um ok, I'll go hunt him down," I said.

I leave the ladies to figure out the problems with our fighters. As I walk into the food court, Mark's standing and talking with Lynsye and Missy.

"Hey guys what's up?" I ask.

"Not much, just trying to figure out how to save some money since we may go broke if you don't find us work," Lynsye says.

"Well, I've solved that problem," I say taking a smoothie.

"You found work that quick?" Mark asks looking amazed.

179

"Actually, work found us. Staff Sergeant Colleen Duran from Saturn Five came up to me while I was at the job board, she's got work for us," I say taking a sip from the smoothie.

"Marines, really?..." Mark says.

"I know, I know, Mittens said the same thing. Look, maybe this is our chance to change all that hogwash history around. Two amazing team's join forces to stop the evil Lab Rat Mafia," I say with my hand sympathetically in the air.

"Ha you're funny, but whatever, work is work and I'm not complaining," Missy says.

"So when do we fly?" Mark asks.

"Two days, I haven't got all of the details yet, Colleen is going to email them to me soon," I said.

"Sounds good. Better get these drinks back to the brains of our operation," Lynsye says.

"Yea, Ichia already drank Mittens smoothie," Missy says

"Crap, I'll catch up guys," I said running away towards the smoothie bar.

I order two smoothies, another one for me and one for Mittens. I swipe my card and I start to stare at the console for payment.

"I hope this works out, we need money and my own bills are starting to pile up," I said to myself typing in my bank code.

The kiosk dispenses the two strawberry and banana smoothies with protein powders in them. Then a little blender arm reaches in and starts to mix them together, almost like a little symphony.

Finally the drinks are complete and the slip shield lifts up and the drinks come out ice cold. I pick them up and start to head back to the flight deck. I get back to the deck and everyone's hanging out in the bomber.

"Hey, took you long enough," Mittens says snatching the smoothie from me.

"Yea, sorry I drank yours and I got myself a refill," I said.

"Well I'm gonna take the rest of the day off. Apooka is playing at the movie theater tonight, Mark and I got tickets to the 9 PM showing. I'm going to work on the fighters tomorrow," Casey says taking a sip from her smoothie.

"That's cool, yea no rush, I wanted to spend tonight with Kat, she gets off early," I said.

"Uh oh, someone's baby making tonight," Lynsye says holding her cigarette elegantly.

"Ha, no, I just want to spend some quality time together. The last few weeks have been rough, might go to the park tonight, Ortega's comet is in view this week," I said leaning on the table.

"Oh yea that's right, I wish Jeffery was home we could watch it too," Mittens says looking down at her smoothie.

"He's been working a lot lately, hasn't he," Missy asks.

"Yea, I see him like one or two days a week. The only time I really get to spend with him is when he goes to his bowling league. But he pays most of the bills so I don't complain. I just try to keep him happy in every way I can, especially when he's stressed out," Mittens says.

"You'll be alright. He'll be taking lots of time off I'm sure when you have your baby," Casey says smiling at Mittens.

"Yea," Mittens says taking a drink from her smoothie.

"Well, when I get the info from Colleen, I'll let you guys know. I'll stop in to see how the repairs are going tomorrow Casey," I said.

"Cool, bring me goodies," Casey says.

"I'll bring your favorite doughnuts, don't worry," I say.

"Alright everyone have a good night," Casey says grabbing Mark by the waist and taking him away.

"I'll see you guys," I say walking out the door.

Later that evening, I'm waiting by the nurses' station. I'm leaning on the counter talking to an older nurse as she's entering information into a computer. I look around, how quiet the hospital gets during the evening.

"Sure gets quiet around here huh?" I said to the nurse.

"Yea, ever since you guys stomped the Lab Rat Mafia it's been really quiet." the nurse says.

"Hey!" Kat comes around the corner, all dressed up. She's wearing a long black dress with one side cut and the other not, so part of her leg is showing. Her hair is down and she's wearing large halo rings on each ear.

"Hey babe, sorry, had to fight to get a shower," Kat says giving me a hug and kissing me on the cheek.

"No problem, I was talking with Mary here," I said.

"Was he bothering you ,Mary?" Kat says smiling.

182

"No, he was just telling me all fun things you two are in store for tonight," Mary says.

"Oh really," Kat says smiling at me.

"You two get on, I'll see you on Monday, Kat," Mary says standing up picking up medical boards.

"See ya," Kat says turning with me and putting her arm around me.

We walk out of the Hospital onto the main walkway into the center of the Space Station. We walk hand in hand, strolling down to the main train station. We step onto the space train, take a seat, and we have an amazing view of Earth from where we sit. It was like if we were falling towards the planet even though we rode the train to our destination.

"So where are we going?" Kat ask.

"Well I figured a nice dinner, then maybe a walk through the park," I reply staring into her beautiful blue eyes.

"Sounds good to me, it feels great not having to worry about anything and getting to dress up again," Kat says holding my hand.

"Yea, I haven't dressed up in while. I feel special, like I'm rich or something," I said while Kat lightly giggles.

"Well, rich or poor I love you, and tonight's going to be a great night," Kat says as she kisses me.

Meanwhile, on the other side of the station is the movie theater.

"Alright, we're early," Casey says jumping up and down.

"You really like watching the previews." Mark says smiling.

183

"Oh yea, and we don't have to rush to get popcorn and Sodi Pop!" Casey says tugging Mark into the movie theater. They pull out their phones and the door man scans their screens with the digital tickets on them. They walk to the giant ballroom with huge chandeliers and kiosks for food. On one side there are two big rooms of arcade games, with lots of stuffed animal crane games. They walk up to food counter kiosk.

"Ok I want the 5 pound bucket of popcorn with extra, extra, extra butter, mwahahahah!" Casey says drooling at the screen.

"Shit I'm going to have to run an extra mile tomorrow," Mark says swiping his card in the kiosk.

"I love you baby, you always feed me right," Casey says putting her arms around Mark giving him a kiss.

"Well, I can't let you starve babe," Marks says.

As the two stare at each other in the kiosk, a sixteen by sixteen inch bucket drops down and popcorn starts to pop and fills the giant bucket. As the bucket is being filled, a one hundred twenty four ounce drink fills up. The popcorn bucket is filled and the machine starts to spray butter onto it, and then it drops a long straw into the drink.

"Oh I'm spoiled as hell," Casey says giggling like a little Asian girl.

"No, just treated right babe," Mark says picking up the giant bucket of popcorn.

The two head over to theater 5 where the movie is going to be playing. They walk in and there are already a lot of people in seats. Casey spots perfect seats, where they could put the popcorn and sit next to each other. They walk around everyone and hop into the seats. The seats are like jelly, squishy and they rock back and forth, too. Where they are sitting they have a mini table that holds the huge popcorn, so they can cuddle and butter each other up.

"Wonder what movie previews we're going to see?" Casey asks.

"I can't wait to see the movie, Apooka Verses the Dark Night. The last Apooka film was great!" Mark says.

"Yea, especially when they went to Disney World, too awesome!" Casey says putting a handful of popcorn into her mouth.

The two cuddle, munching on popcorn as the previews start to roll. Mark has his arm around Casey. Sitting between them is the extra-large Sodi pop and the very large bucket of popcorn is in front of them.

Chapter 16
<u>Dinner for two.</u>

Kat and I walk into the Crystal Scribe. It's a very upscale and classy restaurant. Must be dressed to enter and plan to spend some money. We walk in and the hostess and manger notice me from the news.

"Hey you're from Jupiter Seven, right," the manager says setting down menus at the counter.

"Yea, I'm Ichia." I said.

"I thought so, you saved my restaurant and my family, meals on me tonight," the manager says smiling standing tall holding his hand towards me.

"Um wait, you don't have to do all that," I said waving my hands.

"Nope it's on us, please follow me sir," the hostess says holding two menus, bowing.

I turn towards Kat and I give her a big smile.

"Let's go," Kat says smiling grabbing my hand.

We follow the little hostess thru the restaurant. As we walk through the restaurant, people are looking at us, some people notice me and whisper. We're led to a table next to a big bay window that has a great view of the moon. In the distance you can see the comet, too. The table is covered in a white silk table cloth. On each side there is a plate with a napkin neatly wrapped with forks, spoons, and knives on each side. In the middle is a crystal vase filled with two roses, and on each side two long candles burn. I pull out a chair for Kat, she sits and I help her scoot in, then go to my chair and sit.

"Our specials tonight are Prime Rib from Earth, Cajun Tilapia from Mars, and several Cream Desserts. Your waiter will be here shortly," the hostess says and bows.

"Wow, this is amazing!" Kat says looking at me.

"I know, I figured we'd get crammed into a small corner and have to split a dinner," I said with a smile looking around at the amazing restaurant.

"See, I told you, you're doing great things. Keep doing what you do and eventually things will get better," Kat says.

"I'm glad I found you Kat, ever since I've been with you my life has turned around," I said putting my hand across the table and Kat reached for it.

"I know you've had a few rough patches, between my drama and the attacks. I'm not going to let you down. I'm going to be there for you thru hell and back," Kat says squeezing my hand and smiling back at me.

"Good evening my name in Mario, I'll be your waiter this evening. First I'd like to shake your hand Mr. Chang, thanks to your bravery my cousins are safe on Mercury," Mario says shaking my hand.

"Oh thanks, just doing what I do best with my Team," I said.

"Well, can I make a recommendation on drinks?" Mario asks.

"Absolutely," Kat says smiling.

"The Pineapple Comets are amazing here, I recommend it to everyone," Mario says.

"Sounds good to me," I say.

"Me too!" Kat says.

"Okay, well take your time looking over the menu, I'll be back shortly," Mario says.

We open up our menus and look through the appetizers and start calling off different items. We both point out how everything is almost all handmade and not processed. Most food on the Space Station is pre-processed, but some places still make it by hand. Pre-processed and handmade are still argued on which is better for you and which is safer. Some say there is a difference in taste, and some say handmade has less salts. As for me, food is food, just give it to me.

"Wow, they have real clams from New England, and oh handmade Jalapeño poppers fried in tempura batter and real cheese," Kat says pointing at the appetizers.

"That sounds good, what about the Cucumber rolls with egg and avocado. Oh and the teriyaki steak with rice paste on romaine leaf," I said.

"Yea, that sounds like a good start," Kat says smiling at me.

"Did you see the entrees, oh my gods, this food sounds delicious," I said to Kat holding my menu like I'm looking at a great story in the newspaper.

"Yea, very classy, I don't know what to get. I think I want chicken tonight," Kat says.

"Yea I'm thinking fish, the Tilapia with tartar sounds good," I said.

"Oh they have chicken brisket, that sounds good, it comes with a small salad and fresh vegetables on the side, I wonder if they have baked potatoes. I had one at Wendy's the other day for lunch and it was all flaky, yuck. I still ate it though," Kat says smiling.

"This is turning into an amazing night," I said.

"It's hard to believe sometimes that here we sit above the earth in a space station eating the finest food. Do you think people ever dreamed about these kind of moment's ages ago?" Kat asks me, taking a sip from her glass of water.

189

"Yea, it's all about technology and taking chances. They say it all started on the moon, then Mars. You know one day I wouldn't mind being a captain of Star Ship. It was one of my dreams back then. But I love being a pilot more than anything," I said.

"Space Captain, hmm that would be cool, I wonder what your uncle would say?" Kat asks.

"He'd say, oh you're trying to be like me," I say as we both laugh.

"Well, whatever future you choose I'll be right next to you whatever it is," Kat says holding my hand.

"Thank you."

"Hey what's that white blur out there in the distance past the moon?" Kat says pointing.

"Oh yea, I almost forgot, that's Ortega's Comet. Yea, it's a newly discovered comet, and it's a really bright one, too," I said.

"Is it going to come near the Earth?" Kat asked.

"No, but it's going to pass close to the sun, I heard scientist were going to attempt to catch it," I said looking out the window.

"Really, that would be cool, I guess. Hope they have a big baseball glove," Kat says.

"Sorry about the wait, here are your drinks." Mario says placing two tall glasses onto the table. The glasses are filled with a yellow orange mixture with a large pineapple slice topping the glass with long straws.

"This looks good," I said looking at Kat.

"What have we decided on dinner this evening?" Mario asks with his digital order pad and pen.

"We'll start with an appetizer, we'll have the jalapeño poppers, teriyaki on a leaf, and cucumber rolls," I said.

"Great choices, are you ready to order for dinner too?" Mario asks.

"Yup, Kat you go first," I say pointing at her.

"Thanks, I'll have the Chicken Brisket with vegetables, any chance you guys have baked potatoes too?" Kat asks Mario.

"Best on the station, would you like it filled with butter, sour cream, chives, bacon and cheese?" Mario asks.

"Do it up," Kat says smiling and giggling.

"And you sir?" Mario ask me holding his order pad.

"Otay, I'll take the Tilapia Special," I say.

"Another good choice, I'll have the appetizers right up and dinner will be right behind it, anything else?" Mario asks.

"Nope, thanks Mario," I reply.

Mario takes our dinner menus and heads towards the kitchen. We two lovers sit there holding hands glaring out into space towards the Comet. We sit as if we were under a spell looking at what peace could really be. Within a few minutes Mario comes back with the appetizers.

He first moves the vase and candles towards the other end of the table towards the window. Then he neatly places the Jalapeño poppers down, followed by a long wooden plate that has 6 neatly rolled seaweed and rice cucumber rolls.

Then a half moon shaped white ceramic plate with two romaine leafs topped with teriyaki beef and a rice paste. The food is steamy and it almost looks as if you can see the smell.

"Oh, this smells awesome," Kat says.

"I'll be back shortly with your dinner," Mario says.

"Thanks," I say to Mario.

"Yea, I don't know where to start," I said as I put my napkin on my right leg and use a fork to pick up a seaweed roll. Kat goes for a Jalapeño Popper. She places it on her plate and gently cuts it in half. As she cuts it in two the smell is just amazing like a baked pie, then she takes a bite.

"Wow, this is beyond me, this jalapeño just blew my mind," Kat says to me licking her lips.

"Well I hope I get that chance tonight, too." I say quickly taking a drink.

"Ha, oh I have a plan already for you mister when we get back home." Kat says.

"Does it involve Jalapeños?" I say as Kat laughs and snorts.

"Be patient, we still have to have our main course and desert. I'm craving ice cream lately," Kat says as my jaw drops.

We finish our drinks and appetizers, Mario notices and comes over to our table.

"Would you guys like another round?" Mario asks.

"Absolutely," we both say laughing.

"I'll be right back with your drinks and your dinner will be ready shortly," Mario says taking our glasses and plates.

"Geez, I can't wait for dinner, I'm still hungry," I say holding my stomach.

"Yea I agree, and the food tastes so amazing, I wish we could eat here all the time. This so beats the food court," Kat says.

"I don't know, Taco Bell never fails me when I need a late night snack," I said grinning.

"I don't know how you guys eat that and then fly or do anything, Taco Bell makes me gassy," Kat says.

"Ha, makes me uninhabitable to be around," I said smiling

"Well at least you don't do it around me except that one night where you farted in bed, gods that was bad," Kat says.

"Yea, my bad," I said scratching my head.

"Well, I still love you," Kat says reaching across to me.

"I love you too," I say reaching out holding Kat's hand.

We continue to stare out the large window towards the moon which has moved into view. We watch the Moon slowly grace across our view. Mario comes to the table with a large tray in one hand holding it high over his head and in his left hand he has the tray holder. Like a magician he folds out the holder and places the large tray on top of the stand. He begins to hand out the dishes to Kat and I.

"Wow this smells great! "Kat says ready to drool on her meal.

"Is there anything else I can get for you two?" Mario asks standing tall at the table.

"No, I think we are okay," I reply looking at Kat as she gives me the ok.

"Perfect, I'll check on you two in a little bit, enjoy." Mario says and then takes a bow and heads towards the kitchen.

Kat and I look at each other and then look at our food and we both say, "Let's dig in." We both work on our meals as if it was art. Cutting piece by piece and enjoying the savory flavors.

"Here," Kat says holding a fork full of baked potatoes dressed with a little bit of sour cream, cheese and bacon bits.

I open my mouth and Kat puts the fork in my mouth. I start blushing and almost forget to chew.

"Wow, that's really good! Here try my Tilapia," I say while holding a piece on my fork towards Kat.

Kat bites the Tilapia off of my fork and begins to smile.

"Wow, that's really tasty and it doesn't even taste like fish," Kat says wiping her mouth with her napkin.

We enjoy our meal and watch the comet show from our table. We finish our plates leaving them bare, could have licked them clean if we wanted to, it was so good. Honestly, I haven't had food like this since I was on Mars with my parents.

"Wow, I guess I was hungry," I said rubbing my stomach.

"I'm right there with you, I ate like a pig tonight," Kat says.

"I was thinking, I know they have fancy deserts here but I had something else in mind," I said folding up my napkin neatly.

"What are you thinking?"

"Well there's that new Ice Cream Parlor Shop that opened up on the station near Galaxy Groceries, what do you think?" I ask.

"Sounds good to me, and we can walk a little of this food off, too," Kat says smiling.

Mario comes and cleans up the table for us. I attempt to pay but the Owner and Mario insist it's all on the house. I finally gave up trying to give them any money and shook their hands and thanked them for the wonderful meal. Kat took me by the arm and we both walked out smiling. We exited onto the main floor of the district we were in and we could see Galaxy Groceries, the space stations largest Food and Retail chain store.

We both looked at the indoor monorail then we both looked at the long bridge that leads to the other side of the station.

"Let's take the long way babe," I said.

"Sounds good to me," Kat said giving me a kiss on the cheek.

As we walk the bridge we look up and can see all outside traffic around the space station and the massive center pillar.

Continuing down the long walkway we see different vendors. Some vendors are selling jewelry, food, small crafts. One vendor has an antique popcorn stand and its popping fresh popcorn.

"Oh, that smells delicious," Kat says.

"Yea but the good stuff's at the end of the bridge," I say pulling Kat.

Coming to the end of the bridge we run into Lynsye and Missy on their own date.

"Hey Sexy!" Missy says to me waving her hand high in the air.

"Oh no. Hey, what's up guys, what are you doing up here?" I ask walking over with Kat arm in arm.

"Not much, just enjoying the view, and some popcorn, I take it you two had the same idea?" Lynsye says.

"Yup date night," Kat says holding me tighter.

"You two are too cute," Missy says smiling.

"Thanks," I says looking at Kat

"Well, we are off to the bar, talk to you tomorrow Ichia." Lynsye says grabbing Missy's waist, tugging her away.

"Good to see you again, Kat," Missy says waving bye.

"Those two are awesome," I said watching them walk away.

"How did you meet them again?" Kat asks.

"Long story, we actually met in college before the academy. I accidentally ended up as their roommates because they put males down for their room," I said.

"Hahah, that's funny, at least you guys came out friends," Kat says giggling.

We ended up at the end of the bridge, and right in front of us was Candy's Sweet Shop.

"Oh my gods, this is a diabetic's worse nightmare, I better leave my business cards," Kat says astonished, looking at the candy shop.

"Ha, yea well I'm sure their chocolate sales are thru the roof, that smell of confection is strong! That smell reminds me of Disney World," I said looking in a daze at the shop.

"Let's do this, I'm excited!" Kat says as we walk into the sugar kingdom.

We look around and unlike most shops this one only has 1 kiosk for quick orders. At each display case there are two or three workers making treats for customers. Kat and I walk up to the ice cream counter, we look over the menu and one item catches our eye.

"Hello my name is Mia, I'll be taking care of you today, what would you like?" Mia asks.

"We'll take the Banana Split," I said.

"Good choice! Just give me a few minutes and I'll have it whipped up in a jiffy," Mia says.

We watch Mia do her handy work, as she flips an ice cream scoop and scoops out three different flavors and puts them into a long plastic bowl. Then she hand cuts bananas and strawberries like a sous chef, slicing and dicing them around the long plastic plate and around the ice cream. She tops it off with hot fudge then a mountain of whip cream, topped with three cherries.

"That will be six credits, is there anything else I can get for you?" Mia asks.

"Nope that's it, thanks," I say smiling and then swiping my card through the reader.

I carry the large dish of goodness to a table that's outside of the shop. We sit and start to dig into the mountain of goodness.

"Oh gods, this is good, really good, maybe even better than what we were going to have for dessert at the restaurant," Kat says.

"Yea I would have to agree, and the fruit is fresh," I said scooping a large spoonful into my mouth, it was like heaven on a spoon.

We continue to take on the mountain of goodness. Back on the other side of the station exiting the movie theater, Casey and Mark stroll out full of popcorn holding each other tightly.

"So what's the plan?" Casey asks.

"Well, we do need food for the house, maybe pick up some groceries and call it a night," Mark says holding Casey.

"Call it a night, hey, we don't have to get up that early, hehehe," Casey giggles.

"Well I don't want to tire you out before you have to fix my ship," Mark says smiling.

"Oh, I'll fix ya up tonight, come on big boy," Casey says sexually strutting away.

Mark grins and follows her to the Grocery Store. They grab a small hand basket and pick up the usual essentials. Mark spends a lot of time in the protein aisle looking for better tasting shakes than what he's been drinking. Casey is floating around the snack aisle grabbing candy bars, crackers and potatoes chips. They both come around and throw everything into the basket.

"Hey, what are you buying?" Mark asks.

"Goodies for me," Casey says rubbing Marks shoulders.

"You keep eating that you won't fit into your flight suit," Mark says slapping Casey on the butt.

"Hey down boy, I'll work it off between tonight and tomorrow," Casey whispers into Marks ear.

"Giggidy!" Mark says as he starts to walk to the produce area.

They go to the checkout lines and all the lanes are open for once so getting out is really easy. They put their items on the belt and the machine sorts them, then scans the item. As they pay the machine is bagging the items too. Mark grabs the bags and puts an arm around Casey as they walk out of the grocery store. They stroll over to the main elevator system of the space station and catch a ride up. As the elevator goes up, Casey and Mark are the only two on the elevator and they start to make out. The elevator stops on another floor and the doors open.

"Wow guys, get a room," I say holding Kats arm.

"HEY!!" Mark says jumping off of Casey.

"Is it safe to board the elevator?" Kat asks smiling.

"Hehehe," Casey giggles.

"How was your movie?" I ask Casey and Mark.

"Awesome! I love little Zombie girls!" Casey says.

"Yea the movie was good, how was your date tonight?" Mark asks

"That restaurant was amazing, and we had an amazing view of the comet," I said.

We ride the elevator up to our apartments. The girls chit-chated while Mark and I were going on about game the other day. We get to the 43rd floor, Kat and I step off the elevator.

"See you guys tomorrow," I say waving.

"Yup see you in the morning," Casey says smiling and waving.

We walk around the balcony towards my apartment. Kat is snuggled into me, as we walk I look towards the giant dome that protects us from the vacuum of space. Thinking how we live in an amazing place. We finally come to my apartment, I unlock the door and it slides open. Kat sets her purse on the kitchen counter as I lock the door behind me.

"Boy, those two looked happy as kittens," Kat says walking over to the bed taking off her watch.

"Yea, I think they are a perfect match," I say.

"What about us?" Kat asks, taking off her earrings.

"That's easy, it was fate," I say taking my tie off.

"Well I'm ready to snuggle up like a kitten." Kat says giving a devious glare towards me.

"Well I'm about to make you purr like a kitten," I say smiling getting closer to Kat.

"Show me." Kat says dropping her dress and pulling me down to the bed.

Chapter 17
Marine City Hoorah!

The following afternoon Casey was working with Mittens on the repairs to her fighter and to Marks. They started pretty early, and got ahead of the work that they had in store for them that day. Walking up to them on the platform was Saturn 5, Colleen and two men walked with her.

"Uh oh, here comes trouble," Mittens says sarcastically looking up from the large manual in her hands.

"Hello," Colleen says with a bright smile.

"Hey, what's up?" Casey says lifting off her welding helmet.

"Not much, is Ichia around?" Colleen asks.

"Um, he's running a little late, he'll be here soon," Mittens says leaning on the tool box.

It's almost like everyone's having a stare down, everyone's quiet, as if they are waiting for a pin drop.

"Hey, sorry I'm late!" I yell across the hanger bay waving towards the girls.

"Oh hi, running late?" Colleen asks.

"Yea sorry, had something at home I had to take care of," I said scratching my head.

"What Kat wouldn't let you go?" Mitten says giggling .

"Um yea, it's her day off so... yea good talk. I saw your email this morning on my way down," I said to Colleen.

"Good, its actually a really easy operation," Colleen says.

"Easy?" Casey ask turning her head.

"All you have to do is land the bomber on that station. We'll go in grab the Hydro Processor, then any extra goods we see, and jump the frack out, easy peasy," Colleen says holding two thumbs up like it was a great movie.

"Land my bomber on a what, I better be able to blow something up!" Lynsye says with an attitude walking around the bomber.

"Oh yea you'll be able to blow something up," Colleen says.

"So who's the rest of your crew here?" I ask.

"Oh yea, sorry guys, this is Sam and Frankie, We've all been together since the beginning. There were eight of us but not everyone made it thru the last war," Colleen says tangling a strand of her hair.

"Sorry about your losses, we've been lucky haven't lost anyone, and don't plan on it," I said.

"Well it looks like your team works as one, ours didn't for a while, and those were reasons we lost people," Sam says.

"Yea, people making stupid decisions and getting themselves killed," Frankie says.

"Well enough of the past, ya'll should grab your gear and move it into my ship." Lynsye says throwing her coat over her shoulder.

"Yea, sounds like a plan," Colleen says.

"Hey if you guys are free later, anyone like to bowl?" Sam asks lifting his hat up.

"Um.... Sure I'm down, I haven't bowled in years," I say scratching my head.

"Oh boy, Sam loves to bowl, course I can't talk, I bowl just as much as he does, but I'm not that good though." Colleen says.

"Sure, you guys wanna come along?" I ask my team.

"Maybe Mark and I will come out," Casey says.

"Sorry, Prego can't," Mittens says rubbing her stomach.

"Cool, meet up at Yeti Lanes, we'll be up there at 7:00pm," Sam says.

"Ok," I said.

"Let's grab our gear and bring it down so we don't take up Jupiter's time and space," Colleen says turning towards Sam and Frankie.

"See ya," I say as they walk away.

"Wow, didn't know Jar Heads like to bowl?" Mittens says.

"You really don't like Marines do you?" Lynsye asks.

"Yea, she got rubbed the wrong way with one," I said giving out a loud laugh.

"I hate you, if this baby wasn't in my stomach I'd kick your balls into outer space, bitch," Mittens says pounding her fist on the tool box.

"Well, I'll make some room for their gear, I wonder what they're bringing?" Lynsye asks.

"Probably, lots of guns and grenades," I said.

"Sweet!" Casey says bobbing her head.

Everyone goes about their business, Casey and Mittens continue on the fighters. Lynsye and I clean up the bomber. We get all of the fast food garbage and random papers out of the bomber. We look at the bomber and it hasn't been cleaned in a long time. Lynsye gagged when she pulled out an old smoothie cup from the floor grate. I couldn't help but laugh hysterically, then Lynsye tried to throw it at me but I caught it with a garbage can. We continued to clean it up and restock the egress packs and extra random items. I added a few extra First Aid kits and Lynsye had several blankets and inflatable pillows she threw in storage compartment under the floor. I continued to restock items, then I worked my way over to the mini fridge in the bomber and loaded it up with a case of water bottles. Lynsye told me I should have filled it with beer, I couldn't help but give her a big grin. As we continued to work on cleaning up the bomber there was a knock on the hull.

"Heya, we got our goodies," Colleen says holding an antitank gun that was about 7 feet long.

205

"Jesus Christ, what the hell are you expecting?" Lynsye asks wide eyed and mouth wide open like mine was.

"I've seen shit that will turn you white, trust me. Take everything you can carry because you'll never know what you may need," Colleen says handing ammo cases to me.

Sam, Frankie and Colleen push carts of ammunition and a few boxes of grenades into the bomber. I secure the weapons along the walls. The marines only have eight weapons but a boat load of ammunition. The boxes of ammunition have been stacked nice and neat like Christmas presents under a tree.

"See, this is my baby, AA-k12 automatic shot gun, clear out every mother trucker in the room, hoorah," Sam says holding both of his AA-k12's in the air like Rambo.

"Oh boy," I say shaking my head and giving a big smile right back.

"Stow it Marine, get your shit locked up and stowed," Colleen says pointing and smiling.

"Yes mam!" Sam says neatly locking his gear into place.

"Boys and their guns," Colleen says chuckling with her arms crossed.

"Is that everything?" Lynsye asks wiping her hands on her pants.

"Yup that's everything, cool, well I guess we'll see you tonight?" Colleen asks.

"Yea I'll be there," I said shaking Colleen's hand.

I do a quick walk through with Lynsye, we check turrets and missile posts. We lock up the bomber, and close all the hatches and lock them tight.

"You really going to hang out with Marines?" Mittens asks walking over to me.

"Yea why?" I ask.

"Nothing, I've never trusted Marines, too ego driven," Mittens says.

"And you're not?" I reply giggling.

"Asshole, don't hate the shopping ego," Mittens says punching me in the shoulder.

"Hey, fighters are all set, well as good as they are going to get," Casey says coming over to me and Mittens.

"K, well we fly tomorrow night at 10:00 PM. Hey Casey, you and Mark should come out tonight," I said.

"Come on, Marines, give me a break ok, I'll see ya tomorrow night," Casey says chuckling.

"Ha, see told ya," Mittens says holding her hips.

"Whatever guys, I'm going to make more friends, I'll see you later," I said walking away.

"Geez, don't get your panties in a bunch." Mittens says.

"Pilots and Marines never mix. I don't know why he wants to hang out with them," Casey says pulling her purse on her shoulder and walking out of the hanger bay with Mittens.

"I won't be around tomorrow, so good luck on your mission," Mittens says walking with Casey.

207

"Where are you going to be? You're always here to see everyone off." Casey says.

"I'm going to Mars to see my family, my little sisters' birthday is actually tomorrow so I can't miss that." Mittens says.

"Cool, we'll see you when you get back," Casey says holding her hand in the air.

"Good Luck," Mittens says high fiving Casey as they walk out of the hanger bay of the space station and back to the main part of the station.

Chapter 18

The Brooklyn.

As Kat and I walk into the Yeti Bowling alley, the sounds of pins being knocked down ring throughout the alley.

"Wow, haven't bowled in years," Kat says holding my hand.

"Yea me either, I think the last time I bowled was in college," I said as we walk through the Bowling alley.

"Hey Ichia!" Colleen waves to us holding a beer in her hand. With the bowling alley being lightly lit, Colleen's eyes flash a greenish yellow color.

"Who's that, and what's up with her eyes?" Kat asks.

"That's the leader of Saturn 5, that's Colleen, she's actually half human and half Nephilum," I said waving back.

"Wow, never met one of those before, only heard about them in magazines," Kat says in amazement.

"Hey guys, ready to bowl?" Colleen says hopping up and down like a rabbit.

"Um yea sure, this is Kat; Kat, Colleen." I introduce them.

"Hello, haven't I seen you before somewhere?" Colleen asks then taking a drink of her beer.

"I created the skin cancer cure lotion a few years ago." Kat says.

"Oh yea, wow, you must be rich, good catch, Ichia," Colleen says smiling.

"Ha, um didn't work out that way," Kat says being interrupted by Sam.

"Hey, hurry up, it's your turn Colleen, and the bucket's getting low!" Sam yells standing on the bowling lane.

"Well, let's get some shoes and find a bowling ball, Colleen we'll join you in a minute," I said holding Kat walking towards the retail kiosk.

We pay for additional games to join them on their bowling lane. The kiosk dispenses two pairs of shoes, then Kat and I are on our way to search for a bowling ball. After grabbing our balls, Sam put our names into the machine.

"So, ready for some fun, watch this," Sam says walking up to approach and ripping the ball down the lane. He puts such a spin on it goes straight then cuts like a bat out of hell.

"God damn!" I said sitting with Kat.

"Yea he's a bit of a show off," Colleen says taking a drink of her beer.

"Hey, where's Frankie?" I ask Colleen as I finish tying my shoe.

"He can't bowl, he's got a bad back, I know he's a Marine and has a bad back ,but he's an awesome medic," Colleen says.

"Sweet," I reply.

"Oh, your turn babe," Kat says.

"Okay time to laugh," I said grabbing my ball and standing on the approach. Everyone stared at me as I went to throw my ball. I walk up and pull back and throw my ball down the lane and it goes right into the gutter.

"Hmm, I saw that going differently in my mind," I said to myself.

"Shake it off, use the arrows," Sam says smiling with a pitcher in his hand.

"Yea ha, I'll try," I said walking up again and tossing it down the lane taking out 5 pins.

"Yay, good job," Colleen says.

"My turn!" Kat says walking up, nudging me with her ball and smiling. Kat granny throws her ball and gets a strike.

"Oh my god... really, I love you babe!" I said to Kat.

"Ha-ha Yay!" Kat says jumping in the air.

"Not bad," Colleen says.

211

Kat came back to sit with me and laid back on me like a little kitten as we watched everyone bowl. We continue bowling, we played several games with Saturn 5. Colleen and I got into the mission conversation a little bit. I told her it sounds rather easy, but with the Mafia nothing is easy. Especially when you're trying to steal back from them.

"Over all, we blast a hole into the station, land, grab the goods. Your fighter will cover us from the outside and we jump out of there," Colleen says.

"Yea, I'll be in the bomber, my fighter was destroyed in the last one," I said.

"Maybe we can do a little target practice tomorrow at the gun range," Colleen says.

"I'm good with my side arm, but not with that cannon you

brought on the bomber earlier, that thing was huge!" I said a little tipsy.

"Yea that's my baby. It has homing rounds so I can fire a shot and it will spread and take out five to eight targets at once," Colleen says.

"Yea and I'm awesome with my AA 12's and grenades," Sam says stumbling over.

"Ha, you throw like a girl," Colleen says.

"Yea, how many grenades do you carry at once? You guys brought on like four cases of them," I ask.

"Ha, they're best friends because on all of our guns we can attach them as a secondary ammunition that fires along with it."

"Well, tomorrow should interesting." I said.

"Yup," Colleen says finishing her drink off.

The couples shake hands and change shoes and start to head home after a fun evening of bowling. I wave bye to Colleen and Sam, as I hold Kat tight with my arm.

"They seem cool," Kat says.

"Yea, I don't get why Mittens and Casey are so against working with Marine.," I said walking with Kat back to our apartment.

"Who knows, people can change, hope we get to go bowling again with them some time," Kat says snuggling into my shoulder.

"I plan on it," I said.

Chapter 19

<u>Viva La Pool House.</u>

The next evening I kissed Kat good bye as we both went our separate ways to our jobs. I walked down the hall way to the hanger. I noticed they are doing construction on the station, looks like they are starting to build more housing for people. As if this place wasn't crowded enough. I remember them saying they wanted to build another space station following this one.

Who knows any more, I like my home, I'm not looking to move, I just want to stay with my baby and maybe get promoted to Captain. That has passed through my mind a couple of times lately, don't know why. I guess it's because Kat mentioned it to me the other day about promoting. The money would be better, and I think most of the repair cost, the military would cover.

As I walked down, I ran into Lynsye coming out of a Quicker Mart, which was like a mini mart.

"Hey Chang," Lynsye says mumbling putting a cigarette in her mouth.

"Not much, ready to make some money tonight."

"Hell yea, you know they're going to raise fuel prices again?" Lynsye says.

"Bull shit, how can they do that to us?" I ask Lynsye as we enter the hanger bay.

"I don't know, I mean Jupiter is like an unlimited source of fuel for us. Can't blame the Lab Rats, we scared them all away," Lynsye says puffing on her cigarette.

"If it's not one thing it's always another," I said walking up to the bomber.

"Hey! Alright everyone's here," Casey says leaning on Mark.

We all stand in a circle looking at each other like we were going to cause more mischief than normal.

"Well Casey, Mark did you guys look over the flight plan?" I ask them.

"Yup all set, good thing about this being in the asteroid belt is less fighters," Casey says.

"Yea, it takes great pilots to steer an asteroid field," Mark says high fiving me.

"Yea, let's not bring that up," I said laughing.

"Sounds like it must have been fun," Sam says crossing his arms.

215

"Alright kiddies, we got a water generator to steal or that village is as good as gone," Colleen says slapping Sam on the shoulder.

Everyone grabs their suits. I join the Marines, Lynsye and Missy in the bomber. Mark and Casey hop into their fighters.

The engines fire on the Bomber and it gracefully lifts up into the air and turns towards the large gates of the space station. We are on our way with Casey and Mark following us in their fighters. Then we hit a little orbital traffic to the main gate.

"Why don't we just jump straight to the Asteroid Belt?" Sam asks.

"To many variations. We have to jump outside of it, best bet is the gate," Lynsye says steering us towards the large jump gate.

"Anyone ever break that rule?" Colleen asks.

"Yup, just one person has ever pulled it off," Missy says.

"Who?" Colleen asks.

"You're sitting next to him," Missy says as Colleen turns towards me.

"Wow how did you pull that off?" Colleen asks me.

"It was during the Space War, my fighter had to refuel and rearm. The fleet was already battling it out and the Delphinus was in trouble. Mark and company where busting their butts, but they just kept coming. I took the chance and jumped right into the Asteroid Belt."

"Yea, he showed up just in time to take out two rockets chasing me as I was chasing an enemy," Lynsye said.

"After the battle we learned why not to jump blind, part of my wing had a large rock stuck in it from the jump," I said.

"Wow, I've heard of people like jumping place, miscalculations and ending up in rocks or worse, scary stuff," Colleen says.

"Well our systems are better now, but nothing will ever beat hyper drive. It takes a little longer, but much safer than jumping," I said leaning back.

"Alright, here we go, Asteroid Belt here we come," Lynsye says pulling back on the throttle as the bomber gets sucked into the black void.

We flash in just miles outside of the Asteroid Belt.

"Wow looks like brown sprinkles in space," Casey says over the com.

"Always thinking with you stomach," Lynsye says guiding us carefully through the field with Casey and Mark close behind us. There are Asteroids as big as houses, they gently bump into each other as we drift through them.

"How far Lynsye?" I ask coming up to her cockpit.

"Almost there, as long as we keep close to the Asteroids we shouldn't show up on their radar."

"I don't know why anyone would dare have a radar system in here" I said.

"Hey baby you alright over there?" Mark asks Casey over the com.

"Oh yea, just like flying drunk that's all," Casey replies smiling.

217

All of a sudden we pull around a large asteroid and sitting there is the station we're looking for, but it's partially destroyed and broken into several sections.

"What the hell," Colleen says coming up next to me.

"Um... yea that's the station alright but there's nothing left." Lynsye says.

"God damn military Intel," Sam says knocking his head on the wall.

"I'm not getting any power readings or anything from the station, it's dead," Missy says.

"Um well, how old is this Intel?" I ask Colleen.

"Look at the date, it's dated for four days ago, this is as good as it gets. This is not cool," Colleen says.

"Well on a good note, I guess we got to take a nice tour of the Asteroid belt," Casey says over the Com.

"Yea, on my bill," Colleen says sighing, slapping her forehead with her hand.

"You sure there's not another space station hiding in here?" Lynsye asks.

"Yea, their markings on that one match our Intel. Maybe someone's messing with me again," Colleens says.

"This happen often?" I ask Colleen.

"Never, I quit!" Colleen says crossing her arms.

"Well since nothing's going on can we head for home?" Casey asks over the com.

"Yea might as well, damnit. I'm going to hurt someone when I get home," Colleen says.

"Well guys I'll lead the….." Mark starts to say then a loud ear shattering crash comes over the com.

Mark's fighter gets hit by machine gun fire and more bullets start to spray all around them.

"Mark!!!!" Lynsye yells.

"Shit! Move it people, they got us surrounded!" Mark says trying to recover his fighter.

"I got your back baby," Casey says as she 180's around and starts shooting the enemy fighters coming towards them.

"Everyone fall back out of the Asteroid Belt," I said over the com and pointing a good direction to Lynsye.

All our ships floor it and start making our out way out of the Asteroid Belt. Missy took control of the bomber as Lynsye hopped into the main gunner chair. I took over the secondary robotic guns. We let Casey and Mark take the lead to get Mark farther away with his damaged ship. Lynsye and I started to drop the enemy fighter like flies.

"Baby, you okay?" Casey asks Mark as he pilots his smoking ship.

"Come on now, you know I don't C flat, it's not my tone!" Mark says fighting his fighter and gliding it through the Asteroids.

We continue to fly though and it seems like there's no end to the Asteroid Belt.

"Shit, how much farther!" Casey yells over the com bumping into several basketball size rocks.

"Almost there girl, less than forty two kilometers, then it's clear skies," Lynsye says.

"Um, aren't we in space?" Colleen says smiling.

"Marines," Missy says smiling high fiving Colleen.

"Hey, looks like they gave up," I said looking through my monitor.

"Yea and we outta here," Casey says.

As we exit the Asteroid Belt we glide over a large Asteroid the size of a Sky Scraper. As we come over the giant, we are confronted by a huge battle station. The station is very long, like a Shinconsen Rail Station, with guns mounted everywhere. It sits there looking at us like a Snake ready to snap at its prey.

"What the hell is that?" I said.

"Um we got incoming like it's not funny, Ichia," Missy says looking over at her radar.

"Mark can you jump?" I said over the com.

"Um... nope I'm gonna need a tow if we're gonna do." Mark says then is interrupted.

"Well Jupiter 7, looks like you fell into the wrong trap, this was meant for Saturn 5 but none the less, two birds with one stone is a beautiful thing," an eerie scratchy voice says over the coms.

"Shit, it's that voice," I say.

"Oh great, these ass holes again," Sam says standing up.

"Who is that?" Lynsye asks.

"Dunno but it's the leader of the Lab Rat Mafia and we need to get outta here," Colleen says.

"Agreed, but all exits are kinda blocked," Missy says.

"We got this! We'll clear the runway, with you covering us. Then hook me up and let's get the hell out of here!" Mark says over the com.

"Let's do it on three, they won't expect it." Missy says.

"Right," Casey says sitting up in her fighter, ready to pounce.

I count down to three and we all break into different directions. Mark starts to take out the first wave of fighters, as Casey jumps out from behind him and starts laying fire on the ones he doesn't take out. We take the bomber towards the Station and aim for the fighters protecting it.

"I'll take out the guns, Lynsye keep firing at those fighters," I said as I locked onto several gun towers.

As Lynsye drops several fighters I fire my rockets toward the gun towers and they are shielded. The rocket explosions bounce off like water balloons, and run off spinning.

"Crap!" I said.

"Aim for the doors or radars, their shield will be lesser!" Missy says as she steers us through another heap of fighters.

Mark and Casey are playing cat and mouse with fighters chasing them. Mark has six on his tail, Casey is gracefully picking them off of him. Close behind her are several fighters attempting to shoot her down. Casey activated her rear defense system that she installed long ago when she was with the Alphas. Rockets and homing bullets can't lock onto her and some of the missiles are redirected back at the enemy fighters. Mark takes another hit, but he's still managing to keep his fighter screaming and rocking against all enemy fighters coming at him.

"Come on baby we're almost there, hang in there," Casey says worried over the com.

"I'm good baby, just keep me covered!" Mark says as he is starting to struggle with his fighter.

Coming towards them in the bomber, Lynsye is covering Mark and Casey, as I'm taking out the doors on the station.

"You cannot defeat us," Eerie voice says.

"Does this guy ever shut up?" I say aiming my rockets towards a bay door opening.

A few fighters start to launch as I fire a volley of rockets towards the open door. All of my rockets make it through the shields and cause one hell of an explosion that looks to cripple the station. Several other parts of the station start to explode and you can see the shields start to fail.

"Hell ya, good hit Ichia," Lynsye says.

"Whoa look at that, its starting to move," Missy says.

"Looks like that stations got some engines, let's take em out." Casey says turning towards the station.

"Do it!" I say over the com as Missy turns the bomber towards the station and we keep taking out the fighters.

By now we have stopped over thirty fighters total. Mark and Casey head over towards the engines and start to lock on.

"Hang in there baby," Casey says pulling the trigger firing at the engines.

"I got your back, babe," Mark says shooting down fighters coming at Casey.

Casey dives in and takes out one engine, and two fighters start to give her chase. One fighter hits her back engine.

"Shit, I gotta shut it down and run on one," Casey says.

"Babe," Mark yells as he floors his fighter towards her to take out the other fighters chasing her.

As Mark comes around, one fighter comes out of the Asteroid belt and starts to chase him and hits him hard in the back of his Fighter.

"Shit! My shields are going down," Mark says trying to reconfigure while taking out the fighters chasing Casey.

"We gotta give them a hand," I said.

"Yea, they just keep coming, do we have a solution on getting out of here, Missy?" Lynsye asks locking onto several targets and shooting them down.

"Sixty seconds," Missy says.

"This will be over in thirty seconds, get on it!" Lynsye says firing at more oncoming fighters. Then all of a sudden the station fires a bright beam of light that hits the bomber. The bomber is hit like a baseball by a bat and spins out of control. Inside we're all screaming and getting tossed around like pebbles in a can. Frankie and Sam are thrown hard into the wall and knocked out. Colleen and I are hanging onto the wall straps as Lynsye holds her harness in her gunner chair. Missy is trying to pull us out of a flat spin, she has both feet pressing hard on the brake pedal as she pulls on the flight stick. Casey watches us spin out of control and notices several fighters are going to finish us off.

"I'm coming, hang on!" Casey say racing her single engine fighter towards us.

Missy pulls us out of the flat spin and two rockets hit us hard on the side heavily damaging the hull of the bomber. Frankie and Sam are thrown and slide across the floor like rag dolls. Colleen and I slide over fast to Frankie and Sam and pull them over to the ammunition.

224

"Here, let's use these," Colleen says pulling out two ratchet straps.

"Are you serious?" I ask her looking at her funny.

"I'd do the same and I would expect whatever it takes to get it done," Colleen says as she wraps Sam and starts to ratchet him to the ammunition crates.

I do the same and ratchet Frankie to the ammunition crate. As we finish attaching the marines to the ammunition we get rocked by that beam again. Colleen and I are thrown towards the wall and she lands on me.

"Not cool!" Lynsye says as she opens fire in several directions, taking out on coming fighters.

"Their weapons are powerful, we can't take another hit like that," Missy says.

"Shit, look it's going to finish us off," I said looking over towards my monitor.

"I got this!!" Mark yells over the com.

Mark pushes his broken fighter to the limit and races towards the station avoiding turret fire and heads towards the large rail gun taking aim at his friends.

"Mark, I'm right behind you babe!" Casey yells trying aim in front of him.

Mark and Casey dive towards the station, Mark takes out a large tank that looks to be a generator for the large rail gun. The explosion shock wave swats Casey away like a fly into a flat spin.

Casey gets hit so hard she hits her head hard onto the side console and she is knocked unconscious.

"Baby!!" Mark yells and turns his fighter then is hit by a rocket, ripping apart his left wing.

"Mark!!!" Missy says chasing after Casey's drifting ship.

"Ichia, you guys go, I'm not making it out of this one," Mark says calmly over the com.

"Shut the fuck up and get your ass over here, we're gonna tow you two right now!" I frantically yell over the com, jumping out of my chair heading to main cockpit of the bomber.

"Go, they're about to fire at you guys again, looks like torpedoes," Mark says looking at the station as a part of it cocks like a giant shot gun.

"MARK GET YOUR ASS OVER HERE!" I yell again over the com.

"Never thought I'd go out like this, gods damn wish I had some Taco Bell," Mark says to himself. Then Mark looks to his right and several fighters start shooting up his fighter.

Missy catches Casey's ship, Missy looks into Casey's fighter and she's knocked unconscious.

"Game time." Mark says flooring his fighter towards the station pulling the trigger aiming towards the torpedo launcher.

"MARK!!!" I scream, standing up punching the cockpit glass.

Mark's fighter destroys the launcher and crashed into the station.

"NO!!!" I scream as Lynsye and Colleen pull on me as I fight them.

"MARK YOU FUCK ASS, GOD DAMNIT LET GO OF ME!!!" I continue to scream.

"Ichia!" Lynsye punches me across the face.

"HE"S GONE! We have to get the hell out of here!!!" Lynsye says screaming and crying as she shakes me.

"Prepare to jump… whoa look at the station its jumping away!" Missy says looking in disbelief.

"Yea but them fighters are coming at us!!" Colleen says looking in the gun monitor I was controlling.

"JUMP! GODS DAMNIT JUMP!" Lynsye screams holding onto me.

"RIGHT!" Missy says pulling back on the throttle and punching the jump button. We jump in the nick of time just as three rockets race through where we just were. We jump right in front of ISE and smoke through the gate.

"Clear the deck people! We're coming in hot!" Missy calls to the tower.

"Send medical we have several injured people, too!" Lynsye says over the second com holding me tight as I'm sitting in her lap stunned.

Missy tries her best to land us on the platform right in front of the hospital, but Casey's fighter is dragging us down and both ships slam into the deck and slide towards the ER of the hospital. As we hit the deck we get thrown again towards the cockpit.

227

"Hey, one pilot at a time people!" Missy says unlocking her seat belt.

"We gotta get Casey." Lynsye says.

"I'll get my guys, go get her," Colleen says.

"Ichia…." Lynsye says but I don't respond, I'm sitting like a lifeless doll.

"Ichia, snap out of it," Lynsye tries again.

Missy hops out of the bomber and the medical team is racing towards the crashed ships on the deck. Missy gets over to Casey's fighter, Casey is still knocked out. Missy jumps on the fighter and pulls the emergency rescue release. The fighter cockpit breaks into three sections dumping Casey out like a fish.

"Shit! These things never work!" Missy says sliding down to pick up Casey. Missy puts Casey in her lap and there is blood all over the inside of her helmet. As Missy looks she throws up next to herself.

"Here, we have her, you two check the other craft!" a Doctors yells and directs. The doctor comes over to Casey and checks for a pulse.

"She's still alive, can you help me put her on the stretcher?" the doctor asks Missy.

"Yea," Missy says wiping her mouth and then helps lift Casey onto the floor cart.

Another set of Doctors and Emergency workers arrive at the bomber. I'm on the floor, my heads bleeding while Lynsye is holding her shirt on my head. Colleen helps the workers load her

228

friends onto stretchers.

"Come on, we have to get Ichia to the hospital too," Colleen says to Lynsye.

Lynsye looks up at Colleen as if she's holding her last and only child.

"Ok, we're coming," Lynsye says sniffling, trying to lift me onto a stretcher.

Two ambulances land next to our little crash site and two paramedics grab Lynsye and Colleen. Missy helps the one doctor push Casey into the ER area. Two other doctors and workers push the Marines right behind them.

"Fucking déjà vu," Lynsye says shaking trying to put a cigarette into her mouth.

Chapter 20

<u>Recovery.</u>

I woke up looking at the ceiling, my head is throbbing like someone took a frying pan to me. I look around, it's late because the lights are all dimmed, and holding my hand sleeping on the side of the bed is Kat. As I try to collect my thoughts on what happened, I remember the crash and some of the Asteroid Belt. Then the vision of Mark crashing into that station hits me hard like a gut punch from hell. I start to shake like I've been in ice cold water, waking Kat up.

"Babe, I'm here," Kat says jumping up. Seeing me shake, she jumps up on the bed, puts her arms around me and attempts to keep me warm.

"You're home babe," Kat says softly in my ear.

"Not all of us," I stutter as if I saw a ghost, and Kat holds me tighter.

"Where's Casey?" I ask.

"She's okay, she's in the next room," Kat says rubbing my back while holding me tight.

"We were ambushed, they came out of nowhere," I said beginning to shake more rapidly.

"Babe calm down, you're going to go into shock again." Kat said. But before I could injure myself or go into shock, she hits the morphine button to knock me out.

Lynsye walks into my room quickly after hearing my voice.

"Is he awake?" Lynsye asks.

"I had to put him back down, he started to go into shock again," Kat says holding me tight.

"I thought I heard his voice," Lynsye whispers.

"Yea, he was conscious for a minute or two, what happened out there?" Kat asks.

"It was bad, we were set up," Lynsye says sitting in the chair in front of my hospital bed.

"Damn right you were," Admiral Hitoshi says walking in, taking off his hat.

"Sir." Lynsye hops up. Before she could salute him he grabs her hand and pulls her to him to give her a hug. Lynsye starts to break down in his arms.

"Wow, she was like one of the strongest girls I've ever known," Kat whispers.

"We all have a breaking point," The Admiral says holding Lynsye as she's sobbing.

Kat explains the situation of me going into shock. Then Kat walks over with the Admiral and Lynsye to Casey's room. Casey is laying in the hospital bed with her head wrapped. The right side of her face was fractured and she has a major concussion. There is a nurse keeping constant watch over her, and all of her vitals. The Admiral helps Lynsye sit in a chair in Casey's room, and then walks over to Casey. He looks over her mummified head.

"Is she going to make it?" Hitoshi asks.

"Yea, she'll pull through, I rebuilt her right side and her dental. I did the best I could," Kat said crossing her arms gently.

"When she wakes we can't say anything about Mark right away," Lynsye says.

"Yea, she may go into shock," Kat replies.

"What of Saturn 5?" Hitoshi asks.

"They made it out better than Jupiter 7, one has a broken arm, the other a broken shoulder bone. Besides that, it's all recovery time from here out," Kat says glancing over Casey's vitals.

"Well keep me informed. Lynsye keep an eye on them for me, too," Hitoshi says.

"What about Marks family?" Lynsye asks.

"I'll take care of that, they're just like Ichia's parents, it's my fault they're here, I need to talk to them," Hitoshi says looking down at a spot on the floor.

The next day I awoke to a breakfast laid out. Judging from the looks of it, it has been sitting for a while. The eggs were cold and the potatoes soggy, along with a greasy sausage link. I still ate it, I was starving. As I stuffed my face I looked over and Kat was staring at me.

"Morning," I said with my mouth stuffed with food.

Kat giggled.

"Morning Babe, I didn't even notice, you woke up." Kat said.

"Did you stay the entire night?" I said after swallowing.

"All night? I've been keeping an eye on you and Casey for the past two days," Kat says.

"I'm sorry I require so much upkeep," I say to Kat as she comes over to me.

"It's nice to care about someone who cares so much for everyone else," she says as she kisses me. I drop my fork and slowly put my arms around her, and she holds my shoulders. We kissed, it lasted for seconds and the world stopped around us. Then she backed up and looked at me deep with her blue eyes.

233

"I love you."

"I love you too," I replied.

I finished my food and Kat took the plates to the cart by the door.

"So, am I allowed to walk around?" I ask.

"Yea, but I don't think it's a good idea for you to see Casey right now," Kat says

"I'll be fine, I need to see my crew, babe," I said looking at her to assure her that I was almost ready to handle anything.

"Ok, come on let me help you," Kat says coming to me, slowly helping me out of the bed.

"Oh, floors cold," I said smiling at her.

"Come on," Kat says holding me closely.

As we walked into the hallway the nurses nodded, and waved to Kat and I. We slowly walked into the next room and I could see Casey lying in bed.

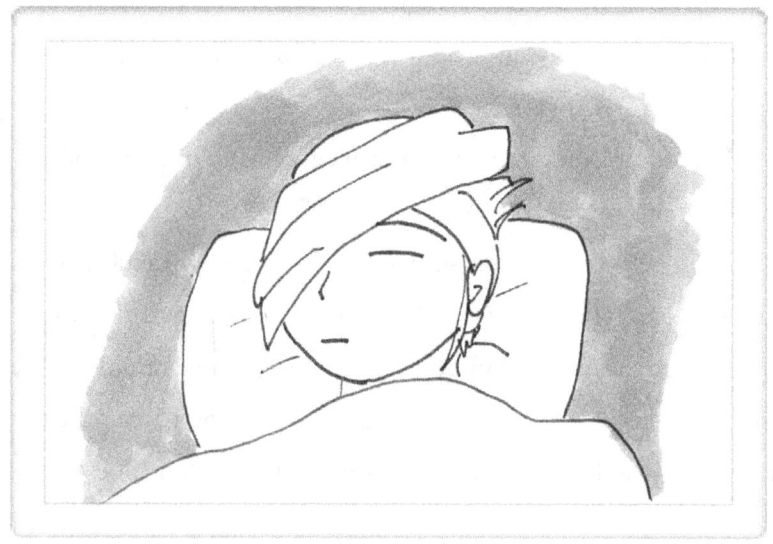

"Is she awake?" I asked Kat.

"Not yet, we are waiting for the meds to wear off."

"I don't know how I'm going to explain this to her," I said leaning on the door.

"It's going to be hard," Kat says being interrupted by Lynsye.

"Hey, you're up," Lynsye whispers giving me a hug.

"Hey," I reply holding her.

"Where's Missy?" I asked.

"She's sleeping, well trying to rest, she's still shaken up," Lynsye says.

"Maybe you were right, shouldn't have worked with Marines," I said looking over towards Casey.

"Its not their fault, both teams were set up." Lynsye says.

"I don't know," I said starting to lose my footing.

"Okay, back to your room babe," Kat says catching me.

Kat and Lynsye walk me back to my room and lay me down.

"Just lay back, ok," Kat says to me.

Kat and Lynsye leave me to rest. Two days later I'm released from the hospital. I'm sitting in Casey's room looking at her helmet. It's completely stained with her blood, the blood has dried and solidified. Two more days pass and I'm still sitting on the couch waiting for her to wake. I haven't really moved to do anything. Kat brought me food or a little snack. Lynsye and Missy would stop by to see how I was doing. They said I looked like a guard guarding a princess. It was about 4 am and Casey began to move and make noises.

"Water… Thirsty…," Casey said with a scratchy voice.

The ICU nurse hopped up and grabbed a water bottle came over to Casey. I hopped up too, I came over to her bed. The nurse let me help Casey drink, I put the tube in her mouth and she slowly sipped from it. After a few minutes she was finished drinking, and looked at me.

"Hey boss, how'd we do?" she asked me.

"We did alright," I said being interrupted by the nurse.

"Don't mention her boyfriend, admiral's orders." She whispers too late into my ear.

"Where's Marky?" Casey asks as I stared at her.

She already knew something was wrong because I paused.

"Is he ok?" Casey asks

"Um, he," I said and paused.

"He's in the next room right, come on Ichia." Casey says.

"He saved us all," I said starting to tear up and shake my head, falling to Casey's stomach.

"Oh come on you're…. you're… no…" Casey starts to tear up.

"He took out that cannon and crashed into the station," I said crying laying my heavy head on her stomach.

"No, no, he can't," Casey says starting to shake.

"She's going into shock," The nurse comes over and hits the morphine button.

236

"Ichia…. Ichia.. please tell me I'm having a night nightmare…." Casey couldn't finish what she wanted to say as she was knocked out from the morphine. I fell to the floor crying realizing again I just lost my best friend.

Three days later Casey was discharged. The side of her face still had a few bandages. I pushed her out of the hospital in a wheelchair. She looked like a lifeless doll sitting in the chair. Her hair was ponytailed up, and her hands were fiddling in her lap. Kat and I decided the best thing for her was to stay with us. As I pushed her through the station Mittens saw us, and was in awe. Mittens just got back from Mars and heard what happened. As she stood there with Jeffery, she dropped her purse and covered her mouth. All I could do was nod towards her and keep walking. I didn't really want to stop and talk, I think she would understand out of everyone. Jeffery picked up her purse and tried to hold her back but she couldn't hold back she ran over to me and gave me a big hug.

"I'm so sorry," Mittens said tearing up holding me tight.

"It's okay," I said putting my arm around her, and the other holding the wheel chair.

"I'll let you guys go, call me later ok," Mittens said.

"I will, thanks Mittens, it's good to see you again," I said and started to walk away.

We arrived at my apartment and Kat was waiting for us. She helped me get Casey onto the couch. We covered her in a blanket and gave her some medication. Casey just lay there, tears rolling

237

down her cheeks. I walked over to the door and locked it and walked back over to the bed and sat next to Kat. I just put my head into her chest, and tears began to roll down my face. She held me, gently rocking back and forth saying it's going to be alright.

"I feel lost, but something's not right," I said weeping.

"You just lost your best friend, I'm going to help you though this the best I can. Just like last time when the station was attacked babe," Kat whispers into my ear and then pulls me down to the bed slowly. Eventually I fell asleep and Kat wrapped me in the sheets. After a little bit she got up to check on Casey. Casey was still awake, tears rolling down her face. Kat kneeled on the floor and laid her arm around Casey's shoulder, and rubbed the top of her head.

"I miss him so much Kat," Casey said crying.

"I know," Kat says.

"I keep wanting him to walk through that door, say it was all a big joke."

"I want him to come in and tell me everything's going to be ok."

"I want him to keep me warm right now."

Casey kept going on, and Kat held her tight as a few tears rolled down her cheek. Kat stayed by her side the rest of the night. I woke up to a video monitor with an incoming call. It was my parents, the last thing I wanted to deal with. I answered, it was my mom and Mark's mom. Kat came and sat next to me to give me strength. I explained everything that happened, my mom held

Marks mom and she wept. She wanted to hear how her son died from his best friend. They also wanted me to come to Mars immediately, but I told our parents I'm needed here right now. It was one of the worst video calls I've ever answered, but managed to get through it, thanks to Kat. We made breakfast, I spoon fed Casey Cream of Wheat. Surprisingly Casey attempted to make a joke.

"What, Cream of Wheat? Is it because I'm part black, ha you forgot the rice for the Asian half," Casey said giving off a little smile towards me, then leaning into me.

Later on Lynsye and Missy came over. She told me my uncle wanted to debrief us on the situation. I said "what's to debrief, we got our asses kicked and we lost a valuable friend."

I didn't have much choice but we all walked down to the military hanger, Kat followed us down too. As we walked in, Colleen was standing there waiting for us. She walked over to me and gave me hug along with Sam. We all walked into the CIC for debriefing. My uncle went over the attack and the Intel that was given to us. Apparently the Intel was forged to screw over Saturn 5, but they got lucky and were unprepared for us when we showed up.

Eventually the part of the debriefing I didn't want to be here for was the video replay. We watched Casey get blasted away from the shock wave, and then Mark crashing into the station. Casey broke down after watching the video, we all decided to end the debrief on our own and signed out. We walked back to my apartment, and as we came to the door, people had left flowers and teddy bears. We just stood there looking at the items left by people. Some people left a sign that said, "He's watching over you now." I just shook my head, unlocked my apartment and walked in.

Chapter 21

Late night stroll.

I couldn't sleep, I told Kat that I was going to head down to the hanger bay to clear my head. She stayed and watched a movie with Casey as I was leaving. It was 3 AM, and the station was quiet.

I walked down to the hanger in my hoody and sweatpants. I walked out, and towards the Kiosk, Mittens was sitting on the ledge.

"Mind if I join you?" I said as my voice echoed in the hanger.

"BITCH! Get over here," she said slurring, waving her hands toward me.

"Looks like you brought our friend," I said grabbing the bottle of Jackie B's Whisky from her.

"Oh there's more where that came from... *BUUUURP!!*"

"Bless you," I said to her, taking a big drink from the bottle.

"Man, I leave you guys and the shit hits the fan," Mittens says slurring waving her hands in the air.

"I know, what the fuck, you leave and it's a train wreck all over again," I reply.

"This is all messed up, you know..." Mittens says and starts to get all choked up.

"I can't believe his dumb ass is gone," Mittens says crying curled up in a ball with her knees to her chest.

I slide over and put my arm around her.

"I need to know what I could have done to make your fighters safer?" Mittens says looking up at me.

"You did your best, we just got jumped on," I said then taking another drink from the bottle finishing it off.

"It doesn't feel right," I said holding Mittens.

"Well, no shit, he's dead," Mittens says wiping her eyes.

"It doesn't feel right, like something's missing or…" I said as she interrupted me punching me several times in my shoulder.

"Marks dead, he's crashed into that thing you guys fought… shit we need another bottle, hold on." Mitten says as she throws the empty bottle at the Job board. The bottle of whiskey shatters all over the place barely scratching the screen.

"Shit!" I said grabbing her as she almost falls face first onto the floor.

"Bingo!" Mittens says as she pulls out a bottle of UV Cake.

"Damn, my kryptonite," I said smiling, taking the bottle from Mittens taking a big swig.

"So, what doesn't feel right, Kat give you the clap," Mittens says taking back the bottle and taking big drink from the bottle.

"No, no. She doesn't do that anymore. No, I don't think Marks dead," I said taking the bottle back from Mittens and taking a drink.

"What, yur talking funny mister?" Mittens says.

"You know that feeling you have when you go on vacation and you think you left something on or behind? That kind of feeling," I said as my words started to slurr.

"Oh, shit hell ya, yea.. yea… I know what you're talking about yea I know, yea I know," Mittens says slurring her words.

"I don't think he's dead," I say shaking my head, then taking another burning drink of Vodka.

"Well, if I were you, but I have no penis, I'd… oh shit." Mittens says leaning forward.

243

"Uh oh, are you about to call some dinosaurs?" I ask finishing off the fifth and throwing it at the Kiosk.

"I'm calling some... Blaaaa..." she says throwing up on the ground in front of her. Talking and throwing up is just one of her special skills.

"OH shit!" I said jumping back.

"Oh god, don't tell Jeffery, I'm so sorry," Mittens says leaning back on the ledge.

"Come on I better get you home," I said helping her off the ledge and avoiding the poison pool she just left on the walk way.

"You're a great friend!" Mittens says hanging onto me.

"You are too, and you're trashed," I said attempting to hold Mittens up, but the alcohol has taken a hold of me too and we both fall on our butts laughing. I attempt to pick her up but slip and fall back to the floor again.

"I'm sorry," Mittens says.

"It's not working, the alcohol is winning Mittens!" I say laughing at her.

"I'm sorry.... No, really I'm sorry, oh my god my head... I'm sorry. Come on let's crawl back to our apartments!" Mittens says trying to crawl on the floor.

"But you live up on 71st, we gotta get you to the elevators!" I said slurring trying to stand.

I manage to get her off the floor, but getting to the main elevators is another story in itself. People are looking at us and laughing as we attempt to get to the elevators. We get to the elevator doors and she throws me into the elevator. I land flat on my butt and slide to the other side of the elevator.

"I got this!" Mittens says as her hand hits Lvl 71 and every button down as she falls to the floor.

"Fuck this is gonna be a long ride," I said laughing.

We start our ascent to the upper floors stopping at almost every floor the whole way up. As we are going up, Mittens pulls out another bottle of whiskey.

"Hella ya, let's do this right!" she yells taking a big gulp then tossing the bottle to me.

"Screw it," I said taking a big gulp too.

We continue to stop at every level. As we keep raising and stopping our stomachs started to hurt. We are feeling the whip lash from stoping, and the high view of Earth isn't helping either.

"Oh, make it stop!" Mitten says.

"I can't you hit all the buttons."

We get to the 53th floor and we both stuck our heads out the door and threw up in front of a bunch of white collar workers.

"Sup," I said then the door to the elevator closed.

"Are you mad at me?" Mittens says

"Oh gods, don't start that shit again."

"Are you mad at me… you're mad aren't you," Mittens says again and starts to cry.

"Come on 71st floor….ugh," I say as Mittens continues to apologize.

"Are you… *burp*!" Mittens says looking at me as if she was trying to hold something down.

We stopped at the 54th floor and repeated the 53rd floor. The doors closed and we continued our upward climb. I stared out of the window of the elevator and I could see Earth. Then I turned towards Mittens, she was starting to pass out on the floor. I start to kick her, but I couldn't get my right leg to move so I flopped like a seal towards her.

"Come on, stay wake, we're almost there!" I slurred slapping her foot.

"I just need to close my eyes for a minute," She said sleepily while stroking my head.

"Wow, your head is poky, you use too much gel!" Mittens says then slaps me.

246

"Hey, come on, gods we stink!" I said.

Not realizing it, we were at floor 7st1 and as the door opened there was Jeffery ready for work.

"Oh my god you guys reek!" Jeffery says holding his arm in front of his nose with brief case in hand.

"Yea, ya see there was this bottle and it's called... *brup*..... Excuse me." I said pausing and turned towards the window of the elevator and threw up everywhere.

"Shit, let me get you guys to our apartment." Jeffery said looking a little frustrated.

He picked up Mittens and I crawled behind him. Lucky for us their apartment was right by the elevator so I didn't have far to crawl. Usually I was the one carrying Mittens up here. Jeffery helped me onto the couch, Mittens was laid out on the bed. Jeffery left a trash can next to both of us and a few bottles of water too.

"Ok, you guys should be ok," Jeffery said shaking his head.

"Thanks man," I said to him as I sprawled out on the couch.

"Well I don't blame you for what you're going through, I have to get to work, so maybe I'll catch you guys later," Jeffery says grabbing his brief case.

"See ya," I say passing out.

Chapter 22

Hang over from hell.

I lay on Mitten's couch, I'm trying to wake up but my eyes are so heavy. My head is pounding, and it's so hard to move, it feels like I just ran a marathon. I attempt to open my eyes and the light coming through the windows isn't helping. It's like staring into heaven, the light is so bright.

"Turn the light off," I say in pain.

"Ugh, I can't reach the window," Mittens says in pain.

"You alive?" I ask throwing a pillow over my head.

"No. What the hell did we do last night?" Mittens says as if she's being tortured.

"Drank... a lot," I replied attempting to pull myself up off the couch.

I manage to pull myself up, and as I sit up my head just spins out of control. My eyesight is gone, everything is spinning and its hard to focus on one point. I slowly lean back into the couch pulling a pillow over my head. Mittens is buried in pillows and blankets, almost looks like she built a little fort. I pull out my cell phone.

"Holy Crap! Its 5pm!" I said trying hard to look at my phone that has 6 missed calls and several text messages from Kat & Lynsye.

I gather my strength to reply to Kat.

I text, "I'm ok, I had a few drinks with Mittens I'm at her apartment."

A few seconds later she texts me back, "I'm glad you're okay I was beginning to worry, Lynsye went out looking for you."

I text Kat back, "I'll be home soon I'm going to try and wake up and head back soon I love you."

She replies, "I love you 2 ☺"

My hand and phone drop to my side, I swing my other hand and arm around and grab a bottle of water and chug it down. I pull myself up onto the couch and look over to Mittens in her fort.

"Hey Eskimo! I gotta go," I said like a pirate.

"Did you just call me fat?" She replies popping her head out of the fort and getting blinded by the light and falling over.

"No, I gotta go, Lynsye is looking for me," I said leaning over the couch.

"How are you going to get home?" Mittens asks through the pillow her face is dug in.

"I'm gonna waallkkk!!!" I said as I flipped over the back of the couch.

"Ouch.." I said on my back.

"Ha, Yea my point exactly," Mitten says.

About a half hour later I've recharged enough like a robot to get off the floor. I say good bye to Mittens, but she doesn't respond so I throw a pillow at her and she yells "Bitch" and starts to snore. I give a grin and grab my wallet, keys and head out the door. I get back to the elevators and ride down to the 42nd level. The last 30 minute power nap I took made me feel awesome, I didn't feel hung over. As the door opened for the 42nd floor, Lynsye was standing there with a cigarette in her mouth.

"Have fun last night?" Lynsye asks me.

"Ha yea um.." I said scratching the back of my head.

"Yea, the cops are looking for the two violators that broke the job board, and left a mess from the hanger bay to the 58th floor," Lynsye says grinning at me.

"I wouldn't know a thing you're talking about," I said and started to walk with her.

"Anyways, I know you don't want to hear this, but Marks mom is coming to the station in two days," Lynsye said.

"I can guess they want to collect his stuff, right." I said.

"Yea that and they want to do a memorial too." Lynsye says puffing her cigarette.

"Hey, I'm going to go see Kat for a little bit, can you load up the footage from the mission? I want to take a look at something," I ask Lynsye

"Why do you want to watch what happened again?" Lynsye asks with her hands in her pocket.

"I just need to see it one last time," I said putting my head down as I walked.

"I'll get it loaded for you, go see your baby, she's worried about you," Lynsye says slapping my shoulder.

"Thanks," I said and continued to my apartment.

I get to my apartment, and I pull out my keys, the door opens and Kats standing in the door way.

"What happened to you last night?" she says as she holds up a newspaper of two shadows in a photo causing mischief.

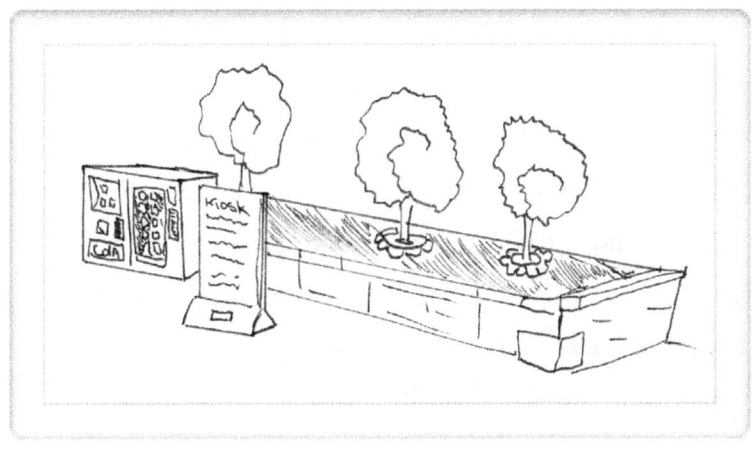

"Ha… ha.. yea we drank a little bit." I said smiling at her as she jumped on me and gave me a hug and pulling me into the apartment.

"Phew you stink. Look, I have to stop by the hospital and do a little paper work, can you watch over Casey?" Kat asks.

"Yea sure, how has she been?" I ask.

"Improving, she's able to sleep now at least," Kat says taking off her tank top.

"What are you doing?" I ask Kat.

"I'm going to shower… wanna join me?" Kat says giving me a sensual grin.

"Don't have to ask me twice," as I jump up stripping off my clothing.

We showered and had a little fun… okay, yes we did for all the pervs out there. We both got dressed and Kat headed out to the hospital. I gave her a long kiss goodbye, I couldn't resist being with something that beautiful. She gives me a heart attack because she's just so adorable. After I closed the door, I turned around and pulled out my cell phone Lynsye texted me "CIC is all set for you."

I text her back, "Cool can you watch over Casey for me?"

Lynsye text back, "Yea sure."

I go around and clean up my apartment, I did the dishes and started washing my clothing and Kats. As I cleaned, I came across my photos of Mark and Ithat I had on my wall. I said to myself, "I know you're not dead bro, I just know it."

As I stared at the photo a light knock came from the door and Lynsye came in quietly with Missy.

"Hey guys," I said folding my uniforms.

"Sup, CIC is all set for you." Lynsye says.

"What do you expect to find?" Missy asks.

"Closure, I hope."

"Well, when you get back we were going to make dinner for all of us, is that cool?" Lynsye asks.

"Yea, Kat will be back in an hour or so, and so should I ,so yea that sounds good," I said pulling on my hoody.

"Alright see you in a little bit," Lynsye says as I go out the door.

I head down to the hanger bay, making my way through the food court. I get to the hanger bay and cut through the part depot to the military bay and check in with the guards. They let me in and I walk into the CIC, it's just me, and it's quiet. I look over, and Lynsye even made me a pot of coffee.

"Best crew ever, and she even left me some Vanilla for it too," I said smiling pouring a big 16oz cup.

I grab the remote and hop in a chair and start running the footage. The footage starts when we all board the bomber and take off. I fast forward the video a little bit, and it starts to play at the point where we get jumped by the hidden fighters. I start to tremble a little bit, breathe in and out and fast forward again. I get to the part where we get hit by the rail beam.

Then I watch as Mark takes out the torpedo launcher and then he slams into the side of the station.

I pause, it looking at it and how he crashes. I pause, looking at the still image, and I can't quite grasp it, but something doesn't look right. I play it again and pause it at the same spot. I look and then I play it again. His fighter hits the side of the station and there is an explosion, but I stop again and replay it. Then last night popped into my head when Mittens threw the bottle at the Job board. Then it hit me, when the bottle hit, the glass went outwards. In the video the explosion goes through him as he crashes. I watch it again and maximize the zoom. I look as he crashes, he is firing his machine guns.

"HOLY SHIT!!!! He doesn't crash, he shot out the wall or window!! Because if he hit the side of the hull, the explosion would have shattered outward like the bottle, not through him or going behind him. He must have shot out a large window or a weakened part of the hull!" I said standing up with excitement.

"Good detective work, Ichia," Hitoshi says as I shit myself and drop my coffee.

"AHHH! How did, what, when did you get in here? "I asked like I just saw a ghost.

"I did my ghost walk, but you have a friend to save. I'll get the good Intel, and find out where that battle station is," Hitoshi says putting his hat on walking towards the door.

"Uncle," I said as he turns towards me.

"Thank you."

"Bring home my other nephew," Hitoshi says nodding towards me then turning and walking out the door.

"Shit," I say running out of the CIC.

I run as fast as I can back to my apartment. I've already been gone forty five minutes, I'm hauling ass running. It almost looks like I stole something, I'm running through the food court and jumping over tables and plant islands. It's about 6pm, a lot of people get off of work at this time and eat dinner down here. I roll through the crowd and get to the elevators.

"Crap, the lines are long as hell," I look to the right where the stairwell is.

"Fuck it!" I say running towards the stairwell.

I run up the stairs, jumping two to three at a time, racing to the 42nd floor. I have so much energy it's ridiculous, I'm jumping around people up the stairwell. I get to my floor and run like I have a bomb to my apartment. I darn near break the door down, Kat left it unlocked and inside everyone was about to eat. Colleen and Sam had come over too. As I stood in the doorway, I looked up at everyone heaving.

"Mark's Alive!" I said bent over with my hands on my knees.

Everyone goes "WHAT!" Kat comes over and brings me a Sodi Pop.

"Here, catch your breath and drink this," Kat says helping me drink from the can and closing door.

"What did you find?" Lynsye asks me standing up from the table.

I go and explain everything that happened. I told them about last night and how we broke the Job Board, then the video. Everyone was in shock from what I told them.

"That sounds too good to be true," Casey says looking around, having a hard time focusing on anything.

"Yea Ichia, there's no way he," Missy says being interrupted by an incoming call from my window screen.

I walk over to the window and press the key pad and it changes to the video monitor and it's my uncle on the screen.

"Uncle," I said.

"Ahh good, you're all in the same room. Its confirmed he's alive and I have the location of the battle station," Hitoshi says as he typing information.

"Are you serious?" Casey asks.

"Very, we have received reports of chatter and a hostage," Hitoshi says.

"Where's the battle station? We all have a bone to pick with these ass holes!" Colleen says pumping her fist.

"Pluto, it just jumped out there less than four hours ago. When you're ready we have a plan to stop the station, but as for getting Mark out," Hitoshi says then being interrupted by Colleen.

"Saturn 5 will handle that with the help of Jupiter 7," Colleen says.

"Yea, the bomber is still loaded with all of your weapons and equipment," Missy says with a smile on her face.

"Then that's it, let's roll right now, damit," I said kicking my bed.

"Be on flight deck in fifteen. I'll have the details for you there," Hitoshi says and the screen cuts out.

"Alright guys, let's bring our friend home!" I say high-fiving Lynsye.

"I'm coming too," Casey says standing up like she could take on Lab Rat Mafia by herself.

"I don't know, you." Kat starts to talk then is interrupted by Casey.

"He's my most precious thing, you'd do the same for Ichia. My baby needs me and if I have to shoot a gun or throw a grenade, you better believe I'm going to do my damn best to be able to hold him again!" Casey says pumping her fist as if she just scored a three pointer.

"Be careful you guys, I'll head to the hospital to get my staff ready for any incoming injuries and Mark," Kat says walking over to Casey and giving her a hug and holding her.

The team runs out in a group and heads down the stairwell. People are all staring at us as we run down the stairs like we are going to start a fight, even though the fight has been brought to us. We get down to the food court where people stop what they are doing and watch us all jog through. You can hear people say, "Isn't that Jupiter 7, didn't they lose someone?" Some people say "Those hero's from Christmas." We jog out to the bomber and my uncle is standing there with a group of people and a very old friend.

257

"Bill!" I said shaking his hand.

"Hey Ichia, I heard you guys could us some support," Bill says with a grin.

Bill was from the Delphinus. He was the leader of the Banshees. They are another fighter group just as crazy as us. Hitoshi pulled everyone over to the bomber and laid out the flight plan. He said we are going to have the jump on these guys, and they will never see us coming.

He explains that the Delphinus and Star Striker will jump in and begin to attack the station. Then support fighters will attack all enemy fighters. During this confusion, Jupiter 7 and Saturn 5 will land the bomber onto the station and rescue Mark. Hitoshi explained Mark is being held in the center of the station with possibly other prisoners. Hitoshi had two cases of armor dropped off for us to use, along with a few extra guns. Colleen started to drool when we opened with supply cases.

"Oh my gods!! Dragon Armor! Look at these boots!" Colleen gave a squeal.

"Time to bring the pain, baby," Lynsye says.

"Payback time," Casey says grabbing the rocket launcher and putting it over her shoulder.

"Everyone ready?" Hitoshi asks.

"YES SIR!" Everyone shouts and salutes him.

"Good, we roll in twenty minutes, everyone to your ships!" Hitoshi says walking to his shuttle.

"We got your back, Ichia," Bill says high fiving me.

"Don't worry, we're going to get em all home!" I said to Bill.

We all grab our armor, extra gear and board the bomber. Lynsye fires up the main systems and begins to take off.

"Ichia, its payback time. You're about to see what Saturn 5 can really do," Colleen says cocking her shotgun single handed.

"Hell yea, no one messes with our friends, let alone tries to make us look like fools in a mission," Sam says locking his AA-12's.

"Let's do this, full ahead Lynsye," I said

"Yes sir." She takes off and follows the Banshee Squadron out of the station to the Delphinus. We land in the bay of the Delphinus and Star Striker, another battle cruiser pulls up and a voice over the intercom comes on.

"All personnel prepare to jump."

"Oh shit, here we go, hoorah!" Sam says.

259

"Express elevator to hell going down!" Lynsye says.

"Ichia, next time someone asks if you're a god you say yes!" Casey yells

"Hell ya girl, that's what I'm talking about, good, bad, we're the ones with the guns!" I say holding my fist in the air, and then both ships jumped.

Chapter 23
The Great Pluto Rescue.

The Battle Station sits waiting as a fuel tanker is docked to it. Several dozen fighter squadrons patrol the station along with two Dreadnoughts and a Large Cruiser. Suddenly the Delphinus and Star Striker jump out of hyperspace. The Star Striker crashes through one of the Dreadnoughts, ripping it in two. The Delphinus opens fire on the Cruiser, and launches all fighters. All enemy Squadrons turn towards the two Alliance ships and begin to fire rockets and machine gun fire. The Star Striker opens up it's defense system and robotic guns begin to fire flak in every direction protecting the itself and the Delphinus from rocket fire. The flak looks like bursts of fire surrounding the large crafts. Bill's team was the first to fly off of the Delphinus and begin taking out the first wave of fighters.

"Jupiter 7 you're clear to launch," a voice says over the com.

"Roger that!" Lynsye says.

"Good Hunting!" Hitoshi says over the com.

We fly out of the Delphinus and head towards the Battle Station. The Lab Rat Mafia is in a panic, the shields of the station are down and several of the bay doors are wide open. As we make our approach, several fighters begin to chase us. Missy opens fire in the big cannon, while I take aim with the rocket monitor. We dodge rockets and gunfire, Bill comes around, clears and gives chase to the fighters that were behind us.

"Alright folks this is it, forty five seconds till we land!" Lynsye says.

"Remember, just keep shooting, ammo is not an issue!" Sam says.

"Thirty seconds!" Lynsye says.

"Baby I'm coming for you!" Casey says locking and loading her large machine gun with the rocket launcher on her back.

"Fifteen Seconds, look sharp!" Lynsye says counting down.

"Time to kick the tires and light some fires," I said locking my machine gun.

"3..2.. 1.." Lynsye counts it down as we land in the hanger bay. As we land, several personnel that didn't launch, start to run towards the bomber.

"LETS ROCK!" Colleen shouts as she opens the door of the bomber and sprays everything that moves towards the bomber.

Two large Mechs come barreling our way firing rockets towards us.

"Oh Hell NO!" Missy yells turning the large cannons towards the Mechs and blowing them away with the rockets like rag dolls.

"Move Marines!... and Pilots heheh." Colleen says waving us forward.

Sam takes the lead hopping back and forth from container to container, taking people out with his automatic shot guns. One bad guy jumped out from behind Sam. The guy tried to stab Sam from behind, but Sam grabbed the guy and used his knife against him slitting his throat.

"Yea, that's how you do it!" Sam screams continuing on.

"Holy shit!" I said.

"Marines baby," Colleen says shooting towards another group of soldiers coming our way.

"We don't' have time for this," Frankie says tossing a belt of grenades.

"Everyone down!" Colleen says grabbing me and Casey and pulling us down.

The explosion rocks the station, all of the soldiers that were firing on us were either dead, in pieces, or attempting to run away.

"Come on, this way," Sam says pointing down a hallway that leads away from the hanger.

"Move in two by two," Colleen says.

We move in twos, side by side, we're going in with little resistance. We come through what looks to be the galley, and sitting in the middle is a water generator, the same one we were originally looking for.

"Son of a bitch!" Colleen says hopping over to it.

"Is that it?" I ask holding my rifle to my face looking for enemies.

"Yup, Frankie get this thing ready to roll, Sam scout ahead, we'll be right behind you," Colleen says ordering everyone.

We continued behind Sam, it seemed as if the station was either being evacuated or everyone was hiding. As we moved through the hallways the station kept shaking as if it was taking heavy hits. We got to the center of the station and sure enough it was a giant prison. There must be ten to fifteen people being held here. A lot of them were Alliance scientists. We sneak up to the bars and there are six guards watching over everyone.

"Okay this is kitten play, Ichia. I'm going to toss a grenade, you and Casey take out the two on the left, I got the rest." Colleen whispers.

"Got it," I said locking my gun softly.

Colleen pulls the pin with her mouth and tosses the flash grenade. She throws it and hits a guard on his head and the moron picks it up saying. "What's this?" The Flash Grenade blows up and we open fire on the guards, killing them quickly without any problems.

"Good Shooting," Colleen says as we run to the entrance of the holding cells.

"Oh, you're Saturn 5 thank the gods," a beaten scientist says.

"Have you guys seen the newest hostage?" I ask him, as I help Casey unlock the gates.

"yes… yes..," a women says.

"I bandaged him up he was from Jupiter 7 right?" the women says.

"YES!" Casey says giving a little squeak.

"He's on the bridge, be careful they are guarding him like gold," the women says.

"How do we get there?" Colleen asks.

"Just head down that hallway and it's the door at the end, be careful, they have big guns," the women says sincerely as Sam runs in.

"Alright, you found the missing scientist!" Sam says high fiving Colleen.

"Did you get the generator back to the bomber?" Colleen asks.

"Yes, and there is a shuttle just sitting pretty, the Scientists can use it to jump out of here," Sam replies giving a thumbs up.

"Alright, get these scientists back to the hanger. Be ready for us because we're going to be most likely running back," Colleen says.

"Be careful babe," Sam says kissing Colleen.

"Whoa, wait you two…." Casey said.

"Come on, like you needed an invitation to figure that out," I said as they smiled at me and the station shook hard.

Sam led the scientists back to the hanger. Casey, Colleen and I rodeo run towards the main bridge. We get to the door and no one was even in the hallway. We put our ears up to the door to listen, there is a lot of panic in the room.

"Alright he's gotta be in there, how are we going to do this?" I asked Colleen.

"First, let's take a peak," Colleen says pulling out a frame and gently places it on the door. She turns it on and you can see everyone in the room. There must be at least fifteen guards, and five or six workers, on top of that, someone is tied to a chair in the far corner.

"That's gotta be Mark in the corner," Colleen says.

"I'm open for suggestions," I say.

"Cat and Mouse." Sam says sliding in like a baseball player to home plate.

"What are you doing here? I said to be ready for us," Colleen says.

"Don't worry, Frankie's got them," Sam says.

"Nice," I say.

"So what's the plan?" Casey whispers kneeling down as we all look at each other waiting for someone to answer.

"Cat and Mouse. I'm going to get them to chase me, you guys go in after they run by, grab Mark and we'll meet back at the bomber," Sam says with a big smile on his face.

"That's stupid, remember what happened last time we attempted that? We need to work our way through the vents and catch them by surprise," Colleen says.

"Screw it, let's do it!" Sam says opening the door.

"Shit!" we all say and duck.

As the door opens, Sam is standing there in the doorway like Rambo with two huge guns on his arms.

"Hey you Zone Dewbies! Any ya'll know where the bathroom is in this shit hole?" Sam shouts as he shoots and kills three guards and runs scrambling away like mouse. All the guards empty out giving Sam chase through the station.

"Holy shit, he pulled it off," Colleen said

"I thought you did that before." Casey asked.

"Yea, the last idiot that did that got shot," Colleen says kicking the door open.

"No one move," as she shoots and kills two of the workers.

"Mark!" Casey yells and runs to her battered boy friend.

"Hey, you guys made it to the party." Mark says tired and sore.

"Hey bro," I say as Casey and I give Mark a group hug.

We untie Mark and help him up, his right leg is busted up and he has to limp. We get him over to the door, and Sam runs through the other set of doors.

"Shit! I'm out of places to run!" Sam yells running towards us.

"Wait, aren't they?" Casey says as we all lift our guns as the guards come barreling in. We open fire taking them out and they start to pile up like zombies.

"Move people! Back to the boat!" Colleen yells as she presses a little red button on a black box measuring about 17"x17"x7"and tosses it towards the center of the room.

267

Casey and I are carrying Mark, Colleen and Sam are covering us. As we make our way back to the hanger bay we are met with more resistance. The station is rocked by a big explosion.

"I think that's cannon fire, Delphinus must be getting bored," I say struggling to carry Mark.

"Look out, to your right," Casey says as a soldier with a gun comes at me.

Sam blows the guy away as another one comes from behind Colleen. I pull my side arm out, taking his head off.

"Nice shot!" Colleen says holding her rifle up.

We continue back through the galley, then back through the long hallway leading back to the hanger bay. We come around the corner and the bomber is sitting pretty, waiting for us. As we make the dash towards the bomber, squads of soldiers come out of every corner in the hanger bay.

"Shit, go, go, go!!" I say holding Mark in one arm and shooting randomly in the other direction.

"Hey, let me help!" Sam says throwing his guns over his shoulder and picking up Mark and running like they just got married.

"Hey, come back with my boyfriend!" Casey says as she keeps up chase with Sam.

Colleen and I are right behind everyone, trying to cover fire. The soldiers keep coming out like ants, out of a hill. Suddenly Colleen stops and sees a dead guard with a data pack.

"Oh, heck yea!" Colleen goes after the data pack. Data packs

basically hold computer data from bank accounts to plans to build weapons to cures to illnesses, or maps to hidden treasures.

"Colleen, what are you doing!?!" I slide and stop for her.

"I'm grabbing a Data Pack!" She screams as she slides in and picks it up.

"Crap! COME ON!" I yell, shooting at everything that moves.

Colleen starts to rodeo run towards me. As she darts towards me she gets hit in her shoulder and blood sprays everywhere.

"COLLEEN!!!" I scream frantically as I duck down behind a crate.

As Colleen falls from being hit, she takes another shot in her butt, and falls to the ground face first. She lies on the ground lifeless bleeding out, I could see her feet from where I was, but I was in a bad cross fire. I looked at the bomber and as Sam was helping Mark in, Sam took a shot through his leg and was hit several times in his back. Casey and Lynsye pulled Sam up onto the ship. As they pulled him up, Missy was pointing at me from the cockpit of the bomber.

"Shit, Ichia is in a cross fire and looks like Colleens down!" Missy screams to Lynsye.

"Get us over to him, and get ready to pick him up hard!" Lynsye yells.

"Here put me into the side gunners chair." Sam says hurting from being shot.

"You're nuts!" Casey says.

"Come on!" Sam yells pulling himself into the side machine gun nest and Lynsye buckled him in.

I'm still caught in the crossfire looking at Colleen and the blood starting to run by her legs. I look at the bomber, and then I look towards Colleen.

"Fuck it!" I said as I jump out from behind the crate. I start to take aim towards the soldiers surrounding me. I empty my clip towards them as I was jumping crates and sliding over barrels. Then I hopped up, locking in my next clip and shooting with one hand, diving over another crate. As I was coming up to Colleen I emptied my next clip, and dropped right next to her. I grabbed her belt of grenades and pulled the pin and with all my might I threw them into the air towards the oncoming soldiers. All I heard was screaming and several loud explosions. I took a glance up and all the soldiers retreated back, only to see as the smoke cleared a large Mech was stomping my way.

"Can I get a fucking break?" I said checking my ammunition levels.

"Ichia.. Ichia is that you?" Colleen says lying in a pool of her blood.

"Yea I'm here, hang in there I'm going to get you out of here!" I said trying to set her up in a sitting position.

"I'm good, I'm not gonna die, I'm a Marine hoo.. haa," Colleen says passing out.

"Don't DIE ON ME!" I said then jumping up from behind the crates. I took aim at the Mech that was walking my way. It's machine guns were firing in my direction, along with small side rockets.

I took aim and started to shoot towards it, I kept hitting the glass in the same spot then, I hit a hose under its arm. Then I took another shot at the Mech and it exploded into a million pieces.

"Yea baby, that's how we do it!" I yelled jumping up and down.

"Hum!" Missy says over the loud speaker of the bomber.

I turn around and look at the bomber right behind be, it was almost like a dragon looking at me seeing if I was worth eating.

"Haters!" I said picking up Colleen.

"Come on get in!" Casey yells, holding out her hand towards me.

As I grab on to Casey pulling myself up, two more Mechs come out and start to fire at us.

"Oh no you don't!" Sam says laying a line of fire towards

271

them, cutting them down.

"Great shooting, now let's get the hell out of here!" Missy says guiding the bomber out of the hanger bay as fast as she can. The bomber flies with great speed out of the hanger bay, avoiding cranes and tankers. As we exit into space we are all caught by surprise. We are orbiting a bright blue planet with land masses, and it's not Earth. On top of that, there are two stars in the distance.

"Um… what the hell, where are we?" I ask everyone.

"Did the station jump away?" Lynsye asks.

"It's possible, but we would of known if it jumped," Missy says.

"Where are the Alliance ships? Where's the Delphinus?" Casey asks holding Mark tightly.

"Get away from the Station as fast as you can." I said giving an order, then being interrupted by a bright beam of light that knocks us towards the planet.

"This isn't good, engines two and three are out, only have one and four working!!!" Missy says.

"I'll try the backups!" Lynsye shouts as she scrambles to the back of the Bomber.

Then one engine explodes and we are now in a free fall towards the planet. We enter the atmosphere and begin to burn up.

"Oh come on, I don't want to become a crispy critter!" Casey screams.

"This isn't good!" I say standing next to Missy in the cockpit, hanging on to her chair.

Suddenly the retro engines fire and I'm thrown to the back of the bomber. I hit my head hard. As I try to recover I can hear Lynsye and Missy screaming at each other.

"We're slowing down!"

"I'll use the egress shoots to bring us down!" Then we are rocked again by another explosion. Another engine must have exploded, we were all thrown to the side of the bomber, I was on top of Colleen and Sam. I was semi-knocked out and I could hear all of the commotion but I could not open my eyes. Then I hear a loud glass shattering, metal crunching, sound. I couldn't feel my body I felt like I was floating in air. I couldn't open my eyes but I could make out the faint sounds of everyone screaming and then everything went silent.

Chapter 24

<u>LOST.</u>

"Ichia, come on wake up, can you hear me?" Casey says as my head is in her lap.

"Uh? What, where are we?" I said coming awake and opening my eyes.

"Good, you're ok, here drink some Sodi Pop, we don't have any water," Casey says.

"Uh thanks, is everyone ok?" I ask.

"Mark and Lynsye have major concussions, I've bandaged them as best as I could. Missy's right leg is broke, I've set it, and taped it, and drugged her up." Casey says helping me sip the beverage.

"What about Sam and Colleen?" I ask looking up at Casey.

"I've managed to stop the bleeding, but I'm no doctor Ichia," Casey says helping me up.

"How long has it been since we crashed?" I asked her rubbing the back of my head and feeling a small bump that had formed.

"At least two days," Casey says.

"Wait, two days and the Lab Rats didn't come after us?" I ask.

"The weather on this planet is pretty rough, it's been thunder storming since we've been here. Not to mention we're in the middle of a forest, the trees dwarf most buildings I've ever seen," Casey says.

I pull myself up from the floor of the bomber and walk past my friends as they lay bandaged and bruised. I pull myself into the other seat in the cockpit. Missy is laying back in the pilot's chair. I look out, and we are surrounded by giant trees that almost look like large buildings with huge fern plants that dress them underneath. Its hard to make out anything in the distance. The fog is laying thick in the distance. Large bugs fly by, scrambling to avoid the rain.

"Must be oxygen out there?" I whisper to Casey.

"Yea, has to be, we have a hull breach. I tried collecting water but its running though a cable and it's full of oil," Casey says.

"Have you opened the side hatch?" I ask.

"No, too scared to," Casey replies pulling a blanket over her and Mark.

"I'd be too, those bugs look huge, how are our supplies?" I ask coming over to look at Lynsyes bandages.

"64 case of Sodi Pop, three MRE's, two day old White Castle burgers, two cases of Hot Pockets and a bag of potato chips." Casey says.

"How do we end up with more alcohol than food?" I ask myself.

"Well, Lynsye did rent the bomber out as a party bus the night before the mission." Casey says.

"Yay," I sighed and popped open a can of Sodi Pop. I looked over to my right and noticed a small green LED blinking.

"Hey what's that?" I ask Casey pointing with my can in hand.

"I checked it, the radar is half working, and we're picking up a very faint signal. Don't know what it is, but it's been blinking since I woke up." Casey says.

"Can't be any enemies, it would be blinking red." I said.

"It might be a part of the bomber, I climbed into the gunners chair and the antenna is missing on the back of the bomber." Casey says.

"Yea, maybe," I said, then Missy turns her chair towards us.

"Hey guys, ugh great landing huh?" Missy says to us.

"You feeling ok?" I ask.

276

"Yea the Meds are working, I can't feel my leg, but I'll take a can of Sodi Pop," Missy says pulling herself up in the chair.

"Ha yea, that's the last thing you'll need," Casey says as I throw her a can.

"Love you, Ichia," Missy say opening the can.

"Really?" Casey says to me.

"Why not?" I said.

Suddenly we hear a loud roar outside of the ship in the distance. We all freeze and slowly look out the cockpit glass. Then another loud shriek in the distance.

"What the Fuck is that?" Casey asks.

"Sounds like a retarded Dinosaur." Missy slurs.

"I think we need to lay low and keep quiet." I say sliding away from the cockpit.

Casey and I carry Missy and sit her next to Lynsye on the floor. Then we take an Egress blanket and cover up the cockpit. I found some candles and lite them with the matches from the MRE's.

"Where did these candles come from? They're vanilla scented." Casey asks smiling.

"I found them with some other items in the storage bin. They must have went shopping and left them in the ship." I said.

"I'm glad they are scented, we've all been in here for a couple of days now. It's starting to get funky." Casey says as thunder crashes and the rain starts to tap on the hull again.

"You know, I'm half tempted to open the doors in the morning to attempt to get some water." I said holding up a water test meter, smiling.

"Sounds good to me, there's two plastic tubs. Want to open the door and toss em out side real quick?" Casey asks with enthusiasm.

"Why not, what do we have to lose, you unlock the door and use this shot gun. I'll open the door and place these the tubs outside of the door." I said grabbing the two plastic bins.

"Okay, here we go." Casey says breathing deeply.

Casey slowly pulls a lever on the door unlocking it, she steps back and cocks the shot gun. I slowly open the door and lightening crashed nearby, lighting up the entire forest. It's raining very heavy, it's like a monsoon outside of the ship. I grab my wits and move both tubs outside of the ship. I slowly close the door and lock it, pushing the lever back into place.

"That was easy," Casey says uncocking the shot gun.

"Ha yea, the air seemed really fresh," I said wiping my face off with a towel.

"I have an idea, we have some old GPS's on here, I could turn one into a motion tracker, it would only track up to 50 yards or so," Casey says kneeling down next to Mark.

"Hmm, that would make it safer to be outside to gather water, and check out the bomber," I said holding my chin in thought.

"This bomber ain't going to be flying any time soon, the

engines are shot. The only thing good is the shield generators. We could tap into them for power but we have nothing we could really run," Casey says sipping a can of Sodi Pop.

"Well, blow out all but one candle if you want to make that tracker tonight," I said pulling out a blanket.

"Ok should only take a few hours, nite Ichia," Casey says.

I said good night to Casey, I pulled up a backpack as a pillow and laid next to Lynsye and Missy. At first I laid there and was wide awake because of the rain. The rain was pounding on the side of the ship. Didn't help that hail was hitting the ship too. Eventually I fell asleep, waking up to Casey coming under the blanket we hung over the cockpit.

"Morning, sleep ok?" Casey asks me.

"Yea not too bad, how's it look out there?" I ask.

"Light rain, and the motion tracker works, I can set it to pick up three types of movement. I was able to pick up those big dragonfly looking things." Casey says.

"Cool, want to go outside?" I ask her.

"Let me get the shot gun, here take the tracker." Casey says handing the tracker to me. The tracker was like a brief case with a radar screen on top. I fold my blanket and walk over to the hatch.

"Ready?" I ask.

"Yup." Casey says cocking the gun.

I open the door and fresh air rushes in, and it's the purest air I've ever breathed. Almost like fresh mountain air that revives you instantly. I turn on the tracker and step out of the bomber. It was almost like a forest on earth, you could hear bird-like creatures chirping, and insects buzzing. The rain was lightly falling, with a mild fog surrounding us. Casey follows me out of the bomber and we walk side by side looking around and inspecting the bomber. The bomber is in rough shape, two of the four engines are gone, along with the starboard wing. Looks like we hit a tree and rode it down to the ground, it must have cushioned our fall.

"Wow, with the bomber sitting the way it is we could almost set up a base camp." Casey says.

"Yea we may do that, at least be outside during the day." I said walking to the over-flowing tubs I set out last night.

"Here lets, check the water." Casey says pulling the tester out of her back pocket. The tester looks like a walkie talkie, she extends the rod from the top and turns on the tester.

"Wow, look at this," Casey says in amazement.

"What? Is it drinkable?" I ask standing next to her.

"It's very clean, there's no acid in it, no chemicals, nothing, its pure water," Casey say looking at me.

"Clean rain water? No iron, or acids, or dust particles?" I ask

"Nothing, it's very pure," Casey says.

"Well here goes nothing." I say as I cup my hands and take a quick drink.

"Well?" Casey say looking at me worried.

"Refreshing, try it," I said as Casey kneeled down to the tub cupping her hands and taking a drink.

"Wow, not even the bottled water on the station is this good." Casey says then taking another drink.

After rehydrating ourselves we bottled as much as we could. We kept the motion tracker on and started to set up a mini camp. Casey used wires as a clothing line, she used one bucket to clean the bloody towels and clothing of our hurt friends. I helped her hang them on the lines, but we realized that as much as it's been raining that nothing would dry. So we ended up moving all the clothing and towels inside to hang. Later that day Lynsye came around, and Mark, Sam and Colleen started to look better, at least with their breathing. It was nice to drink water again instead of alcohol, Casey was able to boil water and make instant potatoes.

"Yay, real food!" Casey says putting some in a bowl for me.

"How long have I been out?" Lynsye asks.

"Couple of days, today was the first day we went outside of the ship," I said.

"Wow, any luck getting a hold of the Alliance?" Lynsye asks.

"Nothing, just a weird signal we're picking up," Casey says, then a loud roar again, we all pause like statues. Then again another roar outside of the ship.

"Is is is... that, that's closer than last time," Casey says trembling.

"What the hell was that?" Lynsye asks.

"No clue but its not the first time we've heard it," I said.

"Have you come up with a plan to get out of here?" Lynsye asks.

"Nothing we can do, the antenna is gone, and last I remember the Lab Rats knocked us out of orbit," I said.

"Maybe you two should go check out that signal," Lynsye says.

"It is only three clicks away," Casey says.

"Maybe, but whatever is out there sounds huge," I said eating my instant potatoes.

"We do have the motion tracker, and our guns., Casey says.

"Yea, and box of grenades," Lynsye smiles slapping the top of an ammo box.

"Well, it would be better than sitting around here. Plus if Mark, Sam, or Colleen's health goes downhill we don't have any proper medical supplies. I've already used most of the antibiotics on them to prevent infection," Casey says.

"Let's do it, we'll pack tonight and head out at first light, 3 clicks should only take two hours in this forest," I said.

"Hopefully the rain will slow down for you guys," Lynsye says.

"Yea, sounds like it's picking up again," Casey says.

"Casey you sure you're ok with this?" I ask.

"I'm good, I'll be thinking of Mark the whole way there and how we are going to get off this rock," Casey says giving me the thumbs up.

"Good news is that we can still talk to you while we're gone. Our compads can connect up to 5 miles, so let's charge the batteries tonight too," I said.

"Oh yea, I forgot about our compads, sweet!" Lynsye says pulling hers out and slides her finger across her screen and opens a game.

We finish dinner and check on our injured friends. I keep Sam and Colleen close together and put an extra blanket on them. Lynsye is keeping Missy warm and Casey is sitting next to Mark cleaning her shot gun. I walk over to the ammo box, grab a satchel and start to look at what I'm going to take for tomorrow. I take six grenades and seven clips of ammunition. I fill up a backpack with water bottles and the Hot Pockets. Double checking the bags, it looks like we are set for our little hike tomorrow morning. I check on everyone, then pull out my blanket and blow out the candles.

Chapter 25

A New Hope.

"This is insane, unsafe and just stupid. Whatever we do deals with sudden death. Small chance of survival, the little shot gun that could and a Hot Pocket, what are we waiting for," Casey says to me smiling.

"Now that's the spirit," Lynsye says tossing a hand grenade to me.

"You know, three clicks really isn't that far," Lynsye says to me.

"Yea, well I don't hit the gym every other day so..." I say smiling.

"You should take those darn egg rolls instead of the Hot

Pockets, they'll make better for throwing stones than food," Casey says giggling.

"Haters," I said.

We grab the guns and the backpacks, and look to everyone.

"We'll be back soon," I said tightening the strap on my bag.

"Hey Lynsye, take care of our babies," Casey says.

"I'll take care of them, you two be careful, watch your Cabooses," Lynsye says giving us the thumbs up.

I open the hatch and a warm humid air rolls in thick. We climb out of the ship and close the hatch behind us and turn towards the signal. We are faced with nothing but a very dense forest.

"This place makes Cambodia look like Kansas," I said.

"Quit quoting movies and lets get a move on," Casey says as she cocks her shot gun.

We begin the long three click hike to hope. The brush, bushes and vines are so thick, I break out my machete and start chopping. As we make our way through, large trees are towering over us like buildings. The sunlight fights to come through the tree tops like on a cloudy day. The trail begins to get rough, we climb over ungodly roots from trees. They breach the ground like stairs. We come across deep grooves in the ground and swing across them. Deeper and deeper we go into the forest, it seems like hours of travel but it's only been an hour. The rain starts to pick up again, we end up putting on some ponchos. As we slowly make our way through the foliage, the trees are acting like pools and create mini water falls.

The sound is almost soothing but it begins to get annoying, because all we can hear is running water. Its like a water logged jungle with all of the rain, plus the thunder doesn't help either.

"Damn, we there yet?" Casey say trying to catch her breath.

"Almost, we made good time, about a click and a few away and we'll be there."

"Thank you Jesus," Casey replies.

After taking a ten minute break getting out of the rain, we begin to continue on, cutting through thick foliage and climbing over roots and down large rocks. As we get closer to the signal, we run across a large carcass. There's some type of furry creature about the size of school bus. Something ate half of it because half of the head was attached to the torn body with the ribs cleanly sticking out.

"OMG, I thought you were bad," Casey says holding her shirt to her face.

"This is fresh, look at the blood, it's still wet," I say kneeling down to look.

"That thing is as big as a dinosaur," Casey says.

"What the hell ki..." I gets interrupted by a screeching roar.

"What the fuck was that?" Casey says pointing her shot gun in multiple directions.

We jump over to the bottom of a large tree and take cover for a minute. In the distance we can hear a large creature trampling through the forest. It almost sounds like a herd of something. Whatever is walking through the forest is breaking large limbs off the trees. The snapping sound is echoing through the forest. Casey has the shot gun aimed and ready to fire, as she keeps looking in multiple directions.

"That shot gun ain't gonna help us here, let's get moving, we're very close," I said with a grenade tightly clinched in my hand.

We continue on, very cautiously through the forest. As we hike on, there are loud bird sounds and in the distance is thunder. The thunder echoes between the trees and under the canopy of the trees. We continue on and under the tree line we run into several large rock faces. We've come to find out that we are actually standing on a mountain and that the trees are larger than the mountain. The other issue we begin to notice is the steam vents coming from the sides of the mountain. Must be a volcano. Sure enough, as we climb down the side, lava is dripping out like water. We come to a clearing with more brush, and some of the larger trees have been knocked down by something large. If things weren't hard enough, a dense fog begins to roll in like a wall. Casey attached the climbing rope to our belts just in case we get separated in the fog.

"You know the first thing I'm going to do when I get back?" Casey ask me, holding her shot gun over her shoulder.

"What's that?" I reply as I cut through the brush.

"I'm going to get a pedicure, oh my god my feet are killing me!" Casey says with a giggle.

"Yea well, when I get back I'm going to take Kat out to dinner and...." I say looking at Casey and then run into something metal.

"Thud!"

"Damn what the hell is this?" I said after being knocked on my butt.

"Holy Crap it's a ship engine, well looks like one. Hard to tell in this damn fog," Casey says looking around.

"I've never seen an engine like that," I say getting up off the ground, brushing the dirt of my pants.

"Let's look for some markings," Casey says.

We start walking around the ship and we don't see any markings. The fog doesn't help much, it's denser on the ground. Casey notices a rock ledge that's sticking out of the fog. We head over to the rock face and begin to climb. As we climb I keep looking behind us to see if I can see the space ship, all I can make out is a blurry shape. We finally climb about hundred feet up to reach the top of the face. I pull Casey up next to me, we both catch our breaths and turn towards the space ship. Looks like the nose of the space ship is sticking out of the fog. Then all of a sudden the fog begins to move and dissipates. The space ship almost looks like its raising out of the fog as it rolls out. We are stunned with amazement to what we find.

"You got to be kidding me right?" I say.

"Wow," Casey says with her mouth wide open.

"Astroliner," I say with a white look on my face.

"This thing was lost over 15 years ago, It was originally a secret weapon-slash exploration ship. It was the first ship to use something to travel faster than warp speed or something," Casey says looking over the ship with her arms crossed.

"I know the Captains grandson who flew this thing, we were in military training together," I said.

"I'm kind of excited, I did several papers on this bad boy back at the academy. Everyone thought I made up my own ship but it's real," Casey says hopping up and down.

"Let's go," I said throwing the rope down the rock face.

We head towards the ship and begin to investigate the outer hull looking for an entrance. Casey remembers her studies, and finds the main entrance to the ship on the port side. We climb over to that side, the ship is somewhat on its side so it makes it easier to get around it. We open the door hatch to get into the ship, it's almost like the ship took a deep breath as we pulled the door open. Air rushed into it like a pharaoh's coffin being opened for the first time in thousands of years. We look at each other with fear, then begin to climb down the ladder into the ship. I put on my head lamp and head into the ship, Casey slowly follows me. I step onto the main floor and it's dark as a tin can, there is a slight musty smell in the air. I turn towards the head of the ship, light is trying to come though dirt covered glass. The entire front of the ship looks to be transparent titanium. I make my way through what looks like a science area, I can see three cockpits. I start to walk slowly up to them and then stop, and Casey bumps into me.

"Hey... what's wrong?" Casey asks grabbing my shirt.

"I just found the crew."

We walk forward and turn, and in each seat lies a skeleton of a crew member. In the middle is the captain seat. The captain's corpse is holding another corpse of what looks like a Nephilum body. I look over the captains remains and I gently put my hand on the headrest. I look towards his lap and notice a paper diary. As I go to reach for the diary my compad falls out of my shirt pocket and hits the floor. We both stop as the sound echoes though the ship. Then out of nowhere it starts to play Amazing Grace from my play list. It just happened to be the last song I had listened to back on the space station. The song was sung by a famous female artist. We look at each other as if we just stole something. Casey starts to break into tears, looking at the skeletons in the chairs as they clung onto what they had. I can't help but stand at attention and Casey follows. As the song plays on, we still stand at attention. The song is echoing through the ship, it can be heard gently on

290

each deck of the ship like a cave. The hull of the ship almost makes it sound like you are in a concert hall listening to the girl singing it. As the song finishes, Casey wipes the tears from her eyes.

"What's the chances of that playing when you dropped your compad?" Casey asks me shivering.

"No clue, I was reaching for the captain's diary and it fell out," I said reaching to pick up my compad off the floor.

"I'm going to go look in engineering and see what's going on," Casey says.

"Yea, I'm going to take a look around up here, this ship was sealed well for some reason. Get back to me as soon as you find something, and keep quiet, don't know what may be lurking around in here or outside," I said to Casey.

Casey heads the other way with her shot gun locked and ready to kill.

I look over to the captain.

"Pardon me sir, please let me read from your diary," I say as I pick up the diary. I go straight to the back of the diary where the writing stopped.

"We've been here for weeks, maybe a month now. The Gamma burst took out all of our power. The shield generator cells are holding. Our only hope of rescue is the probe we shot into space. We dare not go outside the ship. The sound of Marching in the deep jungle, marching, marching in the deep….. They are coming……..Katy I'm so sorry….." The dairy ends and I get a

291

deathly chill across the back as if someone blew cold air along my neck, I about peed myself.

"What is coming?" I said to myself.

I Honor the Dead in the ship and find large long tubs. I carefully lay the remains into the each tub and place the name tags on them. Casey comes running up the stairs.

"Well I found the rest of the crew in the back, but I think I can get us out of here," She says with a daring look on her face.

"How?" I asks.

"If we grab the shield generator from the Bomber and plug it into the Astroliner's shield generators, it will recharge them. These are older generators, but they are well preserved and there's no corrosion. It should be enough to get us back to orbit and then some. It's just a matter of the alternators charging enough to fire the main thrusters." Casey says.

"Hmm, that's a long way to bring a shield generator." I said as Casey interrupts me.

"It's our only chance, better than waiting to die or for rescue. This ship was the pre-design for deep space and miscellaneous adventures. Many ships are designed off of it because of the streamline lay out. I remember they once said it went under oceans," Casey says.

"Oh boy," I said.

"Hey, it's better than a bunch of drunk carneys accidently backing up into a silo and saying, awe shit we can make this a carnival ride." Casey says.

"Alright, well it will give us something to do in the meantime. Plus this looks more secure than our bomber. So if things go south at our crash site we can migrate here," I said assessing the situation, not to mention what the captain wrote in his diary.

"I can unplug the shield generator quickly and we can be back in a few hours, doesn't help it weights 150lbs," Casey says.

"Well, we made a small trail to get here, that should help us move quick enough, we don't have a lot of time," I said.

"Why?" Casey asks me with a confusing look on her face.

"We just have to get a move on, its getting late you know," I said to Casey not trying to give anything away from the diary.

We climb out of the ship and begin to head back. As we head back a bad storm starts to hit. Large hail is coming through the tree tops along with buckets of rain. The water is pouring and we are starting to see flash flooding as we are running. We waste no time with the precut trail we made.

"This is crazy!" I yell as we are running and dodging hail.

Sliding down big roots and swinging our way back, making great time, it only took us about an hour and a half to get back to our crash site. Back at the crash site Lynsye is sitting in the gunner's chair. The gunner is a large dome like on a WWII bomber, but made of Transparent Titanium.

"Where the hell are those guys, three clicks is just under two miles?" Lynsye says to herself looking through the rain drops.

Then large knocking and the hatch swings open. Casey and I dive in and slam the door behind us. We both lay on the floor trying to catch our breath.

"Hey, you guys made it, what was it?" Lynsye ask sliding down the ladder slowly.

"We got a way out of here," Casey says.

"What did you find?" Lynsye asks again.

"Astroliner...pant pant, we found the Astroliner," I said.

"I thought that thing was just a legend or a ghost story," Lynsye says.

"No its real as all hell," I said grabbing a towel and wiping my face off.

Casey and I sit down with Lynsye and begin going over what we need to gather. Casey is drawing the engine design, where to plug in the fuel cells. She shows us what she is going to need. Then I start to go over what items we're going to need between walkie talkies and weapons. I plan to keep what the captain wrote in his diary to myself.

"Okay, Casey and I are going to make a run for it again. We're probably going to spend the night there and come and get you guys in the morning," I said.

"We'll be ready keep your compad's on, batteries are fully charged and we have good range. I'll have everyone ready to be moved when you get back," Lynsye says to me.

As we carry the heavy case out, Lynsye stops me for a second.

"Hey what's making that screeching we hear every now and then?" she asks pulling aside.

I look as Casey hops back into the bomber to check to see if she left anything.

"Look keep this between us," I said as she nods.

"I read the last page in the Captains diary, and the last thing he mentions is marching in the deep forest. Whatever is out there is huge, because we came across a huge carcass. Whatever ate that was no little beast. Stay frosty, first sign of trouble call me and get in that gunner chair," I say to Lynsye who's a little whiter than before.

"Watch your caboose Ichia, I want to be able to share drinks with you and the rest of my friends when we get out of this mess," Lynsye whispers in my ear and gives me a romanic kiss on the lips.

I step back and look at Lynsye confused.

"What was that for?" I ask.

"Good luck, you're the only man I ever trusted, every other so-called man can go to hell. Don't tell Missy," She says winking at me, as I blush.

"Yo, let's go GIJOE!" Casey says hopping outside of the bomber.

I nod to Lynsye, throw my backpack on and help Casey lift the shield generator. We start heading through the forest again. Both of us are carrying one end of the case.

"Damn, this stuff's heavy," Casey says pushing it up a giant root under a large tree.

"Yea, well we're making goo," I say then stop looking to the left of the direction we are heading.

"Casey get down," I whisper.

We both drop down low and look towards a large shadowy figure moving through the trees in the far distance. The Large figure is making a marching sound like a thousand troops marching to war.

"What the fuck is that?" Casey whispers to me, as it shrieks.

"Let's move slowly," I said.

It's a tense moment, whatever the creature is, it stops as it senses something and stays still. We look at each other then towards the shadowy figure which doesn't move. The air is still, and for once the forest is completely quiet as if fear itself has a hold on this area. Suddenly the figure moves further away from us, we pick up the shield generator case and start moving again. As we head towards the Astroliner, Casey has the motion tracker tied to her waist, so she can look at it constantly. We are moving like a cat that has just been scolded by their owner, just looking for the exit.

We get to the rock face and we tie the case with rope, I lower it down as Casey drops down with it. The fog has slightly returned to the area as we make it back to the Astroliner. We use the rope to drag the case up the side of the ship and gently set it into the ship. I close the hatch and help Casey break out the flashlights and then help her carry it to the engineering area. We finally get everything into place. After we set down the case I noticed the other bodies of two more crew members. Shaking off the chill I call Lynsye's compad.

"Lynsye we made it in, we're gonna clean up, take a rest, and then start repairs."

"Sounds good, let me know if there is any trouble," she replies.

"No problem," I reply back.

We unpack the shield generator and set it near the Astroliner's shield generator.

"Hey, let's take a small break, eat something, then fix this thing," I say to Casey holding up a bag of instant hot pockets.

"I'm not hungry for crappy hot pockets, I want Taco Bell. I'm going to get some water and start this," she replies.

"Hey don't' burn yourself out," I said.

"No, I'm going to repair this, everyone's hurting and we need to get out of here. Plus I can't stop thinking about Mark, I finally get him back and now we're in greater danger than before," Casey says grabbing tools with determination.

"True," I said looking down at my hot pocket.

I let her go on her way, as I open an instant hot pocket and take a break. I watch Casey take apart the shield generator. She starts pulling off cables from the Astroliner's shield generator, and disassembles several fuse boxes. After taking a little break I head through the crew quarters and up to the main bridge. I wipe down all of the control panels, instruments and seats. I look through a few of the log books they have. I didn't realize it until now, but it looks like the Astroliner wasn't wired like newer ships with hi-tech computers and AI's. I look around and notice everything is really simplified.

The weapon system looks very different and how it's piloted too. The Captain's chair has the all master controls from steering to weapons, and some other options. The chair to the right has radar and weapons. The left chair has power controls, weapons, and I'm not sure what ION control is. I sit in the captain's chair, I grab the controls and its almost like my fighter. Everything is at my fingertips, almost. I open the Captain's journal again, I flip back to earlier pages and start to read.

"July 4th 2033, We just lit off millions of fireworks for what was the old United States of America. Also celebrating it's Independence was the lunar colonies. Hard to believe that something in history could repeat itself on the same day. Today Katy brought her nieces on board, too. I think it was another try from her sister to get me to have kids with her. I love Katy, we've been married for about four years now. One day when I'm ready to settle down I'll have kids."

"Wow, he was married, Let's see what else he did," I said reading the captains diary, sitting crossed legged in the chair with my head lamp on.

"November 14th 2033, We've discovered a new planetary system with two planetary body's that support life. We met the local people and they are indeed advanced, they have space ships but lack the ability to travel any further than the edge of their systems. Cole has worked with the planet engineers, and their system lacks magnesium, which is a basic fuel for Shield

Generators. Weeks later, we managed to help them reach the stars and they wished to form an Alliance with human kind.

"Wow, so he discovered Kou people, wow," I said then closing the book. I want to read on, but I better go check Casey and see how she's doing. I set the book down in the seat and head to engineering.

The interior of the Astroliner was interesting, it's carpeted, unlike most ships where it's straight metal. I slide down the stairs and see Casey is still working hard on the Shield Generators. I walk up to her to see how she's doing.

"Hey how's it going?" I said and get no reply, I kneel down and she's passed out underneath the generator. I slide her out and pull out a blanket and cover her up. Its been a challenging day. I call back to Lynsye to let her know we are going to sleep for a bit and then get back to work. I head back up to the crew area where we came in and locked the hatch from inside. The rain had returned and it was gently tapping on the outside of the hull. I went back to the captains chair, put my feet up and sat back. The rain was washing the dirt off of the transparent titanium cone. I was able to see outside slightly. It was dark outside, the rain began to pick up and the thunder started to pick up again. My eyes got heavy and I eventually fell asleep in the chair.

Chapter 26

The Astroliner.

Hours later I was still passed out on the chair. The sunlight started to come through the front of the ship, then all of a sudden the ship began to shake.

"WHAT!" I jump out of the chair pointing my side arm in every direction, then I hear.

"Yea, bitches WHAT, yea guess whose good mwahahahahahah!" Casey screams from engineering.

As I stand there, power starts to come on to different parts of the ship. The lights start to flicker, pop and turn on. I think to myself, I'm glad I hired her. I start heading toward engineering as the Astroliner starts to come to life. The sound of computers and fans turning on, lights keep popping on and some screens start lighting up. I slide down to the third level, and as I land Casey jumps on to me.

"I did it, I did it, woo hoo!!!" Casey yells.

"Alright!" I say holding her tight as we both jump up and down like school girls.

"I managed to rig the shield generator to work off of the bombers generator. I had to do a lot of rewiring. Not to mention this tech is a little old, but it's still very compatible with our tech. So with a little ingenuity, bam, we got ourselves a ride!! Oh, and we may need a new power cup link by the time we hit orbit, but I think she'll fly!" Casey say with her hand on her hips.

"Great job Casey you saved us," I say giving Casey another hug.

"How long till we can attempt to fly this thing?" I ask.

"Should be about ten minutes, we just have to get a little juice into the main Generator, let the alternator do it's thing and we should be good to roll. Actually, help me secure this to the bulk head, I'd like it to stay in place so it doesn't come undone. If it does, then we're really screwed."

I help Casey lock the bombers generator to the bulk head. We strap it and rope it the best we can. We clean up the tools and throw everything into the corner. We head back towards the bridge and I call Lynsye.

"Crash landing resort how can I direct your call?" Lynsye says.

"Ha, guess what, we got us a way out of this dump!" I say

301

heading to the bridge.

"No shit, I'll get the ladies ready for you, and tell Casey I'm going to rock her world when we get home!" Lynsye says as Casey gives me a worried look as we are walking back to the bridge.

"She's just goofing around… I hope," I say.

We get to the bridge and everything is lit up like a Christmas tree. I take a seat in the captain's chair and Casey sits in the chair to the left of me.

"Well if I'm reading this right. we have sixty percent power, and I have a green light on shield generator one, but two is only holding at forty percent." Casey says.

"Cool, plug your com pad into the panel so we can contact Lynsye directly. I'm going to see what these controls will do," I said grabbing the controls.

"Lynsye, ETA six minutes to arrival, we just have to get off the ground," Casey says into her compad.

"Roger that!" Lynsye says.

"All right, here goes nothing," I say placing my hand on the pitch control. I pull back on the stick and the ship roars to life. It rumbles like someone left the bass on too loud. The Astroliner begins to lift off the ground, my facial expression is like kid in a candy store. The Astroliner is fully air born, hovering about ten feet off the ground. But then engines are beginning to back fire like Uncle Bucks Cutlass.

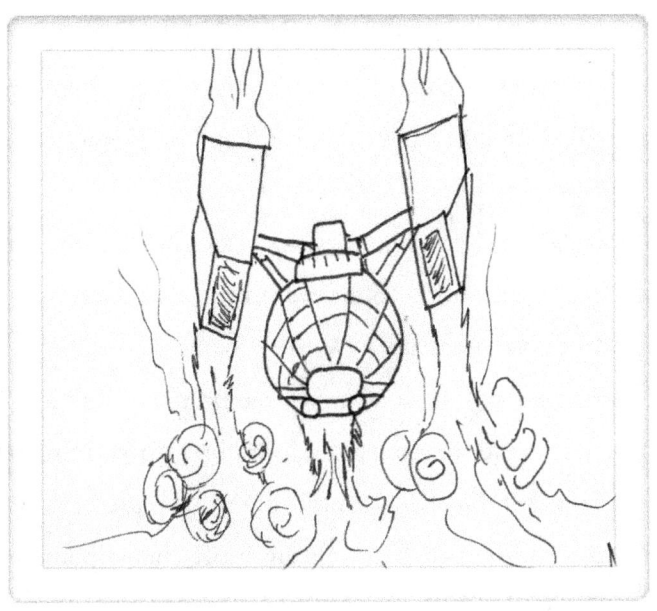

"Casey, I'm losing thruster power in right engine!"

"Right, I'm on it!" Casey says as she jumps out of her chair running towards engineering.

"I'm going to try and make it to the other crash site," I said to Casey as she headed back to engineering. I begin to use both pitch and roll to move the ship around. All of a sudden, *Whammmm!!!!* I run the Astroliner into a huge tree.

"Damn my bad!" I say wiping the sweat from my forehead.

All of a sudden the communicator in the ship comes on.

"Hey, I'm trying to work back here!" Casey says over the intercom.

"Alright lets, try this again, just like my old baby, come on!" I said.

I begin to push through the forest with The Astroliner. The Astroliner is roaring slowly though the forest. Large bugs and smaller animals start to run away as we make our way through.

"Alright looking good, Casey status report."

"Looking good, I patched the leak should be alright. I'm gonna stay back here and keep an eye on the shield generators," Casey says over the Intercom.

Moving forward, I avoided large tree branches and low lying foliage. The Astroliner looks like a football player running with the ball to the end zone. Dodging everything in its path, it's alive. As we scrape through the brush, it's cleaning off the ship and scraping off the moss and dirt, it's getting easier to see outside through the front hull. We finally arrive at the other crash side, Lynsye is in awe looking at the large relic that floats in front of her. She can't help it, but tears run from her eyes as if she was looking at God himself, and knowing they were saved.

"Casey, should I land?" I ask.

"Actually I have a plan B! There's a huge winch in the hanger back here. I think we can lift the bomber and get it in here... I hope," Casey says.

"Sounds like a plan to me," I said turning the Astroliner around.

"I'm on it," Casey says running over to the hanger door, and hits the open button.

The large door on the back of the Astroliner opens like a giant mouth, with two large hydraulic cylinders hissing as it opens.

Casey controls the crane and puts it into position over the bomber. She runs down the ramp and jumps on the bomber, with the cable around her shoulder. She quickly wraps it around the main upper chassis and through a lift loop on top of the ship. As she clamps the cable she gives me the thumbs up to start the rescue.

"Alright hang on, I'm gonna pull ya in," I say over the loud speaker.

From my seat I can control the crane as well. I start the winch from my control panel, while I watch from a camera screen that's projecting on the hull of the ship. As the winch starts to pull, the weight of the bomber pulls the Astroliner back towards the ground.

"Whoa! Hold on," I yell surprisingly.

I push on the throttle and push the rear thrusters to balance the ship, and continue to winch the other ship in. The bomber is gracefully lifting off the ground. The winch is all wound up, I retract the crane and the bomber is dragging on the hanger floor of the Astroliner.

"We're good, I'm closing the door!" Casey says over the intercom.

"I'm coming back to check on everyone," I say setting it to auto pilot to hover.

I run back to the hanger bay, Lynsye comes limping out of the bomber hugging Casey, and me.

"We did it!" Casey says happily to everyone.

"Who's ready to go home?" I say with a hand on each of their shoulders.

"Yea, we need medical attention," Lynsye says.

"We have one of those on here," I said.

"This ship has a medical room?" Lynsye asks raising her right eye brow.

"Yea that's what it said on the door I passed on the way down here," I said.

"I hope it's not a bathroom, heehe," Casey says giggling.

I first grab Mark and put him on a rolling stretcher and take him to the medical room. I open the medical door and peak into the room. As I look around the room, there is tons of medical equipment, two beds and a few chairs.

"Gods, I hope I don't have to pay the bill for this thing," I say to myself.

I roll Mark in, lift him onto the table and strap him in. Right behind me, Casey brings Missy in on another stretcher.

"Wow, hope you don't have to pay for this when we get back." Casey says.

"Hey that's what I was....." then we are interrupted by a loud screech.

All of a sudden the Astroliner gets hit hard, swings violently, and hits a tree.

"What the hell was that!?!?" I said pulling myself off the floor.

"You two get to the bridge I'll take care of these two and the other kids in the bomber!" Lynsye yells at us putting on a leg brace to help her walk.

"Right," Casey says while running with me to the bridge.

As we come to the bridge, right in front of us, is the nastiest monster ever seen by human kind. It stands three stories tall. Bright yellow eyes and drooling from the mouth. Casey and I are stunned, It stands in front of us with its two claws clapping, ready to attach.

Casey punches me in the shoulder.

"ICHIA!!!" Casey screams.

I jump into the captain's chair and grab the controls.

"Holy crap, watch it!" Casey says as the creature hurls a tree stump at us.

Pushing on the throttle, The Astroliner comes to life and veers to avoid the large stump.

"Weapons! Please Gods let there be weapons!" I say to Casey.

"Hell, yea let's try…. Cherry popper? What the hells this?" Casey asks.

"SHOOT, SHOOT!!!!!!" I yell as the creature charges the Astroliner.

"Here it goes!!!!" Casey's says.

I make the Astroliner circle the creature, and on top of the Astroliner the missile pod roars to life and out comes twenty one missiles. They fly into the air as if they don't have a target, then turn towards the monster and slam into it and into the ground causing multiple explosions and blasts.

"HELL YEA, WHO BIG NOW MOTHER F….. Crap," Casey says.

"I think we just pissed it off," I said.

"Agreed!" Casey replies

As the smoke clears the monster stands on its good legs and starts snapping its claws at the Astroliner.

"Let's get out of here!" Casey says.

I begin piloting The Astroliner away from the monster. I turn it into the forest trying to avoid the creature which has not given up chase. Dodging trees, boulders and the monster, the Astroliner is roaring through the forest. All of a sudden I see another creature in the upper canopy of the trees above us. It looks

like it's going to jump on us. I break hard right hitting a tree as the monster dives and misses us and crashes into several trees. As I'm flying the ship I'm looking over the controls again and system information screens.

"Casey I can't connect the engines to the FTL system. I think it's FTL looks older, maybe Hyper drive?" I say to Casey while flying.

"Hold on, I'm working on it, the computer systems a little old. It's a very early FTL but it should work, I just need to charge it," Casey says.

"I hope it doesn't take long, those things are right behind us…..Whoa!'I scream as we exit the forest and end up at the face of a cliff face that's twenty or more stories tall.

"Shit this aint good!" Casey says looking up.

"We're going to have to fight our way out of this. Casey give me the weapon system, Fix that FTL system and get us out of here," I said.

"I'm on it," Casey says furiously typing on the keyboard.

"Come on baby hold together," I said.

I turn The Astroliner around facing the forest, ready for a fight. The two creatures burst out of the forest. I dodge one and it rams hard into the cliff face. I push the laser cannon button and pull the trigger. Two guns fire with rapid fire and I blast the creature in the eye, splattering it everywhere. The creature drops to the ground attempting to cradle its injured eye.

"Oh, that's nasty!" I say as the other monster pulls itself together.

I look above the monster and notice a high extending ledge on the cliff.

"Hope this works," I say switching from lasers to missile pod.

I pull the Astroliner back and open fire. The rockets roar from the missile pod again and they barrage the side of the wall. The monster jumps away from the wall, then it starts to come at the Astroliner with its claws snapping. The ledge on the side of the cliff starts to give way and before the monster has a chance, a large rock slab crushes it and guts go flying everywhere.

"Oh, double nasty," Casey says with her fist in the air cheering me on.

The other creature stands up and begins to charge frantically towards the Astroliner. The creature starts to give us chase. As I'm piloting The Astroliner backwards, I'm looking for more weapons, but run into a little issue.

"I'm out of ammo here Casey!" I say to Casey as we dodge a large boulder from the creature.

"Try ION Cannon, it says it's charged." Casey replies.

"ION Cannon?" I say to Casey while I look at my control panel confused.

I noticed there is a warning label on the button. It reads "Warning wear sunglasses when firing and be prepared to be amazed by the explosion."

"Whatever."

I pushed the red and yellow button. All of a sudden all the chairs in the ship lower down. The front of the ship opens up and large nose cone comes out. The nose cone comes out like a switch blade knife and extends forwards. Electricity starts sparking on the nose cone and the lights go dim. A large bright blue beam of light

310

fires at the creature and it goes right through it melting it.

"Damn!" I say as the monster just stands there with a hole between its eyes. Then I noticed I started a landslide on the entire cliff face. Not only did it melt the monster but I managed to rip half of the cliff apart.

"Casey, today would be good!" I say frantically dodging falling rocks, trying to head for the forest.

"I got it! Hang on, prepare to jump… I think," Casey says typing in coordinates and pressing the enter key.

All of a sudden, The Astroliner makes a loud sound barrier breaking noise and disappears, as the land slide comes crashing down. We are still sitting on the bridge and all of the lights are working. The systems are working, but it's completely black outside.

"Um, are we dead?" Casey says looking around.

"I think we are in jump, should we see like flashing lights of stars and planets passing by? What coordinates did you put in?" I ask Casey.

"I put our home address in for the space station, we should end up near the orbit beacon," Casey says, looking over the log she typed.

"Well this is interesting, wonder if it's broken?"

"Well we um…," Casey says then is interrupted as the Astroliner comes out of jump right in front of earth and the space station.

"OH SHIT!" I said sitting up in my chair grabbing the

311

controls. We both scream as we come barreling towards the space station hanger bay.

"This is ISE station please Identify yourself." A controller says over the com.

"This is Jupiter 7 come in," Casey says over the com.

"Jupiter 7, we thought you guys were taken prisoner?" The controller says as I interrupt him.

"Hey, cut the shit we're coming in hot. Get everything off that deck that isn't bolted down! I yell attempting to control the Astroliner.

"Shield Generator one and two are out! Only back up power is available!" Casey says as she frantically looks for additional power.

The Astroliner engines start to smoke as we barrel through traffic around the space station and head straight for the hanger bay. The gravity from the space station and Earth begin to increase our speed.

"Pull up, you oversize paper weight!" I scream, pulling on the pitch control.

The Astroliner is flying through ship lanes and local enforcement and military are following us in. We speed through the gates of the station, then the retro boosters kick in, and we are almost thrown forward. Thank Gods for our seat belts or we would have had a front row seat.

"Got it! This should slow us down," Casey says fist pumping.

"Oh this is gonna hurt!" I say as I control the Astroliner. I do my best to pull the nose up.

"Pull the landing gear!" Casey says as we come in towards the landing platform.

"Good Idea!" I say pulling the lever for the landing gears. Outcome several large gears with six to eight wheels. I try to keep the nose up but we end up slamming into the deck of the station. We barrel through crates and empty tankers. Sparks start to fly as we skid across the floor, people and vehicles are frantically moving out of the way as we head towards the hospital. As we tear through, we shatter two crane towers, then the shield generators kick in again. The engines kick in again and fire forward, stopping us dead in our tracks. We are mere inches from hitting the hospital, I quickly pull back on the throttle and cut the engines.

"I need a change of under wear," I say smiling looking over at Casey who is still hanging on for dear life.

"Holy Shit we made it! We're home!" Casey says unbuckling

and jumping up and down around the bridge, then she slips and falls to the floor.

"What the hell." I said looking at her on the floor.

"I'm ok…ha ha," Casey mumbles.

Chapter 27

Home coming.

I help Casey off the floor.

"You okay?" I ask, as she dust her butt off.

"Oh yea, butt breaks the fall ha ha," Casey giggles.

"Lets go check on everyone else." I said as we started to head towards the medical room. We walk into the medical room, Lynsye sits in the middle of the room smoking a cigarette and she has everyone strapped, tied, & duck taped down to everything and anything in the room.

"Gods, you two scream like school girls! Hahaha," Lynsye says flicking her cigarette giving us both big hugs.

"You okay?" I ask Lynsye.

"Ichia, I'd have to say that was some of the best flying that I've ever seen you do from a video monitor," Lynsye says.

"Thanks, well I'm sure ambulances are coming, lets cut everyone down and get them checked out," I said with my hand on her shoulder.

We walk over to the hatch and open the door and the smell of the station rolls in. People and emergency crews are coming up to the ship.

"Smells like home!" I said.

"Oh, I think I smell Taco Bell, yum!" Casey says.

Emergency crews pull up with a portable loading dock and help us get everyone out. Mark, Missy, Colleen and Sam were transported straight to the hospital. I was talking with the landing deck manager, he is speechless for what we have discovered. I explained everything that happened, and he said the Lab Rat's said they captured us, even though we escaped. I'm holding a mission log and some random parts. As I'm talking with the manager, I notice my uncle walking through the crowd of reporters and civilians.

"Uncle!" I said jogging towards him giving him a big hug.

"I knew you would make it home," Hitoshi says holding me in his arms.

"I got a story for you uncle," I said.

"Oh, I'd believe it, this is astounding, I haven't seen this ship in years," Hitoshi says looking in amazement.

"Yea, this was one heck of ride, it pilots just like my old fighter," I said.

In the distance in the crowd I hear someone screaming my name. I look around through the crowd and I see my Kat. My uncle waves and tells the guards to let her in. I drop everything and run towards her like I'm being chased. She does the same, she's in a full sprint towards me. We crash into each other's arms kissing and hugging and kissing as if Romeo and Juliet finally met in heaven.

"Oh my god, I thought you were dead," Kat says as we drop to the deck floor kissing.

"You know I can't live without you," I mumble as we are kissing. Kat has me held down on the ground as we make out in front of everyone. My uncle clears his throat and interrupts us as we were about to undress each other on the deck floor.

"Oh, oops," we said as we both looked at each other and then the crowd. We both stood up and everyone started to clap.

"Welcome home, baby," Kat says to me holding me tightly.

"Well I didn't come home alone, I even found something that was thought to be lost," I said to Kat holding her tight.

"Well finders keepers, The Astroliner belongs to you Captain," My uncle says to me as I'm in shock.

"I'll send you the fund to get her repaired and get it space worthy. Jupiter 7 is going to be back in business," Hitoshi says to me nodding his head with a smile.

"Are you sure?" I ask.

317

"Absolutely," Hitoshi says then being interrupted.

"Oh hellllll no, this is going to cost extra and maybe a bottle of Jacky!" Mittens says putting her arms around me and Kat.

"Hey!" I said surprised to see her, I put my arm around her and we had a big group hug.

"Mittens was worried about you, she's been antsy waiting to hear any news," Kat says.

"Heck yea, you still owe me for the last one! Just kidding I can't believe this," Mittens says wiping a tear out of her eye.

"Yea, we crash landed on an unknown planet and we found this hidden in the jungle," I said.

"I can't wait to read the report on this," Hitoshi says.

"I can't wait till I get you home to myself," Kat says making me blush.

I stand with everyone staring at the Astroliner. As I stare at it, it feels like the moment lasted for minutes. The Astroliner stands nearly two stories tall and the light hits the transparent titanium like chrome on a hot rod. It's an amazing site, looks like a phoenix that just raised from the ashes. Minus the smoke coming from the engines, and the blown landing gears. I think to myself for a minute, Gods it's good to be home, but I feel as if something greater is coming my way. Thinking back to the Captains diary. Reporters are still trying to get to me to ask questions.

Kat gets paged with updates on the crew, everyone's okay and they are starting to wake up. My uncle has us escorted to the hospital. As we make our way up the ramp and into the hospital everyone is clapping their hands to me. I blush and we go up to the fourth floor to see everyone. Mark's awake, Casey is holding him tightly. Missy and Lynsye are making out on the other bed, Colleen and Sam are laughing about everything that happened. We're all telling our story about how we crashed and how I walked right into the Astroliner. We took over the ICU, were the only patients in there. Kat had Pizza and Mexican brought up for us from the cafeteria. We all ate like kings for the moment, with large Sodi pops to quench the thirst.

About an hour later, the nurses and Kat were about to discharge everyone to go home. Then my uncle walked in with two other commanders from the fleet, we got quiet really quick. I stood at attention along with Casey everyone else sat where they were.

"Well, it's my honor Ichia." Hitoshi said pulling out a small box.

"What that?" I asked turning my head as everyone turn looking at me.

"Ichia Chang, you are now Captain Chang of the Astroliner, and to continue to lead the Jupiter 7 flight group. The military will fund the repairs of the Astroliner to restore it and upgrade all of its systems. Also we will give you a starting fund, for additional support and crew payroll.

The Presidents of Earth and Mars would like to meet with you as well. You have a new mission now, lead your crew if they are still willing to go on. Take the Astroliner to the stars to search for new worlds, Defend the Sol System, and hunt down the Lab Rat Mafia," Hitoshi says.

"Well I..." I start to say being interrupted by Mittens.

"I think I speak for everyone, we'll follow you to hell and back again. I would like the honor to join your crew, Captain," Mittens says saluting me.

"Yea, Chang I'm with you all the way!" Lynsye says giving me two thumbs up.

"You've shown me how to be a better pilot, and thanks to you I've meet the love of my life. I'll follow you anywhere, and fix whatever needs fixing," Casey says.

"Shit I ain't letting you party by yourself bro, you know I'm in," Mark says giving me a thumbs up.

"I wouldn't miss it for the Sol System," Missy says holding her water cup held high.

"Well, Ichia?" Hitoshi asks me as I stand smiling in a mild shock from listening to everyone. I look at all of my friends and think to myself I've finally made Captain.

"I vow to protect each and every one of you, I promise to never leave any one behind. I promise to lead by example, and on top of that."

I say and turn towards Kat and kneel down. Kat turns bright red and starts to tear up. Everyone's faces just drop and it gets really quiet.

"Will you marry me?" I ask Kat as I'm kneeling humbly on the ICU floor.

"Yes!" Kat says one hand on her chest and one holding my hand.

Too be continued.

About the Author:

Mat Roll is Captain of the real Jupiter 7 in Michigan. Traveling the carnival circuit with the Astroliner.

https:\\jupiter7info.blogspot.com
twitter: @astrojupiter7

Be sure to look for part 2: Jupiter 7 Project Astroliner

Jupiter 7

- Astroliner
- Digital Embroidery
- Screen Printing
- 3D Printing
- Novelist

For Hire!! (Michigan/ Sol System only sorry ^_^).
Astroliner Space Simulator Attraction, check us out
@ jupiter7info.blogspot.com